FRIENDS

FOREVER

www.daniellesteel.com

DANIELLE STEEL

FRIENDS FOREVER

CORGI BOOKS

TRANSWORLD PUBLISHERS
61–63 Uxbridge Road, London W5 5SA
A Random House Group Company
www.transworldbooks.co.uk

FRIENDS FOREVER
A CORGI BOOK: 9780552154796
9780552159876

First published in Great Britain
in 2012 by Bantam Press
an imprint of Transworld Publishers

Corgi edition published 2013

Addresses for Random House Group Ltd companies outside the UK
can be found at: www.randomhouse.co.uk
The Random House Group Ltd Reg. No. 954009

The Random House Group Limited supports The Forest Stewardship
Council® (FSC®), the leading international forest-certification organisation.
Our books carrying the FSC label are printed on FSC®-certified paper.
FSC is the only forest-certification scheme supported by the leading
environmental organisations, including Greenpeace. Our
paper procurement policy can be found at
www.randomhouse.co.uk/environment

Typeset in Adobe Garamond by Falcon Oast Graphic Art Ltd.

2 4 6 8 10 9 7 5 3 1

Printed and bound in Great Britain by Clays Ltd, St Ives plc

This book is dedicated to Nick Traina and Max Levitt, bright shining stars, and the footprints they left on our hearts forever.

And to my precious children, Beatrix, Trevor, Todd, Sam, Victoria, Vanessa, Maxx, and Zara. Please God may you always be among the survivors. I love you so much!!!

Mommy/ds

FRIENDS

FOREVER

Chapter 1

The admissions process to get into the Atwood School had eaten up six months of the previous winter, and driven each of the families nearly to distraction with open houses, meet and greets, intense interviews with the parents, sometimes two of them, and screenings of each child. Siblings had some preferential advantage, but each child was evaluated on their own merits, whether he or she had a sibling in the school or not. Atwood was one of the few coed private schools in San Francisco – most of the old established schools were single sex – and it was the only one that went from kindergarten through twelfth grade, making it highly desirable for families who didn't want to go through the whole process again for either middle school or high school.

The admissions letters had come at the end of March, and had been anticipated with the same anxiety as an acceptance to Harvard or Yale. Some of the parents admitted that it was more than a little crazy, but they insisted it was worth it. They said Atwood was a fabulous school, which gave each child the individualized attention they needed, carried enormous social status (which they preferred not to acknowledge), and students who applied themselves in the high school usually went on to great colleges, many of them Ivy League. Getting a kid into Atwood was a major coup. There were roughly six hundred and fifty students, it was well located in Pacific Heights, and the ratio of teacher to students was excellent. And it provided career, college, and psychological support counseling to the students as part of the routine services it offered.

When the big day finally came for the new kindergarten class to enter the school, it was one of those rare, hot Indian summer September days in San Francisco, on the Wednesday after Labor Day. It had been over ninety degrees since Sunday, and in the low eighties at night. Such hot weather happened only once or twice a year, and everyone knew that as soon as the fog rolled in, and it would inevitably, the heat would be over, and it would be back to temperatures in the low sixties in the daytime, brisk chilly winds, and the low fifties at night.

Usually, Marilyn Norton loved the hot weather, but she was having a tough time with it, nine months pregnant, with her due date in two days. She was expecting her second child, another boy, and he was going to be a big one. She could hardly move in the heat, and her ankles and feet were so swollen that all she had been able to get her feet into were rubber flip-flops. She was wearing huge white shorts that were too tight on her now, and a white T-shirt of her husband's that outlined her belly. She had nothing left to wear that still fit, but the baby would arrive soon. She was just glad that she had made it to the first day of school with Billy. He had been nervous about his new school, and she wanted to be there with him. His father, Larry, could have filled in, unless she'd been in labor, in which case their neighbor had promised to take him, but Billy wanted his mom with him on the first day, like all the other kids. So she was happy to be there, and Billy was holding tightly to her hand as they walked up to the modern, handsome school. The school had built a new building five years before, and it was heavily endowed by parents of current students, and the grateful parents of alums who had done well.

Billy glanced up at his mother with an anxious look as they approached the school. He was clutching a small

Danielle Steel

football and was missing his two front teeth. They both had thick manes of curly red hair and wide smiles. Billy's smile made her grin, he looked so cute without his front teeth. He was an adorable kid and had always been easy. He wanted to make everyone happy, he was sweet to her, and he loved pleasing his dad, and he knew the way to do that was to talk to Larry about sports. He remembered everything his father told him about every game. He was five, and for the past year he had said he wanted to play football for the 49ers one day. 'That's my boy!' Larry Norton always said proudly. He was obsessed with sports, football, baseball, and basketball. He played golf with his clients and tennis on the weekends. He worked out religiously every morning, and he encouraged his wife to do the same. She had a great body, when she wasn't pregnant, and she'd played tennis with him until she got too big to run fast enough to hit the ball.

Marilyn was thirty years old and had met Larry when they both worked for the same insurance company eight years before when she got out of college. He was eight years older and a great-looking guy. He had noticed her immediately, and teased her about her coppery red hair. Every woman in the place thought he was gorgeous and wanted to go out with him. Marilyn was the lucky winner, and they were married when she was twenty-four.

She got pregnant with Billy very quickly, and had waited five years for their second baby. Larry was thrilled it was another boy, and they were going to name him Brian.

Larry had had a brief career in baseball, in the minor leagues. He had a legendary pitching arm, which everyone felt certain would get him to the major leagues. But a shattered elbow in a skiing accident had ended his future in baseball, and he had gone to work in insurance. He had been bitter about it at first, and had a tendency to drink too much, and flirt with women when he did. He always insisted it was just social drinking. He was the life of every party. And after Marilyn married him, he left the insurance company and went out on his own. He was a natural salesman, and had established a very successful insurance brokerage business, which afforded them a very comfortable lifestyle, and plenty of luxuries. They had bought a very handsome house in Pacific Heights, and Marilyn had never worked again. And Larry's favorite clients were the professional major-league athletes who trusted him and were his mainstay now. At thirty-eight, he had a good reputation and a very solid business. He was still disappointed he wasn't a pro ballplayer himself, but he readily admitted that he had a great life, a hot wife, and a son who would play ball professionally one day, if he had anything to do with it. Although his life had turned out differently than he planned, Larry Norton was a happy man. He hadn't come to Billy's first day of school because he was having breakfast with one of the 49ers that morning, to sell him more insurance. In cases like that, his clients always came first, particularly if they were stars. But very few of the other kids' fathers had come to school, and Billy didn't mind. His father had promised him an autographed football and some football cards from the player he was having breakfast with. Billy was thrilled, and content to go to school with just his mom.

The teacher at the door where the kindergarten filed in looked down at Billy with a warm smile, and he gave her a shy glance, still holding on to his mother's hand. The teacher was pretty and young, with long blond hair. She looked like she was fresh out of college. Her name tag said that she was an assistant teacher and her name was Miss Pam. Billy was wearing a name tag too. And once in the building, Marilyn took him to his classroom, where a dozen children were already playing, and their teacher greeted him immediately, and asked him if he'd like to leave his football in his cubby so his hands would be free to play. Her name was Miss June, and she was about Marilyn's age.

Billy hesitated at the question and then shook his head. He was afraid someone would steal his football. Marilyn reassured him and encouraged him to do what the teacher said. She helped him find his cubby, in the row of open cubbyholes where other children had already left their possessions, and some sweaters. And when they went back into the classroom, Miss June suggested that he might like to play with the building blocks until the rest of his classmates arrived. He thought about it and looked at his mother, who gently nudged him to go.

'You like playing with building blocks at home,' she reminded him. 'I'm not going anywhere. Why don't you go play? I'll be right here.' She pointed to a tiny chair, and with considerable difficulty lowered herself into it, thinking that it would take a crane to get her out of it again. And with that, Miss June walked Billy to the building blocks, and he got busy making a fort of some kind with the largest ones. He was a big boy, both tall and strong, which pleased his father. Larry could easily imagine him as a football player one day. He had made it Billy's dream since he was old enough to talk, and his own dream for the boy, even before that, when he was born a strapping ten-pound baby. Billy was bigger than most children his age, but a gentle, loving child. He was never aggressive with other kids, and had made a great impression during his screening at Atwood. They had confirmed that he was not only well coordinated for his size, but also very bright. Marilyn still had trouble imagining that their second son would be as wonderful as Billy. He was the best. And he forgot about his mother as he got busy with the blocks, and she sat uncomfortably on the tiny chair and watched the other children who came in.

She noticed a dark-haired boy with big blue eyes arrive. He was shorter than Billy and wiry. And she saw that he had a small toy gun shoved into the waistband of his shorts, and a sheriff's badge pinned to his shirt. She thought that toy guns weren't allowed at school, but apparently it had escaped Miss Pam's attention at the door, with so many children arriving at the same time. Sean was also with his mother, a pretty blond woman in jeans and a white T-shirt, a few years older than Marilyn. Like Billy, Sean was holding his mother's hand, and a few minutes later he left her to play in the corner with the blocks too as she watched him with a smile. Sean and Billy began playing side by side, helping themselves to the blocks, and paying no attention to each other.

Within minutes Miss June spotted the gun and went to talk to Sean, as his mother watched. She knew they wouldn't let him keep it at school. She had a son at Atwood in the seventh grade, Kevin, and she knew the policy. But Sean had insisted on taking the gun with him. Connie O'Hara had taught school herself before she married, so she knew the importance of school rules, and after trying to reason with Sean to leave the gun at home, she had decided to let the teacher deal with it. Miss June approached Sean with a warm smile.

'Let's leave that in your cubby, Sean, shall we? You can keep the sheriff's badge on.'

'I don't want someone to take my gun,' he said with a stern look at Miss June.

'Let's give it to your mom, then. She can bring it when she picks you up. But it's safe in your cubby here too.' Still, she didn't want him sneaking over to take it and put it in the waistband of his shorts again.

'I might need it,' he said, struggling with a big block and setting it on top of the others. He was a strong boy, in spite of his size, which was no more than average, and he was thin. 'I might have to arrest someone,' Sean explained to Miss June, as she nodded seriously.

'I understand, but I don't think you'll need to arrest anyone here. Your friends here are all good guys.'

'Maybe a robber or a bad guy will come into school.'

'We wouldn't let that happen. There are no bad guys here. Let's give your mom the gun,' she said firmly. She held out her hand for it, as Sean looked her in the eye, measuring how serious she was, and he could tell that she meant it. He didn't like it, but he slowly took the gun out of his shorts and handed it to the teacher, who walked over to Connie and gave it to her. Connie was standing near Billy's very pregnant mother, and she apologized to Miss June and slipped the gun into her purse, and sat down on the small chair next to Marilyn.

'I knew that was going to happen. I know the rules. I have a son in seventh grade. But Sean wouldn't leave the house without it.' She smiled at Marilyn with a rueful look.

'Billy brought his football. He put it in his cubby.' Marilyn pointed to where he was playing next to Sean.

'I love his red hair,' Connie said admiringly. The two boys were playing peacefully side by side without a word, as a little girl entered the corner with the blocks, and she looked like an ad for the perfect little girl. She had long beautiful blond hair with ringlets, and big blue eyes, and she was wearing a pretty pink dress, white ankle socks, and pink shoes that glittered. She looked like an angel, and an instant after she arrived, without a comment, she took the biggest building block out of Billy's hands and set it down for herself. Billy looked stunned but didn't resist. And as soon as she set it down, she saw the one Sean was holding and about to put on his fort, and she took that one too. And she gave them both a look that warned them not to mess with her, and proceeded to help herself to more blocks while the boys stared at her in amazement.

'This is what I love about coeducation,' Connie whispered to Billy's mother. 'It teaches them to deal with each other early, as in the real world, not just all girls or all boys.' Billy looked like he was about to cry when the little girl took another block from him, and Sean gave her a dark look when she took his block from him too. 'It's a good thing I have the gun in my purse. He'd arrest her for sure for that. I just hope he doesn't hit her,' Connie said as both women watched their sons, while the little angel/demon continued to build her own fort, undaunted by them. She was in full control of the block corner and had both boys on the run. Neither boy had ever met or dealt with anyone like her. Her name tag had two names on it, 'Gabrielle' and 'Gabby.' She tossed her long blond curls while the boys looked at her, dazed.

Another little girl walked into the block corner, only stayed for two seconds, and headed for the play kitchen nearby. She got busy with pots and pans and was opening and closing the oven door and putting things in the oven and the pretend fridge. She looked extremely busy. She had a sweet face and wore her brown hair in two neat braids. She was wearing overall shorts, sneakers, and a red T-shirt. She looked ready to play and paid no attention to the others, but all three were watching her as a woman in a navy blue business suit walked up to the little girl in the kitchen and kissed her goodbye. She had brown hair the same color as her daughter's and wore it in a bun. Despite the heat, she was wearing the jacket to her suit, a white silk blouse, stockings, and high heels. She looked like she was a banker, or lawyer, or business executive of some kind. And her daughter looked unconcerned as she left. You could tell that she was used to not being with her mother, unlike the two boys, who had wanted their mothers to stay.

The little girl with the braids was wearing a name tag that said 'Izzie.' The two boys approached her with caution after her mother left. The other girl had scared them, so they ignored her and left the block corner. No matter how pretty she was, she wasn't friendly. Izzie looked easier to deal with as she kept busy in the kitchen.

'What are you doing?' Billy asked her first.

'I'm making lunch,' she said with a look that said it was obvious. 'What would you like to eat?' There were baskets of plastic food that she had taken out of the fridge and oven and arranged on plates, and there was a small picnic table nearby. The kindergarten at Atwood had great toys. It was one of the things parents always loved when they toured the school. They also had an enormous playground, a huge gym, and excellent athletic facilities. Larry, Billy's father, loved that, and Marilyn liked the academics. She wanted Billy to learn something too, not just grow up to play ball. Larry was an astute businessman and a great salesman, and had an enormous amount of charisma, but he hadn't learned much in school. Marilyn wanted to be sure that her sons did.

'For real?' Billy asked Izzie about the lunch order she had requested from him. His eyes were wide as he inquired, and Izzie laughed. All his childhood trust and innocence were in his eyes.

'Of course not, silly,' Izzie chided him good-humoredly. 'It's just pretend. What do you want?' She looked as though she really cared.

'Oh. I'll have a hamburger and hot dog, with ketchup and mustard, and French fries. No pickles.' Billy placed his order.

'Coming right up,' Izzie said matter-of-factly, then handed him a plate piled high with pretend food, and pointed him toward the picnic able, where he sat down.

Then she turned to Sean. She had instantly become the little mother in the group, attending to their needs. 'What about you?' she asked witha smile.

'Pizza,' Sean said seriously,' and a hot fudge sundae.' She had both in the arsenal of plastic food, and handed them to him. She looked like a short-order cook in a fast-food restaurant. Then the angel in the pink dress and sparkly pink shoes appeared.

'Does your father own a restaurant?' Gabby asked Izzie with interest. Izzie was in full control of the kitchen and looked very efficient.

'No. He's a lawyer, for poor people. He helps them when people are mean to them. He works for the ACUUUUU. My mom is a lawyer too, for companies. She had to go to court today, that's why she couldn't stay. She had to make a motion. She can't cook. My dad does.'

'My dad sells cars. My mom gets a new Jaguar every year. You look like you're a good cook,' the angel said politely. She was much more interested in Izzie than she had been in the boys. But even if each sex stuck together and had similar interests, they were in the same classroom and tempered each other in some ways. 'Can I have mac and cheese? And a doughnut,' Gabby said, pointing to a pink doughnut with plastic sprinkles. Izzie handed her the mac and cheese and the doughnut on a pink tray. Gabby waited as Izzie helped herself to a plastic banana and a chocolate doughnut, and they joined the boys at the picnic table, and sat down like four friends who had met for lunch.

They were just starting to pretend to eat the lunch Izzie had fixed for them, when a tall thin boy ran over to them. He had straight blond hair, and was wearing a white button-down shirt and perfectly pressed khaki pants, and looked older than he was. He looked more like a second-grader than someone in kindergarten.

'Am I too late for lunch?' he asked, looking breathless, and Izzie turned to smile at him.

'Of course not,' she reassured him.' What do you want to eat?' 'A turkey sandwich with mayo on white toast.' Izzie got him something that looked vaguely like it, and some pretend potato chips, and he sat down with them. He glanced at his mother, who was just leaving the classroom with a cellphone pressed to her ear. She was giving someone instructions and looked like she was in a rush.' My mom delivers babies,' he explained. 'Someone's having triplets. That's why she couldn't stay. My father is a psychiatrist, he talks to people if they're crazy or sad.' The boy, whose name tag said 'Andy,' looked serious. He had a grown-up haircut and good manners, and he helped Izzie put everything away in the kitchen when they were through.

Miss June and Miss Pam were both in the classroom by then, and asked everyone to form a circle. The five children who had eaten 'lunch' at the picnic table sat next to each other in the circle, no longer strangers, and Gabby squeezed Izzie's hand and smiled, as the teachers handed out musical instruments, and explained to them what each one did.

After the instruments, they had juice and cookies and then went outside for recreation. The mothers who had stayed were given juice and cookies too, although Marilyn declined and said that even water gave her heartburn now. She could hardly wait for the baby to come. She rubbed her enormous belly as she said it, and the other women looked at her sympathetically. She looked miserable in the heat.

Gabby's mother had joined Marilyn and Connie by then, and there were several other mothers sitting in small groups in the corners of the class room. Gabby's mother looked young and was very striking. She had teased blond hair, and was wearing a white cotton miniskirt and high heels. Her pink T-shirt was cut low enough to see some cleavage, and she was wearing makeup and perfume. She stood out among the other mothers, but didn't seem to mind it. She was friendly and pleasant, and sympathetic to Marilyn, when she introduced herself as Judy. She said she had gained fifty pounds with her last pregnancy. She had a three-year-old daughter, Michelle, two years younger than Gabby. But whatever weight she had gained, she had obviously lost it, and had a fabulous figure. She was flashy but a very pretty girl, and the others guessed her to be in her late twenties. She said something about having been in beauty pageants when she was in college, which seemed about right, given the way she looked. She said they had moved to San Francisco from southern California two years before, and she missed the heat, so she was loving the Indian summer weather.

The three women talked about forming a carpool, and were hoping to find two other women to go in with them, so they'd only have to drive one day a week. Judy, Gabby's mother, explained that she'd have to bring her three-year-old with her on her days, but she said she had a van she would use for carpool, so there would be plenty of room for all the kids, with seatbelts. And Marilyn apologetically explained that she might not be able to drive for a few weeks because of the new baby, but she'd be happy to after that, as long as she could bring him along.

Connie agreed to organize the carpool for them, since she had done it before for her son in seventh grade when he was younger. She had been hoping that Sean's brother, Kevin, would take him to school in the morning, but their schedules were too different, and Kevin didn't want to be bothered with his little brother, and had flatly refused to do it. So the carpool made sense for Connie too. It would be helpful to all of them.

After the children came back from the playground and were engrossed in story time, with Miss June reading aloud to them, the mothers were able to leave, with their children's permission, and promised to be back when they got out of school that afternoon. Billy and Sean were slightly uneasy, but Gabby and Izzie were busy listening to the story and holding hands again. While out on the playground, they had agreed to be best friends. The boys had all been running around and yelling, and the girls had had fun on the swings.

'Did you hear about the meeting tonight?' Connie asked the other mothers as they left the building, out of earshot of the children by then. The others said they hadn't. 'It's really for the middle school and high school parents.' She lowered her voice even further. 'A sophomore boy hanged himself this summer. He was a really sweet kid. Kevin knew him, although he was three years older. He was on the baseball team. His parents and the school knew he had a lot of emotional problems, but it was still shocking when he did it. They're bringing in a psychologist to talk to the parents about recognizing the signs of suicide in kids, and prevention.'

'At least that's one thing we don't have to worry about at this age,' Judy said with a look of relief. 'I'm still working on Michelle being dry at night. She has accidents once in a while, but she's only three. I don't think suicide at three and five is a big issue,' she said blithely.

'No, but apparently it can be as young as eight or nine,' Connie said somberly. 'I don't worry about it with Kevin, or I haven't, but he's a pretty wild kid sometimes. He's not as easy as Sean, he never has been. He hates following anyone else's rules. The boy who died was really a sweet kid.'

'Divorced parents?' Marilyn asked with a knowing look.

'No,' Connie said quietly. 'Good parents, solid good marriage, mom at home full time. I just don't think they thought this could happen to them. I think he'd been seeing a counselor, but mainly for problems he had in school keeping his grades up. He always took things pretty hard. He used to cry whenever the baseball team lost a game. I think there was a lot of pressure on him at home, academically. But the family is very wholesome. He was their only kid.'

The other two women looked disturbed by what she said, but they agreed that the meeting wasn't relevant to them, and they hoped it never would be. It was just sad to hear about it happening to someone else. It was unimaginable to think of any of their children committing suicide. It was hard enough worrying about accidents in the home, drownings in swimming pools, and illnesses and mishaps that befell young children. Suicide was in another universe from theirs, much to their relief.

Connie promised to call them when she found two more candidates for their carpool, and then they went their separate ways. All three were driving when they saw each other later that day and waved. Izzie and Gabby bounced out of school holding hands, and Gabby told her mother how much fun they'd had that day. Izzie's babysitter picked her up, and Izzie said the same thing to her. Billy was clutching the football he had retrieved from his cubby when he came out. Sean asked his mother for his sheriff's gun the moment he got in the car, and Andy was picked up by the housekeeper, since his parents were still at work, as they always were at that hour.

All five of them had had a great first day at the Atwood School, they liked their teachers and were happy with their new friends. Marilyn told herself that it had been worth the long, agonizing admission process. As she drove away with Billy, her water broke on the front seat, and she felt the first familiar labor pains, which heralded Brian's arrival into the world. He was born that night.

Chapter 2

By the beginning of third grade, the five best friends had been bosom buddies for three years. They were eight. They were still in the same carpool, with Andy and Izzie's babysitters pitching in when needed, and they often had play dates with each other. More often than not Connie O'Hara, Sean's mother, would invite several of them to her house. Her older son, Kevin, was fifteen by then, and a sophomore at Atwood. He was always getting demerits or study hall for talking in class, or for homework he hadn't done. And no matter how difficult he was to get along with, how much he fought with their parents, or how often he threatened to beat Sean up, Kevin was a hero to his little brother, who worshipped him and thought he was 'cool.'

Connie loved having kids over, both Kevin's friends and Sean's. She volunteered for field trips and various projects at school, and worked for the PTA. As an ex-schoolteacher and devoted mother, she enjoyed her kids and their friends. And Kevin's friends particularly enjoyed talking to her. She was as sensitive to the problems of teenagers as she was to those of her eight-year-old. She was known to keep a cookie jar full of condoms in the kitchen, where Kevin's pals could help themselves, no questions asked. Mike O'Hara was equally great with kids, and loved having them in the house, and had coached Little League and been head of Kevin's Boy Scout troop until Kevin quit. Connie and Mike were realistic about what their kids did, and were well aware of the experimentation with marijuana and booze among kids Kevin's age. They discouraged it, but also knew what went on. They managed to be firm, protective, involved, and practical at the same time. It was a lot easier for them being Sean's parents than Kevin's, but Sean was a lot younger. Things were dicier at fifteen, and Kevin had always been more of a risktaker than Sean, who followed all the rules.

Sean was doing well at school, and his best friends were still the ones he had made in kindergarten. He had gone from wanting to be a sheriff to wanting to be a policeman, then a fireman, and by eight back to the police again. He loved watching any kind of police show on TV. He wanted to keep law and order in his life and among his friends. He rarely broke the rules at home or at school, unlike his older brother, who thought they were made to be broken. They had the same parents but were very different boys. And in the three years since Sean had started kindergarten at Atwood, Mike's business had done extremely well, and he spent a considerable amount of time with both boys, doing activities with them. He and Connie were very comfortable financially. There had been a major construction boom, and he was the contractor that people were fighting to hire in Pacific Heights. It afforded the O'Haras a very secure lifestyle, they went on nice vacations in the summer, and he had built them a beautiful lakefront house in Tahoe two years before, which all of them enjoyed. He had a background in economics, but building houses had always been what he loved. He had set up his own construction company years before, and started small. And it had become one of the most successful private contracting firms in the city, and Connie had encouraged him from the beginning.

Marilyn Norton's life was more hectic than Connie's, with two young boys. Billy was eight by then. Brian was three, and had all the needs appropriate to his age, but was a quiet, well-behaved boy. The big disappointment to Larry, his father, was that Brian had no interest in anything athletic – he didn't even like to throw a ball. At the same age, Billy had already shown his father's love of sports, which he had inherited from him. Brian hadn't. He could sit and draw for hours, was already learning to read at three, and had a strong aptitude for music. But Larry wasn't interested in his achievements. If Brian wasn't going to be an athlete, Larry had no use for him, and barely spoke to the child. It infuriated Marilyn and was often the spark that set off a fight, particularly if Larry had too much to drink.

'Can't you just talk to him?' Marilyn said, looking unhappy, and inevitably raising her voice. 'Just say something to him, for five minutes. He's your son too.' She was desperate to have Larry accept him, and he just wouldn't.

'He's *your* son,' Larry said angrily. He hated to be called on it. Billy was his boy, and they had so much more in common. Billy shared his father's dream for him, he wanted to play pro football, it was the only career goal he ever talked about. He didn't care about firemen or policemen. He just wanted to play sports. But Brian was a quiet, serious, less outgoing child. He was small, and didn't have his father's and brother's talent for athletics. Billy played baseball and soccer at school, and Larry went to all his games. He cheered them when they won, and gave Billy hell when they didn't. He said there was never an excuse to lose a game. His father's exuberance and tough demands made Brian uncomfortable around him and even scared him, but it didn't faze Billy.

Larry's business had been growing too, but his success just seemed to add more stress to their lives instead of less. He was home less often, and he stayed out later when he spent the evening with clients. And most of his clients were professional basketball, baseball, and football players now. Larry spent a huge amount of time with them, and went to Scottsdale for spring training for his clients who played for the Giants. Some of them were now his closest friends, and some of them had a wild side that Larry loved sharing. He rarely included Marilyn in those evenings, and she was just as happy to stay home with her boys. She had gotten back in shape after Brian, and she was looking great at thirty-three, but the girls most of Larry's clients went out with were twenty and twenty-one, and she had nothing to say to them. It was a racier crowd than she wanted to hang out with. She preferred to be with her kids. She almost always went to school functions alone, and when Larry did come, he always had just a little too much to drink, of the wine they served at school. Not so much that the other parents would notice, but Marilyn always knew he had had too much wine, or a couple of extra beers or even a bourbon on the rocks before they left home. It seemed to be the only way he could get through evenings he thought were boring. He wasn't interested in his boy's school, except for sporting events, which he always attended. And more than once he had commented that Judy Thomas, Gabby's mother, was quite a babe. Larry had an eye for pretty women.

Judy and Marilyn were good friends, and Marilyn ignored the comments Larry made about Judy. She knew that however flashy Judy looked, she was crazy about Adam, her husband, and was well behaved. Judy had just turned thirty, and had already had a lot of work done, liposuction, a tummy tuck, breast implants, and regular Botox shots, and although her friends told her she was foolish to do it, she looked great. She had never gotten over her youthful beauty pageant mentality. She had admitted to Marilyn and Connie once that she had entered Gabby in baby beauty pageants at four and five, and Gabby had won hands down, but Adam had had a fit and made her promise never to do it again, and she respected his wishes. Adam adored both his girls, although Gabby was undeniably the star of the show. She had more personality and more spark to her than her much quieter younger sister, Michelle. It was Gabby who Judy was certain would make a mark on the world. She had a dazzling personality. In contrast, Michelle lived in her sister's shadow, but she was only six, so it wasn't fair to compare them.

In third grade, Gabby was taking piano and voice lessons, and seemed to have real talent at an early age. Judy was trying to convince the school's drama department to do a full musical production of *Annie* and put Gabby in the lead role. For the moment, they had decided it was more than they wanted to undertake, and not many of the students were as well prepared as Gabby for a Broadway musical on their stage. Gabby already knew she wanted to be an actress when she grew up, and Judy was seeing to it that she had all the skills she needed. She had been going to ballet lessons since she was three. Michelle loved ballet too, but her abilities weren't as obvious as Gabby's. Gabby was a star. Michelle was just a little girl.

The couple who did the most for Atwood were Adam and Judy, who made big donations to the school, and had both girls there. Michelle was a better student than Gabby and got straight A's, but it was Gabby's many talents that caught everyone's attention. Michelle was just as pretty, but Gabby was more extroverted and infinitely more noticeable.

And Adam was happy to do whatever he could for the school. He had donated a Range Rover from his car dealership for the school auction. The evening had made the school a fortune, and Adam was the hero of the hour. They were flashy and certainly not subtle, but they were nice people and well liked by all, except for a few more reserved parents who thought they were just too showy and could never understand how they had gotten their daughters into a school like Atwood. But they were clearly there to stay, whether their critics liked it or not.

Gabby and Izzie were still best friends in third grade. At eight, they loved each other even more than they had at five. They shared Barbies and traded clothes. Izzie spent weekends at Gabby's house as often as she was allowed. They had carved their initials into Izzie's desk at home, G+I4EVER, which hadn't gone over well with Izzie's mother, and she'd been on restriction for a weekend. Izzie loved staying at Gabby's, where she could try on all her pretty clothes. Practically everything Gabby owned had sparkles on it, and she had two pink jackets trimmed in real white fur, and a pink fur coat her mom had gotten for her in Paris. They wore the same sizes in everything, and traded clothes when they were allowed to, although not the coat from Paris. And Izzie liked Michelle, even though Gabby said she hated her sister, and blamed her for everything whenever she could. Gabby hated it when her mother insisted they play with her, because she wanted Izzie to herself, but Izzie was a good sport about including Michelle in their games, and she even let her win sometimes. She felt sorry for Michelle. She never seemed to have as much fun as Gabby, and her parents seemed less interested in her. Izzie had a strong urge to nurture everyone; she always felt sorry for the underdog, and even took care of Gabby sometimes if she was in a bad mood or had a cold. Izzie was the perfect friend.

Judy always said about her older daughter that she was born to succeed at everything she did, and it seemed to be true. Gabby had modeled a few times for ads for children's clothing, and one national campaign for GapKids by the time she was in third grade. No one ever doubted that Gabby would be a star one day. She already was in her own little world. And Izzie loved being best friends with her, although she loved the three boys in her group too.

Izzie's father, Jeff, took them all out for pizza and bowling sometimes. The girls loved it, although they

could hardly pick up the ball. Once in a while, Izzie's
mother went with them, but usually she had to work late
at night. Katherine always brought a lot of work home
from the office, and you had to be quiet in the house, so
Jeff took them out, or dropped Izzie off at Gabby's, if
Izzie begged long enough. Her mother never minded,
and once in a while she heard her parents fight about it.
Her dad would ask why her mom couldn't take at least
one night off, and then the fight would start. Katherine
always talked about her husband's clients at the ACLU as
the Great Unwashed. Whenever Izzie heard those words,
she knew one of their really big fights was about to
start.

She talked about it with Andy sometimes, because he
was an only child too, and his parents were busy and
worked a lot, like hers. And she wondered if his parents
fought too. He said they didn't, and his mom worked late
if she had to stay out all night to deliver a baby. Both of
Izzie's parents were lawyers, and Andy's were doctors. His
mother didn't come home for two or three days sometimes when she had a lot of babies to deliver, and his
father traveled a lot to give lectures and appeared on TV
for his latest book. He went on book tours when he
wasn't home seeing patients. Andy said his father was
even busier than his mother. He wrote books about

people's problems. But Andy liked their housekeeper, and she lived in the house, so he said it didn't matter to him how busy his parents were. Izzie had a babysitter, but not a housekeeper who lived in. And Andy lived in a bigger house.

Like Izzie, Andy's favorite house to visit was Sean's, because his parents were so nice, but Andy always said that his parents were nice too, they were just out a lot, and the O'Haras were always home, and made time to talk to all of them. Izzie used to like to pretend that Sean's mother, Connie, was her aunt, but she never told Sean about it, she just said it to herself. And Connie always gave her a big hug and kiss when she walked in. Izzie thought all of the moms in the group were nice, except sometimes her own, because she was so busy, had so much work to do, and she came home so tired from the office that she sometimes forgot to give Izzie a hug. But her dad never forgot. He gave her piggyback rides around the house, and took her to movies and the park. Being with her friends made Izzie wish she had a sister or brother sometimes, but she knew there was no hope of that. She had asked her mother about it, and she said she didn't have time, and she was older than the other mothers. Katherine Wallace was forty-two, and Izzie's dad was forty-six. They said they felt too old to have another child, and her father always said that they didn't want one because they knew they'd never have one as great as she was. But Izzie knew it was an excuse, they just didn't want more kids.

It was almost the end of the school year when Kevin O'Hara got into trouble again. Izzie heard about it from Sean, when they traded lunches in the schoolroom. She knew that something bad had happened because Connie hadn't driven carpool for two days. In the end they had kept their carpool to the three mothers, and this week Connie had missed both her days, and when Marilyn and Judy took turns driving for her, neither of them said why. Izzie sensed trouble right away.

'It's Kevin,' Sean said when he traded Izzie her apple for a pink cupcake he didn't want. Izzie always had healthy food he liked better. She gobbled up the pink cupcake and had pink icing all over her lips and nose, which made him laugh.

'What are you laughing at?' she asked him, looking insulted. He teased her a lot, but she liked him anyway, he was her friend, kind of like a brother, only better since he never hit her. He had pushed a fourth-grader once who had called her a name.

'I'm laughing at you. You've got pink icing on your nose.' She wiped it on her sleeve, and he went on. 'Kev got in trouble at the school dance. My dad says he might get expelled. He had to stay home this week. He's suspended or something.'

'What did he do? Get in a fight?' Izzie knew he had done that before. It wasn't unusual for him, and his mother said it was his hot Irish blood. But their father never seemed to get into fights and he was Irish too, just Kevin.

'He took a bottle of my dad's liquor to the dance and put it in the punch. I think it was gin. Anyway, they all got really drunk, and so did Kevin. He threw up all over the boys' bathroom at the dance.'

'It's a good thing you don't share a room with him anymore, if he threw up all over the place,' Izzie said wisely. They had given Sean his own room when he turned six and Kevin was thirteen. 'It must have smelled awful,' she said practically and Sean nodded, remembering how Kevin looked when they brought him home.

'Yeah, and my dad was really mad. The school called him that night, and my dad had to go to pick him up. He had alcohol poisoning, and they had to take him to the emergency room and get him some medicine or something. My mom's been crying all week, she's really scared they're going to kick him out, and I guess his grades aren't so good either.' It sounded serious to both of them.

'Wow. When will you know if they're kicking him out of school?'

'Sometime this week, I think.' Sean wasn't sure. His parents had had endless conversations about it with Kevin, but only one with him. And they were sending Kevin to an outdoor adventure camp for the summer, for kids who'd gotten in trouble in school. Their description of it sounded very unpleasant to Sean. You had to do a lot of really hard things like rock climbing, and hiking up a mountain, and spending a night alone in a forest, which sounded really scary to Sean. He was worried about his brother. He had overheard their father telling him that at the rate he was going, he was going to wind up in jail. Sean hoped that wasn't true, but getting expelled from Atwood would surely be terrible, and their mother had said that if that happened, Kevin would have to go to public school. And if he got drunk again, they were going to send him to rehab. Kevin said he didn't care, and hadn't shown much remorse for the entire event. He said they'd had a lot of fun at the dance till they got caught. And he was on a major restriction for the moment, until the school made its decision, and would be for a long time after. He was in his sophomore year. To Izzie and Sean, it seemed like a lot of trouble to be in at fifteen, but that was Kevin. He was always in trouble for something, at school or at home.

'Your parents must be pretty scared,' Izzie said as they talked about it. Kevin was the only older boy she knew well, and he never paid much attention to her or Sean's other friends, except to call her 'Squirt' when he ran into her in the kitchen when she visited Sean. Kevin never talked to her at school. He was a tall, good-looking boy with jet-black hair like Sean's. He used to be on the baseball team, but he had dropped off the team earlier that year. He said sports weren't his thing, and Sean said their dad had been upset about it. He thought playing sports was good for him.

In the end, the school had agreed to suspend Kevin for two weeks, and put him on probation until the end of the year, but they didn't kick him out. Mike and Connie had gone to bat for him and convinced the school to give him another chance, but Mike had warned him, and so had the headmaster, that if he did something like it again, he would be out. Kevin said he understood, and behaved until the end of the year, and then left for survival camp in the Sierras. He looked stronger and more muscular and healthy when he came back, and was better behaved and seemed more responsible. He had turned sixteen by then, and Mike commented to Connie, when he got back, that he didn't look like a boy any more, he looked like a man.

The survival camp had given him confidence in himself, and they hoped it would turn him around.

'I wish he acted like a man,' Connie said with a sigh and a worried look. For the first few weeks, he was perfect and even helped his mother around the house. But Sean knew it was just an act. He saw Kevin sneak a beer a week after he got home, and he had a pack of cigarettes in his backpack. Sean never squealed on him to their parents, but he saw a lot, more than Kevin knew. Sean knew his brother well. He wasn't fooled.

Sean and Izzie walked in to the first day of fourth grade together when the carpool dropped them off, and the others – Billy, Andy, and Gabby – were right behind them. The five friends were always together, inseparable pals, wherever they went. It had been that way for four years, and they assumed it always would be. All five of them carved the words 'Friends 4Ever' into their school desks every year. It was a sacred pact they had made in second grade. And Connie always referred to them as the Big Five. They had been devoted to each other since kindergarten, and she hoped they always would be. They were a family they had formed on their own. Izzie and Gabby pretended to be sisters sometimes, with new teachers or strangers. And Billy, Andy, and Sean had once told someone at the bowling alley that they were triplets, and the person had believed them. The five of them were like quintuplets, with different parents and one heart and one soul. 'Friends 4Ever' above all.

Chapter 3

Nothing much changed for any of them until they reached eighth grade, and then a number of things began to happen to alter their familiar landscape. First, they all turned thirteen and became teenagers. They would be going to high school at Atwood in a year, which seemed like a major step into adulthood for them. Connie teased them that they were no different than they had been in kindergarten, they were just bigger. Sean was still obsessed with any kind of law enforcement, watched every possible crime and police show on TV, and had taken to reading books about the FBI. Billy was equally obsessed with sports, especially football, and had a huge collection of signed baseball and football cards. Gabby had gotten several more local modeling jobs and was in

The Nutcracker and two school plays, in the leading roles. Andy was at the top of their class with flawless grades, and Izzie was developing a strong social conscience and had done volunteer work at a homeless shelter for families, and collected toys for the children at Christmas. She even used her allowance to buy more toys than the donations covered.

Billy and Gabby were the first to announce a major change. They spent a lot of time together over Christmas vacation, and when they came back to school, they said they were boy friend and girlfriend.

'You are?' Izzie stared at her best friend with wide eyes when Gabby told her. 'What does that mean?' She lowered her voice conspiratorially and glanced over her shoulder to make sure no one was listening. 'Did you *do it*?' she whispered with a look of amazement, and Gabby laughed, that clear bell-like sound that Izzie was convinced would one day make her a movie star.

'Of course not, we're not stupid,' Gabby said confidently. 'We're not old enough to "do it." We're going to wait till high school or college. We just know we love each other.' She seemed absolutely certain, which impressed Izzie immensely.

'How do you know?' Izzie was fascinated. They all loved each other in their tight little group of friends, but she wouldn't have thought of becoming boyfriend and girlfriend with Sean, Andy, or Billy. As far as Izzie was concerned, they were best friends. So how did Billy and Gabby know they were different? What had happened to them over Christmas?

'He kissed me,' Gabby confessed to her, 'but don't tell my mother. We just decided to be boyfriend and girlfriend.' Gabby seemed extremely pleased about it, although she looked no different to Izzie. And they were the only two in the group who had kissed. There wasn't even a boy Izzie liked in eighth grade, and certainly not enough to kiss. 'You and Sean should hook up like we did,' Gabby said, sounding very grown-up and older than her years, but Izzie looked appalled.

'Yerghhhkkk! That's disgusting. He's my best friend!'

'I thought I was,' Gabby teased her, amused at her reaction to the suggestion about Sean. He was getting better and better looking as he got older, although he was still a lot shorter than Billy. But some of the other eighth-grade girls thought he was hot. Sean didn't care. He had no interest in girls yet, just crime shows and sports. And he treated Izzie like a sister.

'You know you are my best friend,' Izzie said uncomfortably. 'You all are. It just seems weird to have a boyfriend at our age.' Izzie looked confused and mildly

disapproving. But Gabby always seemed more sophisticated than the others, and Billy was physically more
mature. Gabby shrugged her shoulders, unconcerned.

'Yeah, maybe. He's nice to kiss, though,' Gabby said,
and Izzie looked a little shocked at that, and after talking
about it for a while, they walked into class together.

Billy had basketball practice that day and was in the
gym, but he had made the same announcement as Gabby
to Sean and Andy that morning. Both looked impressed
and wanted to know how far he'd gone with Gabby. Billy
said they'd made out but hadn't gone all the way. But his
two best guy friends were as shaken as Izzie. It was the
beginning of a whole new era in the group, now that Billy
and Gabby were a couple. It made the others feel like
losers and a little bit left out, since Gabby and Billy had
added an element to their relationship that they didn't
share. It felt very strange to the remaining singles in the
group, but gave Izzie no desire to have a boyfriend among
them, or outside the group. Andy and Sean were like the
brothers she didn't have, and she liked it that way. It
would have felt creepy to single out one of them as a
boyfriend, and she didn't want to.

It took a while for them to get used to thinking of Billy
and Gabby as a couple, but by spring they had all
adjusted and considered Billy and Gabby as a unit. The

romance was still going strong, and had remained chaste. Just 'going together,' hanging out, and kissing was enough. Larry had had a talk with Billy, at Marilyn's insistence, about using condoms and being careful that Gabby didn't get pregnant, but Billy insisted they didn't need them. His father looked disappointed, and his mother was relieved. Marilyn had a long talk with Judy the next day and asked her if she thought their kids were telling them the truth about not having had sex yet. She hoped they were, but she wasn't sure. One heard stories about some kids having sex even before high school.

'Gabby tells me *everything*,' Judy said confidently, and didn't seem worried. 'I want to get her on the Pill before she does anything, just in case.' She seemed surprisingly calm about it, although she hadn't mentioned it to Adam, because she knew how protective he was of his daughters, but he had commented on seeing Billy around more lately, so he was aware.

'They're just thirteen,' Marilyn said with a worried look. 'They're not old enough to handle a serious relationship and everything that goes with it.'

'Sometimes I'm not even sure I am,' Judy quipped, and Marilyn smiled ruefully, but she knew Judy was only kidding, she and Adam had a good marriage and seemed to still enjoy each other after fifteen years.

Marilyn and Larry had had a harder time of it for the past few years. His drinking had continued at a steady pace, and several times she had suspected he was having an affair, but he insisted that he wasn't. He liked to hang out with his important clients and sometimes didn't come home till three or four A.M., but he always swore there was nothing to it. Marilyn wasn't as sure, but she couldn't prove otherwise. And she spent a lot of time at home with her boys, Billy and Brian, who were thirteen and eight, and they kept her busy. It startled her sometimes that at thirty-eight, she had become a homebody. Larry hardly ever took her out any more. He went out with the 'guys.' She complained once in a while to her women friends, but there was nothing she could do about it. And when she said something to Larry, he got nasty and told her to stop whining. He reminded her that he gave her a nice house and plenty of money to spend and if she wanted someone to be around all the time, get a dog. He said he wasn't going to be on a leash for her. He had his freedom, whenever he wanted to get out, and she had the boys.

And he wasn't always pleasant to them either, depending on how much he'd been drinking. He ignored Brian completely because he was indifferent to sports, and the last time Billy had lost a baseball game on the Little

League team he played for, Larry had taken a swing at him when they got home and called him a loser. Billy had gone to his room in tears, and Marilyn and Larry had gotten into a fight that nearly came to blows. She had finally backed down and locked herself in her room. And he had gone out and didn't come back till the next morning. He never apologized, to any of them, and she sometimes wondered if he even remembered what he'd done the night before. Marilyn had apologized to Billy when his father hit him after the game, and tried to explain that his father was so obsessed with winning every game that he didn't know what he was doing. But they both knew he did. And Billy had signed up for the football team for freshman year. He was on a path, the only one that would please his father, and he was determined never to be called a loser again.

Marilyn and Judy talked about their children's relationship often. Marilyn was as worried about Gabby as if she'd been her own daughter, and was terrified they'd lose control and have sex. By contrast, Judy was astoundingly relaxed and confident in her daughter.

'Gabby's too smart for that,' Judy said calmly. But Marilyn knew plenty of girls who had been smart, lost control, and wound up pregnant. Marilyn didn't want that happening to their kids, and hoped they would avert a disaster before it happened. It was a lot to expect at thirteen.

Connie had pointed out to both Judy and Marilyn that Kevin had become sexually active at thirteen, although her younger son, Sean, was far from it. All kids were different and moved at different speeds through adolescence.

For the moment, Connie's worries with Kevin had abated. He was a junior at UC Santa Cruz by then and doing well. He looked like a hippie, with tattoos, piercings, and long hair, but his grades had been decent for two semesters. It gave her some respite, but she worried about him anyway. He called from Santa Cruz from time to time, but not often. He loved being on his own and independent, and Connie concentrated her efforts on Sean, knowing that he needed attention and guidance, and at twenty Kevin would have to be responsible for himself at school.

The star student in the group, among the five friends, was always Andy. It was expected of him, and both his parents never questioned for a moment that Andy would get straight A's. He never let them down, and said he wanted to be a doctor, like his parents. A medical doctor like his mother, not a psychiatrist like his father. Andy wanted to heal people's bodies, not their minds, but he wanted to go to Harvard, like his father. Just like the A's he got in school, that was expected, and he got the science prize every year. Andy had real talent in science, and sometimes Izzie teased him and called him 'doctor.' He actually liked it. He was good in sports now, and had a natural athlete's grace. He was on the tennis team at school, and entered tournaments on weekends. His four friends always went to see him play, just as they went to Sean and Billy's baseball games, and the boys showed up to root for Gabby and Izzie when they played girls' basketball and soccer.

Larry was always at the baseball games, and shouted at Billy during the entire game, telling him what he should be doing. He had a fit after the game, whenever they lost, and Sean tried to intercede for Billy with his father several times, and got Larry angry at him too.

'Mr. Norton, we played a good game today,' Sean stood up to him bravely. 'Billy hit two home runs, which is more than anyone else did on either team.' After the game was over, the coach had even congratulated him for how well he played.

'He screwed up when the bases were loaded, or we'd have won. Or didn't you notice?' he said nastily to Sean, who refused to be intimidated by Billy's father. No one liked Larry, and neither did Sean, who hated to see what he did to Billy. And Mr. Norton didn't even bother to talk to Brian, who came to all his brother's games too. Larry still acted like Brian didn't exist. As far as Larry was concerned, since he wasn't an athlete, he didn't. 'I don't know what you're talking about, O'Hara,' he said viciously to Sean, 'you can't hit the ball for shit. They ought to kick you off the team, and have you play volleyball with the girls.'

'That's enough, Dad,' Billy said quietly, defending his friend. He could see that his father had been drinking, and Billy was mortified by the way he was behaving. He was used to his father's verbal abuse at home, but he didn't want his friends to know.

'You're a pathetic bunch of sissies,' Larry said, stormed off, got in his car, and drove away, as Billy looked at Sean and shrugged. He had tears in his eyes as Sean put an arm around his shoulders, and they walked into the locker room together without a word. Brian was waiting for them when they came back dressed in jeans and out of their uniforms. Brian had watched the entire scene and felt sorry for both of them. He loved to watch them play. None of the three boys commented on Larry's behavior. They were used to it, and everyone had seen him drive away in a rage. As they left the field, Billy caught up with Gabby, who was waiting for him too. Billy put an arm

around her waist and hugged her when she compli-
mented him on the two home runs.

'Yeah, whatever,' he said, brushing it off, trying to
forget his father, and smiling down at her. Billy was six
feet tall at thirteen, and looked more like sixteen than the
age he was, and Gabby looked older too, with a grown-
up haircut and the little bit of makeup her mother let her
wear. They were a cute couple and a familiar sight now.
And Gabby always gave him support about his difficulties
at home. They met up with the others then for hamburgers and ice cream after the game, and Billy took
Brian along, which made his day. The Big Five were
always great to him.

The five best friends spent spring vacation fooling around
together with nothing much to do. They went to baseball
games, and swimming at a friend's pool in the Napa
Valley, when they were invited up for the day. Connie and
Mike O'Hara organized a backyard barbecue for them,
and the day after, they got a call from UC Santa Cruz,
and the police. Kevin had gotten arrested for possession
with intent to sell and use of marijuana at school. He was
accused of selling it to fellow students, even though they
had no proof. He was in jail, pending arraignment. The
police sergeant Mike spoke to said he could be facing as

much as four years in prison, and he was being expelled from school. Kevin was twenty, and something like this was exactly what his parents had feared for years, and Mike had predicted. Kevin lived by his own rules, and no one else's. Not his parents' rules, or the school's, or even the state's.

He called them from jail that afternoon, and Mike had already called his lawyer. They were going down to Santa Cruz the next day for the arraignment. Kevin wanted them to bail him out of jail that night, but Mike told Connie it would do him good to spend the night in jail and think about what he was doing. They were terrified for him, and so was Sean. His brother's free and easy ways didn't coincide with Sean's passion for law and order. He still dreamed of joining the police force one day, and lately had said he wanted to work for the FBI or the CIA after college. His ideas were as far as you could get from Kevin's.

The next day Sean looked glum when he went to stay at Billy's house, while his parents went to get Kevin out of jail. And the lawyer made a strong case for dismissing the charges and sending Kevin to rehab. The judge had been open to it, and set a hearing for two weeks later, which gave them very little time to find a rehab program for him, and present the option to the judge. And much to his parents' despair, his days at UC Santa Cruz were over for good. They were devastated by the situation he was in.

Kevin looked cocky when he got home, and didn't seem shaken by his night in jail, the charges, or his expulsion from school. They had brought his things home, and Sean saw that he was keeping a backpack close to him. Sean was sure there were drugs in it, and he thought Kevin looked stoned late that afternoon, but their parents didn't notice. Sean was furious at him. Kevin had no respect for their parents, their home, or even himself. He had just gotten out of jail and had used drugs again. Sean was sure.

'You're going to kill Mom and Dad,' Sean said miserably when he slipped into his brother's room an hour later. Kevin was lying on his bed, listening to music with the TV on. Sean didn't know what he'd taken, but whatever it was, he seemed happy.

'Don't give me any of your pious bullshit lectures,' Kevin said, looking at his little brother standing in the middle of the room. There were worlds between the two brothers. 'You're not a cop yet, even if you think like one.'

'Dad's right,' Sean said quietly. He had lost all respect for his brother, and hated what he was doing to their parents. Their mother had been crying for two days, and their father had cried when he told her what had happened. They felt defeated and didn't know what to do to stop him. 'You're going to wind up in prison.' He had seen the scenario a thousand times on the TV show she watched.

'No, little wimp, I'll probably wind up on probation. This isn't the big deal they make it out to be. It's just marijuana, for chrissake, not crystal meth or crack. Just a little weed.' But not so little – he had had a considerable amount on him and in his car when he ran a red light and they suspected him of being under the influence.

'It's illegal,' Sean said, still standing there and watching him. Kevin looked perfectly relaxed, stretched out on his bed. He had been so stoned when they arrested him that he hardly remembered the night in jail, and had slept like a baby. 'Maybe next time it will be crack, or crystal meth, or mushrooms or LSD, or some of the other crap you do with your friends.'

'What do you know about what I do with my friends?' Kevin asked angrily. His brother was turning into a narc.

'I hear things.'

'You're just a baby, Sean. You don't know what you're talking about.'

'Yes, I do. And so do you. I swear, I'll kick your ass when I'm older if you do this to them again,' Sean said.

He was trembling with rage, and his older brother just laughed at him and pointed to the door of his room.

'I'm shaking in my shoes, little guy. Now get your ass out of my room before I kick yours.' He was like someone who had come from another world, another family. He was a stranger in their midst and always had been. Kevin would always find a way to do what he wanted. He always had, no matter what the consequences to him and everyone else.

Sean left his room quietly, and for the next two days his parents met with counselors and lawyers. They had found a drug rehab in Arizona that would take him, and the lawyer was going to make a presentation to the judge asking if Kevin could plead to a lesser charge and be sent to rehab as probation with no jail time. It wasn't a sure thing, and the day before they went to court, his father made him cut his hair and shave his beard. Kevin objected, but he had no choice in the matter. His father handed him a suit and told him to wear it. Mike's eyes were smoldering when he did. 'I don't want you doing this to your mother ever again,' he said through clenched teeth, barely able to control his temper, and Kevin nodded. Mike handed him a shirt and tie to go with it, and a pair of his own dress shoes since they wore the same size and he didn't want to go downtown with him to buy new ones. For two weeks, Kevin had hung around the house, and they wouldn't let him go anywhere. He didn't like the plan they had in mind, but it sounded better even to him than four years in jail, if they threw the book at him.

The ride to Santa Cruz was long and silent. It took nearly three hours to get there in traffic from San Francisco, and they had agreed to meet their lawyer outside the courtroom. They had an official letter from the rehab in Arizona, accepting him, and it was becoming more real to him as they walked into the courthouse. Kevin looked scared, though not as much as his parents. They had dropped off Sean to stay with Billy, and Marilyn was going to take both boys to baseball practice that afternoon.

The judge listened to what the O'Haras' attorney was suggesting, and made no comment as he looked over the letter he handed him, with the description of the rehab and what it offered.

'You're a very lucky young man,' he said to Kevin after he read the information about the rehab. 'A lot of parents would turn their back on you and let you go to jail. And it might do you a world of good, if they did,' he said sternly. 'What I'm about to do, I'm going to do for them, more than I am for you. And you'd better make good use of it, or you will wind up in jail. I'm sentencing you to six months at this rehabilitation facility in Arizona, which sounds like a country club to me. You'd better stay there for the entire six months. If you leave one day early, I'm sending you to jail. And I'm giving you two years' probation. If you break the law at any time during those two years, you're going to jail. Is that understood?' Kevin nodded, barely able to conceal his anger. Six months in rehab sounded like a nightmare to him, and all thanks to his parents, for whom he felt no gratitude at that exact moment. He was screwed. The judge said he had twenty-four hours to turn himself in to the facility in Arizona, and he wanted proof that he'd been admitted. He asked Kevin if he had anything to say for himself, and he didn't. Mike spoke up in a hoarse voice instead and thanked the judge for his compassion. 'Good luck with your boy,' he said gently, as tears swam in Mike's eyes, and ran down Connie's cheeks. It had been an agonizing and terrifying two weeks.

The drive back to San Francisco was as silent as the trip down. Mike had his secretary make reservations on a flight to Arizona at seven A.M. the next day. He was flying Kevin there himself, to be sure he got there and didn't run away.

Kevin went straight to his room when he got home, and openly smoked a joint in his bedroom. They could smell it but didn't go in. The nightmare was almost over, and he'd be in rehab the next day, as long as he didn't walk out while facing the rigors of the program, or forget that if he did, he would wind up in jail.

Once Kevin went upstairs, and she and Mike changed out of their court clothes, Connie went to pick up Sean at Billy's. They had just come home from baseball practice. When she drove up, Sean looked at his mother with worried eyes. His brother acted like a jerk sometimes, but he loved him anyway. He was his brother after all, and Sean didn't want him to go to jail.

'Did he go to jail?' Sean asked in a voice filled with panic, and his mother shook her head. She looked exhausted and beaten.

'No, they're sending him to rehab in Arizona for six months, and he got two years' probation, so he'd better behave. If he leaves the rehab or screws up again, he'll go to jail.' It was good news, but didn't feel like it to her yet. She was only too aware of the risks, and she had no idea to what degree Kevin would cooperate or for how long. They would be going down for family weekends, to engage in therapy sessions with him, and Sean might even have to go too. Kevin was putting them all through the wringer. It was the worst thing he'd done so far, and it wasn't over yet.

'He'll be okay, Mom,' Sean said to reassure her, but he didn't fully believe it himself.

While Connie was talking to Sean and Billy, Marilyn came outside to ask what had happened, and Connie told her with a tone of immense relief. He had gotten rehab, not jail. Marilyn could see how strained and exhausted Connie was, and put her arms around her friend and gave her a hug. Connie looked as rocky as she felt. Billy stood there silently watching them, he didn't know what to say. He gave Sean a friendly slap on the back and a shove before he left, which was his way of saying how sorry he was. Sean looked up at him with a grin. And Izzie called Sean at home that night, to ask him what had happened.

'So is he going to jail?'

'No. Not this time anyway. But if he screws up again, he probably will. I don't know what's wrong with him, he's always been a pain in the ass,' Sean said, sounding tired himself. He had worried about his brother all day, and about his parents, who were so visibly devastated by what Kevin had done and by what could happen to him.

'Some people are just different, I guess,' Izzie said quietly. 'Even in the same family. How's your mom?' They had all been worried about her. Kevin's arrest had been such a shock.

'She's a mess. She's not saying anything, but she looks like she was hit by a bus. So does my dad. He's taking Kev to Phoenix tomorrow.'

'Is Kevin scared?' Izzie asked, impressed by what was happening. He was the first person they knew who was going to rehab.

'No, I think he's pissed. He's not saying much, and he came down to dinner tonight stoned off his ass. My parents didn't see it, but I could tell. Dad told him he had to come down for Mom. She cried all through dinner.' It sounded awful to Izzie, and she could hear the strain of it in Sean's voice, who hated to see his parents so upset.

Mike and Kevin left the next morning before Sean got up. Connie got up to say goodbye to her son and tried to hug him, but he shook her off and turned away, and that was more than Mike could take, and he grabbed his arm, hard.

'Say a decent goodbye to your mother,' he said through clenched teeth, and Kevin hugged her as she cried. They left then, while it was still dark, and she lay in bed and sobbed. Mike came back alone late that night, and he burst into tears when he sat down on their bed, and Connie took him in her arms and held him to comfort him.

'How was he when you left him?' Connie asked about Kevin.

'He looked like he hated me. He just turned his back on me and walked away.' Kevin had already forgotten that a judge had put him there, not his parents.

The O'Hara house seemed instantly too quiet without Kevin, although he'd already been away at college. But his recent presence had seemed larger than life, with his hostility, his clandestine drinking and dope smoking, and the stress he caused everyone around him. At first the peace without him seemed unnatural and unfamiliar. Sean missed the idea of a big brother, but the reality of Kevin was never what he hoped.

Sean alternated studying and distracting himself by watching TV. His favorite shows were still the crime shows, and Izzie came over to study with him a few times. She baked him his favorite cookies, and cupcakes for him and his parents. It was hard to know what to do to help: she could see the sadness in their eyes, even Sean's.

Sean was quiet for the next few weeks, and was starting to feel better when they had midterms to get through. Izzie was halfway through studying for them when her father knocked on her bedroom door and asked her to come into the living room one night. She followed him out of her room with a look of surprise, and was instantly scared when she saw her mother waiting on the couch, looking tense.

'Am I in trouble?' Izzie asked, looking from one to the other. She couldn't think of anything bad she'd done, but you never knew. Anything was possible. Maybe school had called to say she'd flunked all her tests. If they had, it would have been a first.

'Your mother and I have something to tell you,' Jeff said quietly, after he sat down. Izzie was sitting in a chair, and everything about the scene was strange. Her mother wouldn't look at her, and the room was so quiet that Izzie could hear the antique wall clock ticking in the hall. She couldn't remember ever hearing it from the living room before, but no one was talking. 'We're getting a divorce,' Jeff said with a look of defeat.

Izzie stared at them with wide eyes, with no idea what to say in response. *How awful? How could you? Why? Don't you love each other? What's going to happen to me now?* A thousand thoughts raced through her mind, but nothing came out of her mouth. She wanted to scream or cry, but she couldn't do either. All she could do was stare from one to the other, and finally her mother dragged her eyes to hers.

'Whose idea was it?' was the only thing Izzie could think of to say. But she was sure it was her mother's. She always acted like she didn't really want to be there.

'Both of ours,' her father answered as Katherine looked

at her husband and daughter like strangers. She had felt like a stranger in their midst for years. She had never wanted children and had told Jeff that when they married. They had met when they were both in law school, and he had had big corporate ambitions then, but he later changed his mind and fell in love with the work he was doing for the ACLU. He took a summer job with them and never left, and turned it into an internship while he continued school.

Katherine's ambitions and goals had never changed, but Jeff had become a different person over the years. He had thought that having a baby would help their marriage and be good for them, and had promised to do everything he could to help her, and he had. He had been far more attentive to Izzie than she was, and Katherine knew it. But even after Izzie was born, much to her own horror, she had never warmed up to the idea. As far as she was concerned, it was a terrible mistake. And there was a human being involved. Izzie was a wonderful little girl, but Katherine didn't feel like a mother, never had, and still didn't now. She knew it was some important piece missing in her. She couldn't bond. She felt guilty about it, and she hated Jeff for forcing her to do it, or talking her into it. He had been so convincing. Katherine's own parents had always been cold with her, and nothing in her background had taught her how to be a mother, and in her heart of hearts she didn't want to learn. She felt like a monster every time she looked at her own child, and she knew that Izzie knew it too. Jeff had denied it for as long as he could, but although he hadn't admitted it to Izzie, he had asked for the divorce, and Katherine had been relieved.

'Your mother has a very important new job,' Jeff explained. 'She's going to be the senior counsel for a very large corporation, and she's going to be traveling a lot of the time. That's not the way that either of us want to be married. Sometimes things change between two people,' he said, looking at his daughter. 'Our marriage no longer makes sense with your mother's work.'

'So you're dumping us for your new job?' Izzie said to her mother with an anguished expression, and Katherine felt a knife slice through her heart. She had always known that she shouldn't have children, and Izzie was paying the price for it now. Even she knew how wrong that was, but it didn't change how she felt about it, or the maternal instincts she didn't have. And Izzie knew that most of all. She had never been able to win her mother's affection, or even more than a small slice of her time. She had grown up feeling like an imposition, and in many ways, in her mother's life, she was. Jeff tried to make up for it, but he was her father, not her mother, and Izzie had been starved all her life for a mother's love. And now she was leaving. For a job.

'I'm not dumping you,' Katherine said, looking at her daughter, knowing she should hold her arms out to her, but she couldn't. 'Your father and I have drafted a very fair agreement. You'll be spending three days with him every week, followed by three days with me, when I'm in town. And you can spend Sundays with whichever of us is available. Or we can just do three days straight and three days on a revolving schedule, whichever you prefer.' It sounded sensible to her, for a business deal, but not for a child.

'Are you serious?' Izzie asked with a look of horror. 'You expect me to bounce between the two of you, like some kind of ball you're throwing at each other, or a dog? How am I supposed to live any kind of life like that? I'll be packing my suitcase every three days. I'd rather be an orphan and live in an institution. I can't live like that. It's insane.'

Katherine looked surprised, and Jeff didn't say anything. The difficulties for Izzie had occurred to him too, but Katherine thought it was 'fair.' 'I suppose we could alternate weeks, if that works better for you,' she said to Izzie, like a client she was trying to satisfy.

'I don't want to go back and forth between the two of you,' Izzie said as tears sprang to her eyes. They were destroying her life. 'You're both crazy. I can't live like that. It's not my fault you don't love each other, and you got a new job. Why are you taking it out on me?'

'But that's what joint custody is all about,' Katherine said calmly, trying not to react to the distress in her daughter's eyes. She would never have asked for the divorce – she had made her peace with the living arrangement they had. But when she told Jeff about the new job, he had asked for the divorce. And when she thought about it, it made sense to her too, and Izzie was old enough to understand.

'I'm not a piece of furniture that you can shove back and forth at each other and expect to move twice a week.'

'You'll get used to it. It may even have some advantages for you. I just found a very nice apartment downtown, near my office, in a building with a pool.'

'I don't want a pool. I need a mother and a father and a home. Can't you work this out, or something?' But the moment she asked the question, they both shook their heads.

'We both deserve a better life than this. Our marriage hasn't worked for a long time,' Jeff said sadly. 'And I'm sorry this is hard on you.'

'A year from now, when you're fourteen, you can tell the judge what you want. But right now, it's up to your father and me to come up with an equitable arrangement,' Katherine explained again.

'Equitable for who? Doesn't it count what I think?' They both stared at her blankly, and didn't know what to do. 'I think joint custody sucks, and so do you,' Izzie said, and ran into her room and slammed the door. She called Gabby and burst into tears and told her what had happened. Gabby couldn't believe it and told her that she could stay with them as often as she liked. But Izzie didn't want to stay with Gabby, she wanted her own home. She called Sean and Andy after that, and they were both sorry for her.

Izzie lay in her bed and cried all night, and the next day at breakfast her father told her that they would try to set it up some way that was easier for her.

'Maybe you can do a week at a time with each of us, or two weeks, or a month. You could stay here all the time if it were up to me, but you have to see your mother too.'

'Why? She's going to be traveling all the time anyway. Why don't you two alternate, and let me stay here all the time? I've heard of parents who do that.'

'I think that would be pretty uncomfortable for us,' Jeff said unhappily, hating what they were putting Izzie through, but the marriage had been over for years. He had been going to group therapy for a year, and he didn't want to live in a dead marriage anymore, with a woman who didn't love him, and whom he no longer loved. But Izzie was the casualty of it now too.

'But it's okay to make me uncomfortable, I guess,' she said bitterly as she pushed her cornflakes around the bowl with a spoon. And then she looked at him unhappily. 'Just don't blame me if I flunk out of school. I can't get decent grades and be moving three times a week, because you and Mom don't like each other anymore. And the minute I turn fourteen, I'm going to tell the judge that I won't go back and forth between the two of you, so you'd better figure out something else.'

'We'll try,' her father said sadly, but he couldn't think of anything yet. And a moment later he heard the front door close, as Izzie left for school.

The only thing that comforted her that day, and for the next many months, was her friends. She spent as much time as she could at the O'Haras', being loved and nurtured by Connie, and she stayed with Gabby now and then, which helped too. Judy was a warm person, and she had always been very fond of Izzie, and felt sorry for her in the divorce. And Gabby and Michelle were very sympathetic and supportive, as were all her friends.

The custody arrangement with Katherine never really worked. She was out of town almost every time Izzie was supposed to stay with her, and eventually they dropped the plan of having her go back and forth between her parents, like a tennis ball. Instead, she stayed with her father, and went to her mother for a night once in a while on the weekend. Katherine took her to dinner, and let her bring Gabby over to swim in the pool. Sometimes Izzie went for a month without seeing her, or longer, but even when she saw her, Izzie knew that her mother had never really been there. What she had to sustain her was a father who loved her, and four terrific friends. And Connie O'Hara, as a loving adopted aunt. It wasn't everything you were supposed to have in life, but all put together, it seemed to work for Izzie.

Chapter 4

The first big event of sophomore year in high school was that Billy and Gabby 'did it,' the weekend before Thanksgiving. She confided it to Izzie the next day, and to her mother the day after. She assured her mother that they had used a condom, and she admitted to Izzie that it hadn't been quite as fabulous as she'd hoped. Billy had gone off like fireworks on the fourth of July, a little faster than either of them had expected, and it had hurt, a lot. They were both virgins, but the best part was the tenderness between them. They had been 'going together' for two years, had never cheated on each other or looked at anyone else. They were crazy about each other, and Gabby said that having 'done it' strengthened the bond they shared. And her mother was very nice about it. Judy

was concerned about the responsibility they'd under-
taken, but grateful that Gabby was honest about it, so she
knew what was happening in her daughter's life.

By the end of the weekend, all of the Big Five, as
Connie still called them, knew. Billy didn't brag about it,
but something about the way they stood even closer to
each other, looked at each other as though they had a
secret, let everybody know what had happened. Izzie still
thought they were too young to have sex with each other,
but Gabby and Billy never doubted for a minute that
they loved each other and felt ready to take on the
responsibilities that went with it. He was responsible
about using condoms, and Gabby told her mother she
wanted to go on the Pill, so she didn't get pregnant. They
managed to do it two more times, at Billy's when his
mother was out, his father was at work, and Brian was in
school. They had a break in their school schedule over
lunchtime, and the second time it was better, and the
third time it was great. They were glad they had finally
decided to add sex to their relationship.

Judy took Gabby to Planned Parenthood the day
before Thanksgiving and she got the Pill, and the others
suddenly felt very immature and as though they had been
left out. None of the others had a girlfriend or a
boyfriend. Andy spent all his time studying, Sean was

quiet, not as massive in size as Billy, and he always complained that girls never even looked at him. And Izzie had spent the last two years surviving her parents' divorce. She hardly ever saw her mother, although Katherine called her frequently from other cities to see how she was, and once in a while they spent a weekend together, but not very often. And in some ways, Izzie missed her. It was weird to no longer have a mother in the house, and one she hardly ever saw. It felt sad sometimes. Jeff tried to make up for her mother's indifference and absence. But there were times when she really missed having a mom she saw every day, no matter how busy Katherine had been before the divorce.

Jeff hadn't met anyone he cared about deeply yet, but he'd been dating for about a year. Whenever he brought someone home, he had to live with Izzie's editorial comments, and she was usually right. He had no desire to get married again, but he would have liked to find a woman he loved enough to live with, particularly when Izzie left for college in two years. He knew just how lonely he would be when she did, and he had no illusions that she would stay in San Francisco. Izzie wanted to see more of the world, even if she came back to the city after that. And Jeff realized that he would have no personal life without her. Everything he did revolved around his daughter.

For the past few months Jeff had been dating a woman at work whom he seemed to like, and he brought her home to have dinner with Izzie. And Izzie hated her. He was fifty-three by then, and the young lawyer he was dating was in her early thirties, and Izzie pointed out to him the next day that she was too young for him, and he looked embarrassed. It had occurred to him too, but it was awkward having it pointed out by his fifteen-year-old daughter, who was closer to her age than he was, though not by much. But women his own age didn't appeal to him.

'I'm not marrying her. She's just a date,' he said to Izzie.

'Just keep it that way,' Izzie said sternly. 'Besides, she's not as smart as you are.'

'What makes you think that?' He looked startled.

'She kept asking what things mean, things that she ought to know, as a lawyer. Either she's playing stupid, or she really is. Either way, you deserve better,' Izzie said as she rinsed their breakfast dishes and put them in the dishwasher. She was very much the woman of the house now, and had a comfortable adult relationship with her father.

'No one is ever going to be as smart as your mother,' he said matter-of-factly. 'I'm not sure I was either.

Probably not.' Or as cold, he thought to himself, but didn't say it. 'I'm not sure I need to be with a genius, or even want to. Just a nice, friendly woman,' he said, and Izzie looked at him from across the kitchen.

'You need a smart one, Dad. A dumb one would get boring.' Her mother was dating someone too, the CEO of the company she worked for. He was recently divorced. Izzie hadn't met him yet, but her mother had told her. In the two years since her parents' divorce, she had grown wise beyond her years.

They had no particular plans for Thanksgiving, so he accepted an invitation for both of them from one of his co-workers at the ACLU, a nice divorced woman with two children roughly the same age as Izzie, and she had invited about a dozen other people. It sounded like an easy invitation and a nice way to spend the day. Katherine was in New York on business, and spending the holiday with friends there.

The O'Haras were planning to entertain relatives and friends and had much to be thankful for this year. Kevin had done well in rehab, and returned as the boy they always hoped he would be. At twenty-two, he was going to City College, getting good grades, and hoping to graduate the year. It was an enormous relief to them, and the two boys were getting on well. Kevin had apologized to Sean in a family therapy session in Arizona for being such a bad brother to him until then. He had been a different person when he got home.

Andy and his parents were visiting relatives of his mother's in South Carolina. Judy and Adam were going to the Fairmont Hotel with Michelle, and Gabby was spending Thanksgiving with the Nortons. Marilyn had planned a family dinner with Larry, her two boys, and Gabby. It was a meal Marilyn always prepared, and she did it well, and Gabby had promised to help her.

Gabby got to Billy's house early enough to help Marilyn get things ready. She had taken out her best linen tablecloth, and Billy and Gabby set the table together. They set it with Marilyn's best china and crystal, and the turkey smelled delicious as she basted it. They were planning to have six o'clock dinner, and Larry had gone to watch football at a friend's, and said he'd be home in time for dinner. But at six o'clock he still wasn't back and didn't answer his cell phone when Marilyn called him. They waited for him until seven. The turkey was getting dry by then, and Marilyn was fiercely upset.

They sat down to dinner at seven-thirty, an hour and a half later than planned. The biscuits were slightly burned, and the turkey and stuffing were undeniably dry. No one mentioned Larry's absence during dinner, and Marilyn served pumpkin and apple pies for dessert, with home-made vanilla ice cream. And after they got up from the table, the boys and Gabby helped her clean up. By ten-thirty, everything was put away, and Gabby pretended not to notice Marilyn crying as she walked upstairs, just as Larry walked in, trying to act as though nothing had happened. The kids disappeared like mice, and went down to the playroom in the basement to watch a movie.

Marilyn turned and looked at him from the stairs. Her voice was flat, but her eyes were blazing. He looked as though he'd been drinking all day.

'Where were you?' She had been worried about it all night.

'I had dinner with a friend,' he said, as though it were any other day and not Thanksgiving. But he wasn't fooling anyone but himself.

'You missed Thanksgiving dinner,' Marilyn said, as their eyes met.

'Sorry, I had something else to do,' he said brusquely, pushing past her on the stairs, and as he did, she could smell liquor on his breath and see lipstick on his collar, a great smear of it that felt like a slap in her face.

'You're disgusting,' she said under her breath, and as soon as she did, he grabbed her arm and yanked her toward him.

'I don't give a damn what you think,' he said, and then pushed her away. She nearly lost her balance and fell down the stairs, but caught herself with the banister before she did.

'Did you have to do that tonight?' she said, as she followed him to their bedroom. He looked disoriented for a minute, and she realized just how drunk he was. He walked across the room unsteadily and sat down on the bed. He had been with another woman all day.

'I'll do it whenever I damn well want to. I don't give a damn about Thanksgiving anyway. Or about you,' he added for good measure, and she was grateful that the boys couldn't hear him. As she looked at him, she wondered why she had stayed for so long, why she had put up with the insults and the degradation, the drinking and the disappointment, and the pain of knowing or suspecting he was cheating on her all the time. She had told herself she did it for the boys, but now she wasn't sure. Maybe she was just afraid to be alone, or to lose a husband she hadn't loved in years. There was nothing in Larry to love, and she knew he didn't love her.

'Go back to wherever you were today. I don't want you here with the kids, in the condition you're in,' she said calmly.

'What are you talking about?' He looked unconcerned and lay down on the bed. She could tell as she looked at him that the room was spinning for him, and she didn't care.

'I'm telling you to leave,' she said, standing over him and looking down. He took a swing at her and she moved out of range. 'If you don't get up right now, I'm calling the police.'

'My ass, you will. Just shut up. I'm going to sleep.' She picked up the phone and started to dial 911. She wouldn't have done it, but she wanted him to think she would. He was off the bed in seconds, and ripped the phone from her hands and threw it at the wall, and then he backhanded her across the face before she could get away from him. He hit her hard, and she looked at him with a hatred she never knew she had in her. There was a thin trickle of blood running down her cheek.

'Get out, Larry. Now!' Something in her eyes told him she meant it. He grabbed his jacket off the bed, walked out of the bedroom, hurried down the stairs, and slammed the front door a moment later. She was shaking from head to foot, and she quietly closed her bedroom door so the kids wouldn't see her when they came upstairs. And she burst into tears as she sat on the bed. It was over, and should have been years before.

She called Larry the next morning. Before he could come home again, and told him not to come back.

'You can pick up your things next week. I'm changing the locks today. I want a divorce.' Her voice was unemotional and cold.

'You pissed me off last night. You shouldn't have done that.' He had blamed her dozens of times before, when he slapped her, humiliated her, flirted with other women, or came home too drunk to stand up. And she had put up with it. The boys had seen her treated in ways she never should have allowed, and she suspected that he had been cheating on her for years.

'I'm done, Larry. I'm filing for divorce.'

'Don't be insane.' He tried to brush it off. 'I'll be home in a couple of hours.'

'I'll call the police if you come near this house. And I mean it.' He could hear that she did, and with that she hung up.

When she heard the boys stirring, she went downstairs to make breakfast for them. She had called the locksmith by then, and he changed the locks in less than half an hour. She asked for extra keys for the boys. She handed them their new keys after she had served them breakfast, and then she sat down at the kitchen table with them.

'Don't give that key to your father when you see him.

We're getting a divorce.' Neither of them looked shocked when she said it. Billy looked sad, and Brian seemed relieved. His father had belittled him for years because he didn't want to play sports.

'Because he didn't come home last night?' Billy asked her quietly. 'Maybe he was with an important client.' Billy always made excuses for his father, he was incredibly loyal.

'For all the reasons that all three of us know. His drinking, the other women, the way he treats me and Brian, and even you sometimes,' she said, looking at Billy. 'I hope he deals with his drinking now, but whether he does or not, I'm done.' It had been too many years of being disrespected and abused. She had let him do it, but she just couldn't anymore. Hitting her the night before had been the last straw. 'I don't want him back in this house. You can visit him when he gets his own place.'

'Do I have to go?' Brian asked her quietly, and she shook her head.

'You can't just throw him out like that, Mom,' Billy said, near tears. 'This is his home too. He has nowhere else to go.'

'He can afford a hotel.' And then as she turned toward him, Billy saw the thin mark on her cheek and the bruise around it, and he knew that his father had gone too far.

He got up from the table and went to his room. He didn't call Gabby, he called Izzie, and she could tell something was wrong the minute she heard his voice.

'Are you okay?' she was quick to ask him, and he started to cry as soon as she did.

'I think my dad hit my mom last night. He's done it before. He didn't come home for Thanksgiving dinner. They're getting a divorce. I'm just like you now,' he said, sounding like an anguished child. But no one had struck anyone at Izzie's house. Her parents just didn't like each other anymore, and it had been simple and clean. But Izzie knew that no one liked Billy's dad, he was a jerk and a drunk, he was even mean to Billy, who was crying for him. 'What's it going to be like now?' He was scared, and he felt as though all the responsibility was on him. He was the only ally his father had left.

'It'll be better,' Izzie reassured him. 'Your mom will be happier, and she won't be so upset. And it'll be good for Brian too.' She had seen how cruel Mr. Norton could be to his younger son. 'You'll be okay. I promise. It's actually better now for me too. It took me a while to get used to not having my mom here, but she was never really here anyway. And your dad isn't either. He's always out with clients or friends, drinking. You said so yourself.' She could hear Billy calm down as they talked.

'It's going to be really strange to not have him here,' Billy said sadly. He didn't like the idea of his parents getting divorced, but he didn't like how his dad treated his mom either, and she was unhappy all the time, and had been for years. There was no pretending any more.

'Yeah, it'll be weird for a while,' Izzie agreed with him, there was no point in lying, and she never did, 'but then it will be good.' He didn't answer for a long time, and then they talked some more for a few minutes. Izzie was supportive and comforting as she always was. They all considered her the wise woman in their midst and the person they could count on for reassurance and emotional support. It was just like when she'd made them all lunch on the first day of kindergarten, to make them feel comfortable and at home. Izzie was there for each of them when things got though for them. Billy looked and felt better by the time they hung up. There was so much to say, and to worry about. All Billy knew for sure now was how grateful he was to have his friends. He couldn't have gotten through any of it without them. They were the greatest gift he had.

And when he saw his mother a little while later, she already looked better, and Brian was smiling when he came downstairs. And Billy wondered if Izzie was right.

She usually was. Billy went to see Gabby then, to tell her the news. She wasn't surprised. They talked for a long time that morning.

Chapter 5

A year later, during junior year of high school for the Big Five, Brian and Billy had become latchkey kids, they were old enough to handle it. Billy was sixteen and kept an eye on Brian, who was eleven. Billy usually had football practice after school, but when he did Brian hung around to watch. He loved watching Billy play. His big brother was the star quarterback. Gabby came to watch him too. They were still the only real couple in school, but they handled it responsibly, and even the teachers were touched by how devoted they were to each other. Gabby had helped get Billy through the divorce, and so had his other friends. Izzie was his adviser in all matters relating to the divorce, since she'd been through it herself. And the only thing Izzie hadn't prepared him for, because she hadn't experienced it herself, was that his mother started dating right away, which upset him. And his father was going out with hordes of young girls, most of them only a few years older than Billy. Larry made no secret of the fact that he was sleeping with every hot young body he could lay his hands on. In fact, he bragged about it to anyone who would listen, even his son, and his drinking hadn't improved. It had gotten worse. He was out of control, and Billy worried about him.

Marilyn had gotten a job almost immediately selling residential and commercial real estate. She had passed the exam and was doing well at a large firm, learning the ropes, and she seemed to have a knack for it, and enjoyed it. She had gotten their house in the divorce, and after seventeen years of marriage, Larry had to pay her spousal support, and although he complained about it to Billy, he could afford it. Marilyn's whole life had turned around. The divorce had been final for six months, and as soon as it was, she had met Jack Ellison, a good-looking man in his late forties, divorced, with two boys of his own in Chicago. He owned a successful restaurant downtown that was a popular meeting place for businesspeople for lunch or dinner. It wasn't chic or trendy, but it was a solid business. He had opened a second equally popular restaurant in the Napa Valley the year before.

Jack was nice to her boys, and she was crazy about him. Brian was thriving on his attention and kindness to them, and although Billy grudgingly admitted that he was a nice guy, he felt an obligation to dislike him, in order to be loyal to his father. Billy spent as little time as possible with Jack and his mother, and spent most of his time with Gabby. Larry hardly ever made time to see him, he was always too busy, and he made no effort whatsoever to see Brian. He was having too much fun. And on weekends, when he wasn't working at the restaurant in the city, Jack took Marilyn and Brian to his ranch in Napa, so he could check on things there. And sometimes he took them out on the bay in his boat, which Brian loved. He thought Jack was a hero. Marilyn was truly happy for the first time in years. She told Connie that she felt like a miracle had happened in her life. The only one resisting it was Billy, but she was sure he'd get used to Jack in time. Jack's genuine niceness was impossible to resist.

The biggest problem Billy had during junior year, other than his mother's boyfriend and his father's disappearance from his life, was that his grades suffered from all the changes he'd been through, and his adviser warned him that he would never get a football scholarship with his grades, no matter how well he played. He had no idea what to do about it, and junior year was crucial for his acceptance to college and getting a scholarship, which was his goal. It was an exciting year for him, and recruiters had come to watch him play since the beginning of junior year. Florida, Alabama, Tennessee, LSU, USC, and Notre Dame were all contenders, and desperate to have Billy accept their offers. Larry had put video clips of Billy's best games on the Internet, which they all saw. But his adviser said he had no chance of getting in with his GPA as low as it was. It was crucial for him to get his grades up, so he could get into one of the schools recruiting him.

Marilyn hired a tutor, who only made everything seem even more complicated to him. He explained about it to Izzie one day over lunch.

'My father will kill me if I don't play football in college,' Billy said glumly. Gabby tried to help him do some of his assignments, but her grades weren't stellar either. Gabby had never been a great student, and she didn't want to go to college. All she wanted to do was go to L.A. after graduation and become an actress. It had been her dream since first grade, and now it was only a year away. But she was no help to Billy with his schoolwork.

'Do you even want to play football in college?' Izzie asked him seriously, and he looked shocked at the question. 'Or were you just going to do it for your father?' Izzie's mother wanted her to go to law school, but it was the last thing she wanted. Although she admired what her father did at the ACLU, she knew it wasn't for her. She had no idea what she wanted to do as a career. She had thought of teaching, or majoring in psychology, or maybe nursing, or the Peace Corps. She liked taking care of people, but she didn't know what form she wanted it to take yet. She liked what Connie O'Hara did as a wife and mother. She was Izzie's role model, and she had been a schoolteacher. But Izzie knew her mother would be upset if she didn't choose a more glamorous career. Katherine wanted her to go to an Ivy League School, which Izzie didn't want to do either, although her grades were good enough to get in. She wanted to stay in California, and her father told her to do what she wanted. He said she didn't have to go to Harvard or Yale to get a good education, which was liberating for her, despite her mother's pressure.

'Of course I want to play football,' Billy said with a look of determination. 'That's all I've ever wanted to do. What else would I do? They're offering me a terrific deal at all those schools.' And Billy knew it was what his father expected of him, and he didn't want to let him down.

'Well, then I guess we'll have to help you,' Izzie said

matter-of-factly. She had well-organized study habits, and good grades. She was stronger in English and history, and Andy was the top science student in school, and between the two of them, Izzie figured they could get Billy's grades up, if he was willing to work hard, and he said he was. Billy was determined to do anything to get into a top school to play football.

They organized a study program for him. Andy tutored him during his free periods at lunchtime – they met in the library every day. And Izzie worked with him after school. Billy's two friends stuck with him with unwavering dedication for the rest of the year, helping him with papers, preparing him for quizzes and tests, and breaking down the material into digestible chunks he could understand and manage, and by the end of the second semester, Billy was in the top third of his class with a strong B average in almost every subject, and the occasional A on a science quiz, thanks to Andy. They had done a heroic job tutoring him, and Billy was where he needed to be to qualify for the scholarship he wanted. It was a major victory for all three of them, and Sean had joined in to help him in Spanish, since Sean had become fluent. And by the end of Junior year, Billy's adviser couldn't believe what he'd done and the improvement he'd made. He had no idea how Billy had gotten there.

And Marilyn was ecstatic too. Billy was on his way to having his dream come true. And so was she. Jack Ellison asked her to marry him in June, and she accepted.

They didn't want to wait, and they agreed to get married at his ranch in Napa in August. She told the boys the morning after he'd asked her. She wanted them to be the first to know. Brian was thrilled, he loved Jack more than his own father. And Billy stayed drunk for two days. He told his mother he had stomach flu, but Izzie, Gabby, and the others knew the truth of how upset he was, and how he had reacted to the news. He was devastated. It was the first time he truly understood that his parents would never get back together, his father would never sober up, and even if he did, Marilyn didn't want him. She was going to marry Jack.

Billy's childhood ended that summer. He was so distraught about his mother's marriage that he began drinking in secret and smoking marijuana when he was alone. No one knew what he was doing or even suspected. He hid it well. And he got so drunk at his mother's wedding that he passed out, and Sean and Andy had to carry him to his room, with Izzie and Gabby helping. They thought it was just a one-time excess. Marilyn was so happy and excited that she didn't even notice he was missing as they cut the cake. The party went on until four in the morning, and she told Connie she had never been as happy in her life.

'Where's Billy?' Connie asked Sean later that night, when she saw him talking with Izzie at a quiet table far from the dance floor that had been set up for the occasion. Jack's Napa restaurant had catered the event and the food was great.

'I don't know, Mom,' Sean said vaguely, glancing at Izzie, his partner in crime. 'Maybe he got tired and went to bed.' He didn't tell her that Billy had passed out hours before, and was unconscious in his room.

Connie and Mike danced a lot that night. It was a beautiful wedding, and made everyone feel romantic to see how happy the bride and groom were. Marilyn had confided in Connie that they wanted to have a baby. She was forty-two years old, and thought she still could. They were going to start trying right away. Connie had a strong feeling Billy wouldn't like it, but by the time the baby came, he'd be leaving for college, and Marilyn had a right to lead her life, she'd been unhappy with Larry for a long time. And Jack was good to her. He was down-to-earth and easygoing, and crazy about Marilyn and her boys. His sons were at the wedding too, and seemed like nice kids.

The O'Haras genuinely liked Jack and enjoyed

spending time with him and Marilyn. Gabby's parents, Judy and Adam, were at the wedding too, and had brought Michelle, who seemed astonishingly thin, but looked very pretty. She looked a lot like her older sister, Gabby, only paler, smaller, and less vivacious.

Andy's parents had declined, because they were both working. His mother was on call, and his father was in L.A. doing a TV show to publicize his new book. Andy had come with the O'Haras. And Jeff Wallace, Izzie's father, had come with a new woman he was dating, whom Connie knew Izzie didn't like. None of the kids wanted change in their lives, they wanted everything to stay the same, but it couldn't. Two sets of parents had already gotten divorced, and who knew what other changes life had in store for them. And the kids were changing too. In another year, they'd all be leaving for college.

The only things everyone agreed on were that they had never liked Larry, and how much they liked Jack. And unlike Larry, Jack treated Marilyn like a queen.

There was a brunch at Jack's restaurant in Yountville in the Napa Valley, the day after the wedding, and all their good friends came to see them off on their honeymoon. Jack was taking Marilyn to Europe. They were starting in Paris, and he had chartered a sailboat in Italy. He had invited the boys to come, but Brian got seasick and Billy didn't want to go, so both boys were going to stay with the O'Haras, and his own sons were going back to Chicago to their mother.

After brunch, the bride and groom left, and everyone drove back to town. Brian chatted animatedly with Sean on the way home – he was blossoming with his stepfather's kindness and attention. And Billy barely spoke. He was too hung over from the night before to say anything. Connie just thought he was tired, and he went right to bed in Sean's room as soon as they got home.

Connie smiled to herself as she thought of the first time she'd ever seen Marilyn, on the first day of kindergarten, the day Brian was born. It amazed her to think that Marilyn wanted to have another baby, and start all over again. Connie couldn't imagine doing that herself. She and Marilyn had been friends for twelve years. It seemed hard to believe, it had all flown by so fast. And it was even more amazing to realize that the kids' school career, the five best friends, was almost over. The twelve years since they'd all met in kindergarten had passed in the blink of an eye.

Chapter 6

Marilyn and Jack came back from their honeymoon three weeks after the wedding. It was already mid-September, Brian had started seventh grade, and the Big Five were all seniors. They were in the home stretch of their high school careers.

Marilyn took Connie to lunch to thank her for taking care of the boys while she was gone, and Connie insisted it had been no trouble. She and Mike loved having them, and so did Sean.

'Our house is so overloaded with testosterone, with Mike, Kevin, and Sean, believe me, two more guys isn't a problem. I wouldn't know what to do with a girl.' And then she thought of Gabby's sister, Michelle. 'Did you notice Michelle at your wedding? She gets thinner every time I see her. I was worried about her. I wanted to say something to Judy, but I didn't want to upset her. She's always focused on Gabby, I'm not sure she sees what's happening. Michelle looks anorexic to me.'

'I did notice,' Marilyn admitted. 'I've seen it for a while. I keep wondering if I should mention it to Judy, or mind my own business.'

'That's kind of how I feel too. But I've always been grateful when people told me things about Kevin, when he was in trouble. Sometimes you're too close to see it, or they hide it from you.'

'I know. How's he doing, by the way?'

'Terrific. He's still at City College. He's getting there slowly. He should graduate next year. It's taken longer than we hoped, but his grades are really strong, and he's still sober. He's in good shape . . . which reminds me,' she said with a serious look. 'I found a few beer bottles under Billy's bed. I think he and Sean may have partied a little one night. They're nearly eighteen, but I gave them hell about it anyway. They both apologized but I wanted you to know. I think he's still kind of upset about your getting married. He likes Jack, but he feels torn between him and Larry. He doesn't want to be disloyal to his father, but he's happy for you. Jack is a great guy. He's ten times the man Larry is.' Marilyn knew that too.

'That's why I married him,' Marilyn said with a slow smile. She looked peaceful and happy, and Connie was pleased for her. 'I think Larry puts a lot of pressure on Billy, so he doesn't bond with Jack. Brian had no relationship with his father, so he threw himself into it with Jack. But it's a lot harder for Billy. I think it will be good for him when he goes away to school next year, and gets away from his father. Larry is such a mess, I don't know how he keeps his business together.' He was still making money hand over fist, from everything Connie knew, but drinking more than ever, and dating girls less than half his age. It was pathetic. And she knew Billy didn't like it either, although he rarely criticized his father, but he had made a few oblique comments.

'Billy says he's still trying to decide what school to go to,' Connie said with interest. The schools with the best football teams had been recruiting him since the spring of junior year, which was exciting for him, and for Larry. 'He says he's still serious about a career in pro football, and he's certainly got the skills for it. Mike promised him we'd go to all his big games, wherever he is.' Marilyn smiled at her faithful friend of so many years. And she knew they would go to Billy's games. She, Jack, and Brian were planning to go too. 'It sounds like he might do USC, so he can be close to Gabby, and it's a great school for him.' He had the pick of them all, and recruiters had been doing everything possible to get him to accept their schools' offers.

'Jack is worried that he only wants to play pro football to impress his father,' said Marilyn. 'It's the only thing Larry ever cared about since the day he was born. Jack tried to ask him if there was any other career he might like to pursue. I don't think Billy's ever even thought about it. And that's a tough life, a short career, with a lot of pressure, and a lot of injuries. I can see Jack's point.'

'I don't think you'll get Billy to change direction now,' Connie said, 'especially with all the top schools after him. Who could resist that? And he's been headed that way for too long. You have to see how he does in college, of course, and if they draft him, but Mike says he's got what it takes to be a star quarterback and have a fabulous career in the NFL. He's a lucky kid. It's every boy's dream.'

'Jack thinks so too. He just wonders if he'll be happy doing it.' It was a reasonable question to have asked him, and Marilyn was glad he had.

'It's what Billy wants,' Connie said quietly. 'His eyes glow full of dreams whenever he talks about it. The way Sean's do when he talks about law enforcement.' But Billy's was a much bigger dream and a lot harder to achieve, sometimes at a very high price. They both knew that not all of Larry's important sports clients were happy people, and some led very empty lives, particularly when their careers ended, or they got badly injured on the field. The risks were high, no matter how good the money was, and Marilyn knew better than most that there was a seamy side to that life too, that she didn't want for her older son. But the die had been cast, by his father, ever since he was a little boy. And Larry wanted Billy to live out his own dreams, so he could live vicariously through his son. And Marilyn knew she couldn't change it now, especially not with all the top schools recruiting him.

'So how was the honeymoon?' Connie asked her as they finished lunch. It was what she had really wanted to know, but she could see the answer in how relaxed and happy Marilyn was.

'Fantastic! Paris was unbelievable, and the boat in Italy was like a dream honeymoon in a movie. Jack is such a sweet guy. We spent a few days in Rome after the boat, and then drove to Florence. And we came home through London. It was an incredible trip. He spoiled me rotten.' He was a very loving man, and excited to be with a good woman he loved so much, and he loved both her boys, and she loved his too. They made a perfect family, despite Billy's reticence about it, which they were hoping he would get over eventually, and figure out that he could enjoy Jack and their family without feeling disloyal to his father. 'I've got some news to share with the boys, but I don't want to say anything too soon.' Marilyn's whole face lit up as she confided in Connie. She had been dying to tell her ever since she got home.

'What kind of news?' Connie looked instantly suspicious, as Marilyn beamed at her. Just looking at her expression, it was easy to guess.

'I'm pregnant, only about three weeks, but I saw the doctor yesterday, and she said everything is fine.' By coincidence, when her own doctor retired after Brian was born, she had become one of Helen Weston's patients – Andy's mother – and she liked her very much. She was a good doctor, and she was very attentive to her patients. She wasn't concerned about Marilyn being pregnant at forty-two, although she had told her that she might want to wait until after the twelve-week mark before she started announcing it, since the risk of miscarriage was higher at her age, and a possibility for all women. But she saw no reason for concern – she said she had lots of patients older than Marilyn having babies these days. 'I have to go back for a sonogram next week, but she thinks everything is fine. The only thing she warned me about, other than miscarriage, is a higher possibility of multiples at my age. Jack would be thrilled if they were girls. With four boys between us, he really wants a girl.' She was beaming as she looked at Connie, who was excited for her.

'Wow! I didn't think it would happen this soon.'

'Neither did we. It happened in Paris. I'm due the week of the kids' graduation in June,' she said sheepishly, and Connie laughed out loud.

'You'll be ending Billy's school career the way you started it, giving birth, like you did with Brian on the first day of school.'

'I thought of that too,' Marilyn said, looking concerned. 'I think Brian will be okay with it, because he's so crazy about Jack, but Billy will be pissed.' She looked genuinely worried about it. 'He hasn't even gotten used to the idea of our being married, and now we're having a baby right away. But at our age, we didn't want to waste any time. I'm lucky I got pregnant this fast, without having to take fertility drugs or any kind of intervention. Jack is as excited as I am, but we're both a little worried about Billy.'

'He'll be fine,' Connie reassured her. 'He's a great kid, and he loves you. And he's leaving for college two months after you have it. He'll be off on his own life. After college, they hardly come home again, if everything is fine. Once Kevin graduates and gets a job, we won't see him either. You'll be lucky if Billy comes home for Thanksgiving and Christmas, especially if he's playing college football. A baby at home won't make much difference to him, but it'll be great for both of you.' She looked nostalgic as she said it. 'You make me want to start again too, especially with Sean leaving for college next year, and Kevin will be gone by then too, once he's working and can afford to pay his own rent. It's over so damn fast, before you know it. But I'm three years older than you are, and I think at forty-five, I'm too old to start again. I'd be practically seventy when the kid graduated from college. And Mike would kill me. He has all kinds of romantic notions about chasing me around the house naked when the boys leave, and trips he's been waiting twenty years to take with me, and we can afford it now. I don't think a baby's on the cards for me.'

'I didn't think it was for me either,' Marilyn said, sitting back with a blissful smile.

Marilyn was scheduled the following week for a sonogram, and Jack went with her. They were both excited to catch a first glimpse of their baby, and find out that it was healthy, had a strong heartbeat, and the right number of everything. Marilyn held her breath and Jack held her hand, while the technician moved the metal wand around her belly, and all three of them watched the screen. They saw the image appear, and the technician continued to move the wand through the gel on Marilyn's abdomen and said nothing. She smiled brightly at them both then, said she'd be right back, and left the room, as tears filled Marilyn's eyes and she looked up at Jack in panic.

'Something's wrong,' she said in a hoarse whisper, as they both glanced at the screen again, but they couldn't see anything. It looked like a section of a gray blur to them. It was too early to be able to make out the shape of the baby without some explanation from the technician, and she hadn't said a word. Tears rolled down Marilyn's cheeks as they waited, and Jack gently stroked her fiery red hair that he loved and then bent to kiss her. He was as alarmed as she was but didn't want to show it. He had waited a lifetime for this woman and he loved her. He didn't want anything bad to ever happen to her again, and he knew how miserable she'd been with Larry and how badly treated, and he hated him for it, although he never said it in front of her sons, out of respect for their relationship with their father, as minimal as it was.

Jack was holding tightly to Marilyn's hand, with the wide diamond wedding band he had given her, as Helen Weston walked into the room, with a broad smile that encompassed both of them. Marilyn was both frightened and reassured when she saw her. Obviously, something serious was going on if the technician had called the doctor in to look at the sonogram, but at least Helen would tell them what was happening. Marilyn liked her a lot as her gynaecologist and obstetrician, and they shared the additional bond of their sons who were close friends.

'Let's take a look here,' Helen said, smiling at both of them, in her white doctor's coat with her name on it, and a stethoscope hanging out of the pocket. It was the kind of stethoscope that allowed her to hear a baby's heartbeat.

'What's wrong?' Marilyn said miserably, as tears continued to roll down her cheeks. She was braced for the worst, maybe a deformed baby, or maybe she had already lost it, without knowing. She knew that happened early in a pregnancy sometimes, that a fetus began to form, didn't attach properly, stopped growing, and then died or even disappeared.

'Nothing's wrong,' Helen said gently. 'I get to be the bearer of good news too.' She smiled at both of them calmly, and Marilyn's tears stopped for a minute as she squeezed Jack's hand harder. 'Elaine just wanted to be sure I agree with what she's seeing. It's still early days here, and I think it's great news. I hope you will too.' She turned away from the sonogram screen and looked at both of them with a kind expression. She liked them both and was sorry she hadn't been able to go to their wedding. She had been on call, and Robert, a somewhat well-known media shrink, had been in L.A. for a TV appearance. 'It looks like we're going to be having a double birthday here. You're having twins,' she said, and Marilyn burst into tears again and threw her arms around Jack's neck in relief. She was sobbing openly then, and he had tears in his eyes too, when he looked back at Helen. It was great news to them both. They had talked about wishing they had time for two babies, not just one, but at forty-two, Marilyn didn't think they'd be lucky enough to have another one after this. It was possible, but seemed unlikely, and now they had their wish. Two babies, twins, in addition to the four children they had from their first marriages.

'Are you sure?' Jack looked thrilled.

'Yes, I am.' Helen beamed at him. 'That's why Elaine called me in to look.'

'Is it more than that?' Marilyn said hopefully, and Helen laughed.

'Let's not get greedy here. I think two will keep us plenty busy. You could end up on bed rest toward the end if the babies get too big. You've never had a history of early deliveries, and both your boys were pretty big, so you should be able to carry them to term without a problem, but you're a little older now than you were with Brian, so we'll have to see how things go. But I don't foresee any problems. You're healthy, and your babies should be too. Do the boys know yet that you're pregnant?'

'I wanted to wait till we knew everything's okay,' Marilyn said, looking dazed by the news. She hadn't let go of Jack's hand since she lay down on the exam table.

'I'd give it a few more weeks. It will be harder to hold out till twelve weeks with twins on board. You'll probably start showing fairly soon. Maybe you could wait till then.' Jack and Marilyn both agreed. She gave Marilyn more vitamins, some instruction sheets with simple dos and don't about her pregnancy, all of which was familiar to her, and a book about delivering twins and what to expect in the first few months afterward.

Twenty minutes later they were in Jack's car on the way home. He had kissed her passionately as soon as they left the doctor's office, and told her how much he loved her. They were both incredibly excited, and it was going to be hard not telling anyone right away, but it seemed wiser to wait. And Marilyn was still mildly worried about telling the boys. She was almost sure Brian would be okay about the baby, even two of them, but she was concerned about Billy, and he had so much on his plate right now, keeping his grades up, and deciding which school he would allow to recruit him. It was a major turning point in life for him, and she didn't want to complicate things, or upset him. Jack reassured her on the way home, and she called Connie as soon as they walked into the house and told her it was twins. She was as excited as they were.

'Holy shit! That's fantastic!' Connie said enthusiastically. 'Are you okay with it? You said you wanted another one anyway,' she reminded her.

'We're thrilled! The technician left the room without saying anything, and I thought the baby was dead or deformed or something, then Helen came in and told us it was twins. I was scared to death until she did, but everything is fine.' She was talking a mile a minute. Jack stopped in the doorway and blew her a kiss before going back downtown to the restaurant.

'Bye, Mom!' he said, and then left as Marilyn talked to Connie.

'I hope I don't wind up on bed rest, especially for Billy's graduation. I *have* to be there. But sometimes twins come early, so maybe I'll already have had them by then.'

'As long as you don't have them at the ceremony, you'll be fine. I can't wait to see them!'

'Me too.' They talked excitedly for a few minutes, and

Marilyn said she hoped they would be girls, but she'd be happy with anything, just so they were healthy. And for the rest of the day, Marilyn felt like she was floating. Her whole life had turned around. After years of painful marriage, she had found a wonderful man, and now she was having his babies. It was almost too good to believe. Jack called her twice that afternoon to see how she was feeling, and her answer was 'Ecstatic!' So was he.

By the beginning of November, her belly was getting harder and harder to conceal. She was wearing loose blouses and sweaters. She was eleven weeks pregnant by then, by medical standards of computation, which always added two weeks to the real number, and Helen said she was doing great, and she felt fine. She was a little queasy in the morning, but nothing major. The only noticeable change was that her breasts felt enormous and were growing by the day. Jack said he liked it.

And two weeks before Thanksgiving, Billy made his big decision, and chose USC from among the schools recruiting him, and accepted their offer. He had talked to Gabby at length about it, and his father. It was a great school, with a terrific football team, and by staying in L.A., he'd be close to Gabby, working on her acting career there and modeling. He had been tempted to accept Florida or LSU, but he actually liked USC better, and their star quarterback had been injured recently, so they really needed him and were going to let him play freshman year. And Gabby was an important part of the equation for him. He told her even before he told his parents, and she was thrilled. Her parents were getting her an apartment in L.A., and he could spend weekend nights with her. Life was just beginning for them, and it was looking very, very good.

And with that decision behind him, life became a celebration for Billy. He was a hero at Atwood and among his friends, and Marilyn decided that it was a good time to tell him about the twins. Billy was in a great mood, and his father was over the moon, and planning to rent an apartment in L.A. so he could go to all his games.

Jack and Marilyn took both boys out to dinner, at his restaurant, the week before Thanksgiving. And he had promised to cater their Thanksgiving meal – he didn't want Marilyn doing any extra work right now, and he was doing everything he could to help her. The food was delicious, and Jack ordered a bottle of champagne at the end of dinner. He gave Billy half a glass, and Brian barely more than a thimbleful, since they were in the restaurant's private dining room and this was a very special occasion. And then, after smiling at Jack, Marilyn told them.

'We have something to share with you,' their mother said, and both boys could see that it was important.

'You're getting divorced?' Brian said with a look of panic.

'Not if I'm pouring champagne, Brian,' Jack explained with a smile. 'If that were the case, I'd be handing out hankies and crying. You two and your mom are the best thing that ever happened to me.' Brian looked relieved the minute he said it. He loved Jack and didn't want to lose him.

'This is a good announcement,' Marilyn said to them, took a breath and leaped in. 'We're having a baby . . . well, actually,' she corrected herself, 'two of them. We're having twins. In June. We wanted you to be the first to know.'

Both boys looked at them in astonishment, and then Brian broke into a slow, shy grin.

'That's weird,' he said, smiling at Jack, but he didn't look unhappy about it. 'Aren't you both too old?'

'Apparently not,' Jack said, smiling at him. Billy hadn't said a word and was looking at his mother, stone-faced.

'You're kidding, right? This is a joke, isn't it?' He looked like he was about to burst into tears.

'No, Billy, it's not. It's for real. At least they won't keep you up at night – you'll be in school.' Marilyn already had plans to re-model their guest room and turn it into a nursery for the twins. Jack had moved into her house, because it was familiar and easier for the boys. And it was big enough to work for two more children too.

'I think that's really stupid,' he said. 'You've got enough kids. And what if you decide you don't like each other in two years, what happens to them? You each take one?' Billy was still smarting from the divorce and his mother's remarriage, and it showed.

'Hopefully that won't ever happen,' Jack said calmly. 'I think your mother and I knew what we were doing when we got married. We wouldn't have more children if we weren't sure.'

'You may be sure now, but you don't know what will happen later. Look at Izzie's parents, and you and Dad,' he said directly to Marilyn. 'Now Dad's a mess, and you're married to someone else and having more babies.' She didn't tell him that his father had been a mess before she divorced him. She could see that Billy needed to express his feelings, and she felt bad for him, and for a moment as though she had betrayed him by getting pregnant. He was a senior in high school and nearly eighteen years old, but he was still a little boy.

'I'm sorry you're upset, Billy,' she said softly, and tried to reach for his hand but he wouldn't let her. He said nothing until they stood up to leave, then he strode out of the restaurant and waited for them at the car. As soon as they got home, he went to Gabby's, without a word of congratulation to Jack or his mother. He looked like a storm cloud, and Jack found Marilyn crying in the kitchen a few minutes later, rubbing her stomach. The end of the meal had given her terrible indigestion.

'Are you okay?' Jack asked as he walked in and put his arms around her. 'I'm sorry Billy took it badly. He'll be okay. I guess in a lot of ways he's still a kid.' She nodded and clung to her husband. The last thing she had wanted to do was upset Billy. He'd been through enough with the divorce, and all the pressure put on him by Larry. 'He'll be fine when he sees them. It's an adjustment, and he'll be in L.A. anyway,' Jack was hugging her and rubbing her back when Brian walked in with a curious expression.

'So do you know what they are yet?' Boys, girls, one of each?' He looked as though he was ready, and his mother and stepfather laughed and turned to smile at him.

'We'll let you know as soon as we do,' Marilyn promised, relieved to see him so matter-of-fact about it. 'Any preference?'

'Of course,' he said, rolling his eyes. 'Two boys. Jack

and I can teach them to play baseball.' Brian was already liking his role as older brother, and he exchanged a knowing look with Jack.

'You can teach girls to play baseball too, you know,' Marilyn reminded him, as Brian rolled his eyes again, helped himself to a cookie, and sat down at the kitchen table.

'Girls are such dorks.'

'You won't always think that,' Jack said confidently, and after that they turned off the kitchen lights and went upstairs. Unlike his older brother, Brian had taken their announcement extremely well. Billy had felt it as a personal affront, and that night he said as much to Gabby, who thought it was going to be cute to have babies to play with, twins, whenever they came home from L.A. Billy looked unhappy when she said it, and the next morning Marilyn found two empty beer cans under his bed. She didn't say anything, and decided to give him some slack, but it wasn't reassuring, if he was responding to stressful situations by drinking beer. She didn't want him to turn out like his father, but two beers were not enough to panic about yet. She told Jack about it, and he suggested they keep an eye on Billy and try not to over-react, and she agreed.

* * *

Thanksgiving at the Norton-Ellison household was a lot happier than it had been the year before. Both of Jack's boys joined them, as did Gabby. She helped Marilyn set the table, and Jack had the entire meal catered by his restaurant, with two waiters to serve them and clean up afterward. All Marilyn had to do was sit down and eat, and the dinner was delicious. It was a traditional Thanksgiving meal, and everyone was in good spirits, except Billy, who said nothing. Jack's boys tried to engage him in conversation about playing football for USC, and Billy gave them short, terse answers and retreated to his room after dinner with Gabby. He surprised her by taking out a bottle of tequila and pouring shots for each of them. He had been hiding the bottle in a drawer in his dresser. Gabby looked shocked when she saw it, and refused the drink.

'That's not cool, Billy,' she said softly. 'I know you're upset about your mom having a baby, or two of them, but getting drunk isn't going to change anything.' Except his scholarship if he got caught.

'I'm not going to get drunk on one shot. I don't care about my mom and her babies, and it's Thanksgiving, for chrissake.' He had never spoken to her that way before, and when she refused the shot glass he handed her, he drank hers too. She had seen him get drunk before at parties, on beer, but she had never seen him have a serious drink, or do it because he was unhappy, not even during his parents' divorce. It had only started once his mother had decided to marry Jack.

'You can't do that when you're in training,' she reminded him with a look of disapproval.

'Don't tell me what I can do, and don't be such an old lady,' he complained, and for a minute he sounded just like his father. Gabby was upset about it and left a few minutes later. Marilyn was surprised to see her leave so soon. But it had been easy to see that Billy was not in a good mood. It had almost ruined Thanksgiving dinner for her, except that Brian had been so sweet, and so was Jack. But Billy made it clear that he was not willing to share in their happiness. They told Jack's two sons about the twins before dinner, and they were surprised but pleased. They hoped it would be two boys too.

She found the two used shot glasses in Billy's underwear drawer on Monday morning, when she put his laundry away, and the bottle of tequila when she dug a little deeper. She felt her stomach turn over as soon as she found them, and called Connie immediately, and told her what she'd found.

'Shit, I don't want him to turn into an alcoholic like Larry. I think he's been drinking ever since Jack and I got married. And now he's upset about the twins, so he's doing it again.'

'That's not a good enough reason,' Connie said, sounding unhappy at her end too. 'I found a bottle of vodka in Kevin's closet this weekend. He's been sober since rehab, and he's an adult now. I could say something, but he'd accuse me of snooping. He's twenty-four years old, he's a man living under our roof. But if he starts drinking again, his life will go right down the tubes. Mike wants him to start working with him now, and come to work full time when he graduates. But Kevin hates construction work, and he never likes working for his father. Mike is tough on him – he thinks it's good for him.'

'I swear, sometimes I think they're trying to kill us,' Marilyn said with a sigh, and Connie laughed. But it wasn't funny to either of them. They both knew only too well that their sons' futures were at risk. And Billy had so much at stake now. All his dreams were about to come true. 'Let's just hope it's a bad phase and they'll get their shit together soon. Are you going to say something to Kevin?'

'Mike's going to talk to him tonight and lower the boom. He's going to tell him that if he wants to live here, he has to stay sober and work for him in his spare time. And if he doesn't like it, Mike says, he can move out. So it's showdown time around here. What about you and Billy?'

'Billy is in training. He's not supposed to be drinking. Maybe he just has 'senioritis.' Everyone says that their kids go nuts for a while, once they get accepted into college. For Billy, the pressure is off now till he gets to USC. Unless he flunks out of school. I'm going to keep a close eye on the drinking.'

'Me too,' Connie said, sounding discouraged. She had been convinced that Kevin was home free, and the bad days were over. Now she wasn't as sure. Kevin was definitely at risk, of using drugs or booze, and getting lost along the way. After all, he had very nearly gone to jail, and in a similar situation, the next time he would. She was less concerned about Billy having a couple of beers and a shot of tequila in his bedroom, although they weren't happy about it, but there was no denying that kids Billy's age drank from time to time, even good kids. But Kevin was no longer a kid, he was a man.

There was good news and bad news during Christmas vacation. Connie and Marilyn ran into Michelle at the manicure salon one day and were horrified by what they saw. She looked frighteningly thin. There was no denying that she was anorexic, and when Marilyn finally got up the guts to mention it to Judy, she said that they had been to the doctor that week, and Michelle had just started outpatient treatment at an eating disorder clinic. Judy was very upset about it. Marilyn was relieved to hear that Michelle was in treatment.

The best news of the season was that on the day before Christmas vacation, Andy got the letter he'd been waiting for from Harvard. He had gotten in on early decision, in pre-med, and it came as a surprise to no one but him. Izzie let out a scream that resonated down the halls when he told her, and Sean and Billy picked him up and carried him on their shoulders, while Gabby grinned. He was a hero to them, and all his teachers were elated for him but not surprised.

He called his mother in the office to tell her, but her cell phone was on voicemail, which meant that she was with a patient or delivering a baby, so he sent her a text to find whenever she was free, and he got hold of his father between patients. He sounded busy, but pleased with the news.

'I'd only have been surprised by anything less,' his father said calmly. 'You didn't really think they'd decline you, did you?' Robert sounded amused at the thought, particularly since he had gone to Harvard too. And with Andy's grades and test scores, Robert considered him a shoo-in. Only Andy himself had been deeply anxious about it, and hadn't slept well in weeks. But Andy never let it show. The only one whom he had confided in about his nervousness was Izzie. He had had nightmares about not getting accepted, on early decision or ever, and being banished by his father as a result. His mother would have forgiven him and understood, but his father never would. He had always expected the 4.0 GPA that Andy always delivered with ease, although sometimes it wasn't as easy as Andy made it look.

'Thank you for helping me with my application essay,' Andy whispered to Izzie as they left their last class of the day. 'I think that's what got me in.' He was grateful and relieved.

'Are you insane?' Izzie looked at him in amazement. 'With your grades and scores, you think my help got you in? Andy Weston, wake up! You're practically the genius of our class.'

'No, silly, that would be you. You have one of the best analytical minds of anyone I've ever met. You even make more sense than my parents, and they're both really smart, and my father writes books and is considered brilliant.' Izzie knew his father's books were successful, but she had always considered him a cold person. She liked his mother a lot better.

'Trust me, you're a genius, and you're going to be a terrific doctor one day. Any ideas about what you're going to specialize in?' she asked him as they left school.

'Probably research. I hate seeing people in pain. And I'd never want to make a mistake that cost someone their life. That's too much responsibility for me.' After twelve years in school together, one thing she knew about Andy was that he never wanted to hurt anyone, in deed or word. He was a very thoughtful, cautious, caring, compassionate human being, and Izzie admired him enormously. Although she loved all of them in her group, he was the friend she respected most. And now he had gotten into Harvard on early decision. She was thrilled for him.

She was going to finish her own applications over Christmas vacation. Her first choice was still UCLA, and she was excited that Gabby and Billy would be in L.A. too. She just hoped that she'd get in. Most of her other choices were back east, at schools where she really didn't want to go, although one of them was Boston University, and now Andy would be close by at Harvard, so there was some comfort in that. She hated to think of all of them going their separate ways in six months, and she hoped that they would always see each other and come home for holidays. She knew they all really meant it when they said they were friends forever, and she hoped their lives would cooperate to help them stay that way.

But if Andy got good news, Izzie got bad news over the holidays. Her father came home with a new girlfriend, and she could tell instantly that this one meant something to him. No other woman since her parents' divorce really had. Her name was Jennifer, she was a social worker he had met at work. She had gone to Columbia and come to San Francisco two years before Jeff met her, and she was thirty-eight years old. Jeff was fifty-five. They had a seventeen-year age gap that Izzie thought was ridiculous. Jennifer was a nice woman, and she could see why her father liked her: She was smart, pretty, she had a great body, and a good sense of humor, and she looked about twenty-five years old. He took Jennifer and Izzie out for a Mexican dinner in the Mission, and Izzie realized that she spoke fluent Spanish, and had grown up in Mexico, because her father was a diplomat, so she had a little touch of the exotic about her that made her even more appealing. She was smarter and more sophisticated than anyone Jeff had gone out with, and Izzie recognized instantly that she was a serious threat to the peaceful life she had shared with her father for the past five years. She saw her mother every once in a while, but Katherine was spending most of her time in New

York now, for the corporation she worked for, and all pretense of joint custody had gone out the window. And Izzie liked her life with her father exactly the way it was.

After dinner, Jeff took Jennifer home, then came to see Izzie in her room. She had been talking on the phone to Gabby, and she hung up the minute her father walked in.

'So what do you think, Iz?' he aside, about Jennifer, and Izzie hesitated before she spoke. She wanted to be careful about what she said. She didn't want to hurt her father's feelings, but she thought Jennifer was too young for him. She had mentioned at dinner that she wanted to have children, and Izzie had nearly choked. As far as she was concerned, her father was much too old to start another family, at least she hoped so.

'Don't you think she's a little young, Dad?'

'Not really. We get along very well.' He didn't look worried.

'How long have you known her?' He had never mentioned her before, until she suddenly appeared. But there had been stars in his eyes every time he looked at her during dinner. It scared the hell out of Izzie. Jennifer was a major threat to her.

'About three months. We worked on a case together, a discrimination case at a day-care center. She really knows her stuff.'

'That's nice,' Izzie said, pretending to be calmer than she was. 'She's a really nice person and I can see why you like her. I just think she's going to want to get married and have kids one of these days, and I don't want you to get hurt.'

'I'm not too old to have kids,' he said, looking insulted, as his daughter felt a cold chill run down her spine. She felt new compassion for Billy when it did. 'Marilyn is having twins, for God's sake, with her new husband, and Billy is the same age you are.'

'Yeah, but they're in their forties. You're fifty-five. Would you want more kids, Dad?' she asked, with a tremor in her voice.

'I've never thought about it. Maybe with the right person, I might. I don't know. You're going to be gone pretty soon, and it's going to be very lonely around here.' He looked sorry for himself as he said it, and Izzie felt terror in her heart.

'For God's sake, Dad, get a dog, don't have a baby. That's a life-time commitment, and you hardly know this woman.'

He seemed stubborn suddenly as he replied, 'I like her a lot.'

'Then date her, but don't marry her and have kids. I just think she's a little young for you, that's all.'

'She's very mature for her age. She thinks like someone my age.'

'No, she doesn't,' she corrected him. 'She thinks like someone my age. I felt like I was talking to a kid all through dinner.'

'She's very versatile and good with people,' he insisted, and Izzie saw she wasn't getting anywhere.

Izzie couldn't wait to talk to Sean about it the next day, and she was worried.

'I think my dad met someone he really likes. She's seventeen years younger than he is, and all I need is for him to marry some bimbo while I'm away.'

'Is she a bimbo?' Sean looked surprised. Izzie's father had always seemed very sensible to him, like his own parents. He couldn't imagine him running off with some disco girl.

'No, she isn't. That's the trouble. I even like her.' She sighed as she looked at Sean. 'I just don't want anything to change, for us, or them. It's hard enough leaving without worrying about everything being different when you come back.'

'It won't be,' he reassured her. 'Your father loves you, and he's a great guy. He's not going to do anything stupid while you're gone. He probably just likes her as a date.'

'Yeah, maybe,' Izzie said, but she wasn't so sure. She

knew how lonely her father had been at times in the last five years, and there had been no one serious in his life.

'Just relax, everything's going to be fine. They'll probably stop dating by next week,' Sean comforted her, when she complained to him again about her father and the new woman.

'Whatever,' Izzie said. It was hard to worry about everything, and impossible to control their parents' lives. Marilyn was proof of that. Divorced, remarried, and pregnant with twins all within a year. Things had moved very fast in Billy's life, and they both knew he was still upset.

'How's your brother, by the way?' she asked him about Kevin. Sean didn't talk about him often, but Izzie knew that he was still worried about him, more than he admitted.

'I don't know,' he said honestly. 'I get a weird feeling about him. He looks okay, but I don't think he is. He acts like he's sneaking around again, and he's in such a good mood every time I see him, I get the feeling he could be doing drugs again. I hope not. He's working for my dad right now. But if he screws that up, my dad will be really pissed.'

Izzie nodded, and they talked about other things then.

They all wanted to go skiing in Tahoe over the winter vacation, and the O'Haras had offered to let them stay at their house for a few days. Izzie had her last college applications to do too, and the vacation would be over before any of them could catch their breath. They were headed straight for graduation in six months, which was the scariest thought of all.

Chapter 7

The O'Haras gave the whole class a graduation barbecue in their backyard. It was a major event. Everyone was invited, and they hired a chef from Jack's San Francisco restaurant to cook steaks, hot dogs, hamburgers, ribs, and everything that went with them. It was a terrific party, and everyone had a ball. They were a wholesome, happy group, although a few people arrived drunk and weren't allowed in and were sent home in cabs. The O'Haras were vigilant about it. They had had T-shirts made for everyone, with the names of the entire graduating class on them. Everyone put on a T-shirt as they came in, and the Big Five stuck together, eating and talking and laughing. Sean thought Billy was high and asked him about it, but Billy denied it. When Sean asked Izzie what she thought, she said he seemed fine to her, and Sean was relieved.

Marilyn and Jack came by for a little while too. She had been on bed rest for a month, just at the very end, but with her due date only five days away, Helen had let her get up so she could attend graduation and the surrounding events. They knew that both babies were girls, and Marilyn said she had never been so ready in her life. Having Brian had been a breeze compared to this, but she had no regrets, they were thrilled, and Jack was waiting on her hand and foot, which she said was a good thing since she hadn't seen her feet since Christmas, and she was so big now, she couldn't get out of bed without help. He was being wonderful to her. And Billy had stopped complaining about it. He was focusing on school, and leaving home a month early for football practice at USC.

Judy was planning on taking Gabby to L.A. in August to help her find an apartment and get everything set up for her. Michelle was looking a little better, after her treatment at the clinic, and Judy had told Connie and Marilyn that she was better now, although she didn't look much heavier than she was before. She seemed happier and more relaxed as she hung out with Gabby's group. Judy and Gabby were busy making plans for L.A., and Michelle would be staying with a friend while they were away, setting up Gabby's apartment.

Izzie had been accepted at UCLA and every other school she'd applied to, so she had a choice in the end, but UCLA was her favourite school, and she loved knowing that Gabby and Billy would be nearby. They promised to see each other whenever they could. And Sean had decided on George Washington University in Washington D.C., because he said he wanted to major in political science and foreign policy, with a minor in Spanish. He had a real gift for languages and had won the Spanish prize in their class. He didn't tell anyone except Izzie, but he was trying to tailor his major to what was required to apply to the FBI. He had been carefully studying the qualifications they looked for and reading about them online. Connie and Mike thought he'd chosen an ambitious program and were sad he was going so far away, but it was a wonderful opportunity to see more of the world than home base. He had turned down Georgetown, Columbia, and MIT and insisted that GW was the right school for him. He was a very smart kid.

Kevin showed up at the graduation party, and said he had plans and was meeting friends later. But he was much older than Sean and the others, and a bunch of high school seniors celebrating their graduation wasn't his cup of tea. He left very quickly.

The party in the O'Haras' backyard went on until

three in the morning, although they had to turn the music down at two. The food kept on coming, they didn't serve alcohol since no one was legally old enough to drink, but the kids had a great time anyway, and even Marilyn and Jack stayed till midnight to keep the O'Haras company. And Izzie's dad, Jeff Wallace, came with his girlfriend, Jennifer. Izzie didn't look too pleased when she saw her, but she was always polite to her. Helen Weston came, and had to leave after a few minutes for a delivery, but Andy's dad didn't come, he never did. He was too busy with his practice, or books. Helen spotted Marilyn on the way out and stopped to say hello.

'What are you doing here?' Marilyn asked her in surprise. She very rarely attended school-related events and didn't have time. She was always working.

'I dropped by to see how you're doing, and I thought I'd do a home delivery while I was here, between hot dogs and hamburgers,' she teased. 'How are you feeling?' she asked her more seriously. Marilyn looked pretty good, but her feet and ankles were swollen like balloons.

'Like I'm going to explode any second,' Marilyn said with a grin, as Jack stood with his arm around her.

'Well, keep your legs crossed till tomorrow afternoon. We all want to be at the graduation tomorrow. I'll deliver you in the parking lot if I have to.'

'That'll work,' Marilyn said, looking relaxed. She had contractions constantly now as her body got ready for the big event, but none that were worrying her particularly. They were frequent but not hard, just practice runs, although Jack was watching her like a hawk. He was afraid of not getting her to the hospital in time, although Helen had reassured him. They went home just after midnight, and Marilyn got a good sleep that night, in spite of how uncomfortable she was. She was used to it by now. She felt as though her body had been taken over by aliens. But she could hardly wait to see her little girls. They had already named them. Dana and Daphne.

When all the parents had left, except Connie and Mike, who were discreetly supervising, the Big Five disappeared one by one for a few minutes and slipped away to Sean's room. They had talked about doing something more dramatic, like getting a tattoo that said 'Friends 4Ever,' just as they had carved in their school desks for years, but Gabby said her mother would kill her, and Izzie didn't want a tattoo either. The boys had been more enthused about the idea. Instead, as she so often did, Izzie came up with a compromise solution that satisfied them all. It was less impressive than a tattoo, but they agreed that it would mark the occasion and seal the pact between them. Prepared as usual, Izzie had brought the supplies.

And as soon as Sean closed and locked the door to his room behind them, Izzie brought out a package of sewing needles, and handed one to each of them with alcohol pads she had brought too. They looked appropriately solemn, as Izzie made a little speech and spoke their vows. It had been her idea, and all had agreed, even though at first the boys had thought it a little silly and would have preferred the tattoo.

'We are gathered here,' she said officially, 'to make a solemn vow to each other, to never forget each other, never lose each other, always be there for each other, wherever we are. We promise to love each other till the day we die and be best friends forever.' She paused then and looked at each of them, as they watched her with serious expressions. 'Now we all say "I do,"' she prompted them, and a chorus of 'I do' filled the room, and then she pointed to the sewing needles. They knew what they had to do. Only she and Gabby used the alcohol wipes – the boys didn't bother. They each pricked their finger, and as a bright bead of blood appeared, they pressed their fingers together and said the familiar mantra aloud. 'Friends forever!' they said loudly, and then Izzie handed each of them a superhero Band-Aid, which she helped them put on. She was still taking care of them thirteen years after kindergarten. She put a Wonder

Woman Band-Aid on Gabby's finger, and Batman on the boys as they laughed, and then they all hugged. The blood pact had been made. They had been planning it for months.

'Okay, you guys, we're done. It's official,' Izzie said, satisfied with the result. They left the room as a group, each wearing their superhero Band-Aid, and went back downstairs talking and laughing. Connie saw them as she came out of the kitchen.

'Uh-oh, what have you all been up to?' They looked victorious and euphoric, but she was pleased to see that all of them were sober.

'Nothing. They were signing my yearbook,' Sean was quick to answer.

'Why is it that I don't believe you?' she said, smiling at them, but whatever they'd been doing, it was probably harmless. They were all good kids. She was going to miss them terribly in the fall, almost as much as she knew they would miss each other. 'I just put your favourite cheesecake out on the dessert table, and some pies,' she told them, and they all went outside. They were looking very smug about something, and as all five helped themselves to cheesecake a few minutes later, they exchanged a long, mysterious smile. Friends forever. It was real – the pact had been sealed in blood.

And at ten o'clock that morning, they were all seated in chairs and lined up. An area had been roped off in Golden Gate Park, near the museum, for the graduation. It was the day they had all waited thirteen years for, from kindergarten through twelfth grade. And everyone was there, parents, grandparents, old friends, new ones. Izzie's father had invited Jennifer, which infuriated Izzie since he hadn't asked her, and her mother was there too and didn't seem to care that Jeff was with a woman. It had been five years since their divorce, and she had her own life. She hugged Izzie and told her how proud she was of her and looked as though she meant it. Larry Norton was there for Billy, and had brought a young bimbo with him, who looked like a hooker he had rented for the occasion. Billy knew she was just typical of the women he went out with, and his eyes glazed over when he saw her. Brian was there, sitting with his mother and Jack, four rows ahead of Larry and the woman he had with him. Kevin was sitting with his parents. Michelle was wearing a pretty, long-sleeved flowing print dress that hid how thin her arms were. She was still struggling with her weight but looking better. And for once, both of Andy's parents were there. His father had flown in from an important psychiatrists' meeting in Chicago the night before, and his mother let Marilyn know where she was sitting just in case things started to happen quickly. The parents who had cheered them on for thirteen years, and the teachers they had grown up with, were all there.

The class was waiting to file in, in the procession, and the head of the school and president of the board were waiting onstage to give out diplomas. The seniors had on their caps and gowns, ready to toss their hats in the air when the ceremony was over. And then the music began, and the teachers filed in and took their seats in the front rows. Two hundred cameras were pointed and poised at the ready when the procession came by, and to the strains of 'Pomp and Circumstance,' the senior class filed in, looking grown-up and dignified, and took their places onstage.

Andy was the valedictorian and made a moving speech. It was eloquently written, and his classmates cheered for him when it was over, and all through the audience parents were starting to cry with the emotions of the moment. This was a long-awaited day, and the beginning of their lives as adults. As Andy had just said in his speech, life would never be the same for any of them again.

Izzie made a speech as class president then, and reminded them all to remember how important they were to each other, and how much they had shared as they grew up. She wished them all a safe journey, and encouraged them to come home often. She promised each of them she would never forget them, and she looked at her four very special friends as she said it. 'I've loved you since kindergarten,' she said, 'and I don't intend to stop now. So go out there, make something of yourself, be important, and Billy Norton, you'd better be the best damn quarterback in college football!' Everybody laughed when she said it, and then she addressed the class again. 'But no matter how important any of you get, or how far you go, or how big a deal you become or think you are, always remember how much we love you,' she said in conclusion, and then went back to her seat next to Andy, since they were Wallace and Weston, the last two names on the alphabetical list of their class. And then the diplomas were distributed, and it was over. Their hats flew in the air after they removed the tassels to save them. They all ran around hugging each other and crying. It was happy chaos in the park, and Izzie couldn't believe it was over. Thirteen years at Atwood were finished.

They all had plans with their families for lunch and had promised to get together that night. There was a rumor that someone was giving a party, and they all waved at each other as they drove away. Brian and Billy were going with their mother and stepfather to Jack's restaurant. And they had invited Larry and his date to join them, just to be nice. He ordered scotch on the rocks the minute they got to the restaurant, and a bottle of expensive wine for lunch. His date said she was twenty-one years old, had never gone to college herself, and drank her way through a whole bottle of champagne. They both left the table early and said they had to be somewhere, but at least Larry remembered to tell Billy how proud of him he was. He said he could hardly wait to see him in his first college game, and Billy was just as excited to play it. He had wanted Gabby to come to lunch, but she had to be with her own family that day, and Billy had promised to meet her after lunch.

After Larry left, the cook brought out a graduation cake for Billy, with a football player on it in the Trojans uniform in scarlet and gold, and after that they went home. Billy drove over to see Gabby, Brian went next door to play with a friend, and Marilyn walked up the stairs to their bedroom, and felt as though she couldn't walk another step as she collapsed on the bed and looked at her husband.

'Thank God we didn't have triplets. I can hardly carry these two around anymore.' Helen had told her they were a good size, and they didn't seem to be in any hurry to be born. Jack sat on the bed and smiled at her and rubbed her ankles.

'Why don't you stay in bed the rest of the day?' he suggested. She had been up since early that morning, helping all of them get ready and celebrating Billy. She had taken a thousand pictures of him during graduation. She was so proud of him, and she had cried when they handed him his diploma. She closed her eyes to take a nap then, and it was nearly dinnertime when she woke up, and felt like there was a war inside her. The twins were hopping all over the place. It took a major effort to go downstairs and see where Jack was. He was making himself a bowl of soup in the kitchen, and he said the boys were still out. Brian was having dinner at his friend's next door and then going to a movie, and Billy was at Gabby's, and had called to say he was staying there for dinner. There was nothing much happening at their house these days, since Marilyn could hardly move now, and it was nice for her and Jack being there together, with everything so quiet.

'So, are we going to meet our girls tonight?' Jack asked her with a hopeful expression, and she laughed and shook her head.

'I think they're having some kind of dancing party, but I don't think they're going anywhere. I'm hardly having any contractions. Maybe I should run around the block or something.'

'Maybe not,' Jack said, and offered to make her something to eat, but she wasn't hungry. There was no room to fit even food into her body. She was always full now after two mouthfuls and had heartburn even looking at food. It really was time for it to be over. She kept saying she was ready, but apparently the twins weren't.

She kept Jack company while he ate his soup, and then she lumbered back upstairs, feeling like an elephant, and Jack put a movie on the TV in their bedroom. She got up to go to the bathroom before it started, and was saying something to him about the movie as she walked into the bathroom, and the instant she did, she felt as though there had been an explosion, and she was being hit by a tidal wave of water. It felt like it was everywhere and for a minute, she didn't know what happened, and then she remembered.

'Jack . . . ,' she said in a small voice and at first he didn't hear her. 'Jack . . . um . . . my water just broke . . .' She was looking dazed as he walked into the room to hear what she was saying.

'What? . . . Oh my God—' Everything she had on was soaked from the waist down, and she looked like she'd been standing in the shower. 'What happened?' And then he knew too, but wasn't sure what to do next. Marilyn started laughing.

'I look like I've been swimming.'

'Lie down or something,' Jack said nervously, and handed her a stack of towels. She took her wet clothes off, put on a terrycloth robe, went back to the bedroom, and lay on the towels. She could still feel the fluid leaking, but it seemed like most of it was gone. Jack was cleaning up the bathroom and came to check on her. 'Are you having contractions?'

'Not one. But the girls have gotten very quiet. No one's moving,' whereas half an hour before they had felt like they were dancing. Maybe they knew what was coming and were resting.

'I think we should call Helen.'

'She's probably having dinner, and I'm not having contractions. Why don't we wait awhile and call her later? She won't want me to come in if I'm not having contractions.'

'I think twins are different,' he said cautiously, looking nervous.

'Yeah, they take longer,' Marilyn reminded him. 'Let's watch the movie.' Jack had lost interest in the movie, but he turned it on to relax her and lay down next to her, watching her closely.

'Stop looking at me, I'm fine.' She leaned over and kissed him as she said it, and at that moment, she felt like she had been hit by a bomb. The worst contraction she could ever remember having ripped through her, as she grabbed Jack's shoulder and couldn't speak for a full five minutes. The minute it was over, Jack jumped out of bed and grabbed his BlackBerry.

'That's it, we're going. I'm calling Helen.' As he said it, she had another one, and she reached for him again. She squeezed his hand tightly while he called, and the minute Helen saw his name come up on her own BlackBerry, she answered.

'Hi there, what's happening? Any action?' Helen sounded calm and cheerful.

'Yeah, a lot of it, all of a sudden. Her water broke about ten minutes ago, and she just started having huge contractions, about two minutes apart, long ones. They lasted about five minutes.' Helen was frowning as she listened to him.

'It sounds to me like your two little ladies are in a hurry.' She thought for about two seconds and made a decision. 'Just let Marilyn lie there. Don't do anything. I'm going to send you an ambulance. They can take her downstairs on a gurney. I'm sure nothing will happen, but I'll feel better getting you to the hospital in an ambulance, just in case they're in a bigger hurry than we think. I'll meet you there.' She cut the connection, called an ambulance, and this time as the contraction hit, Marilyn screamed, and he wouldn't have admitted it to her, but Jack was scared. Everything was happening much faster than they'd expected.

The ambulance was there in five minutes. Jack let them know it was twins as he followed them upstairs, but Helen had already told them. They got Marilyn on a gurney and were out the front door, with Marilyn and Jack in the ambulance, less than three minutes after they arrived.

Marilyn was clutching Jack's arm and screaming now with every pain, and they never seemed to stop. The siren was on, and they were whizzing through the streets toward California Pacific Medical Center, where Helen had promised to meet them.

'I can't do this,' Marilyn said, panting between contractions.

'Yes, you can,' Jack said quietly. 'I'm right here. You're going to have them really soon, baby . . . It'll all be over soon.'

'No, I can't—' she insisted. 'Too much.' And as she said it, she screamed again, and when she laid her head back on the gurney, her eyes rolled back in her head. Jack was panicked, and the paramedic gave her oxygen and her eyes opened again. Her blood pressure was low, but she wasn't in any danger.

'You're doing fine,' he said to reassure them both, and then they were at the hospital, and Helen was waiting for them. She took in the scene with a practical eye, and smiled at both of them.

'Well, I can see you didn't waste any time,' she said to Marilyn. She could tell from looking at her that she was probably already dilated to ten, or close to it. She would have had the babies at home, if Helen hadn't sent the ambulance for them. 'If you don't mind, I'd like to get you to the delivery room, so no pushing,' she said to Marilyn in a firm voice, as Marilyn's face contorted, and she screamed again. 'Fast!' Marilyn said to the men who took the gurney out of the ambulance. Helen led the way at a dead run, they followed her, and Jack was running next to them, holding Marilyn's hand. She never stopped screaming from the ambulance to the delivery room, and Helen had a team waiting for them. They barely got Marilyn's terrycloth robe off, slipped a gown on her, and lifted her onto the delivery table, when she screamed such a fiercely piercing wail that Jack thought she was dying.

And what he heard instead seconds later was a long cry replacing hers, and a little face with a mane of red hair had appeared between her legs. Their first daughter had been born. Marilyn was smiling at him through tears, and Jack cried as he held her hand, and Helen cut the cord and handed the baby to a nurse. They still had work to do, and within seconds it all began again, the hideous contractions, the agonizing pain, Marilyn screamed as Helen helped her this time with forceps, and then another wail. Both babies had been born in less than ten minutes, forty-five minutes after it had all started. Helen said it was the fastest delivery of twins she had ever seen, but she also knew how hard it was when it went that quickly.

Marilyn was shaking violently, alternately crying and smiling and clinging to her husband, who kept looking from her to their beautiful babies. One of them had red hair like Marilyn's, and the other one had dark hair like his. They were fraternal twins, not identical, and they decided immediately which was Dana and which was Daphne. Jack still looked stunned. He had never seen anyone in so much pain, but it was all over so quickly.

'Thank God you sent the ambulance,' he said gratefully to Helen. 'She would have had them at home.'

'I think so,' Helen said, smiling at them. 'You certainly made things easy for me. You did all the work here,' she said to her patient. Marilyn still looked shaken, but she looked instantly better when they handed her the babies, and Jack looked at them proudly.

They kept Marilyn in the delivery room for another two hours, and put the babies in an incubator just to warm them. They each weighed just under eight pounds, and were strapping babies. Jack called all their children then and told them that their sisters had arrived. Billy thanked him somewhat tersely after asking if his mom was all right, and Brian wanted to know how soon he could see them. They were going to keep her in the hospital for two or three days.

It was ten o'clock that night when they rolled Marilyn into a room with her babies in little plastic bassinets on wheels. A nurse pushed one of them, and Jack was pushing the other, and he looked at Marilyn with open adoration. It had been a moment in his life he knew he would never forget, and the look of love that passed between them touched Helen's heart. It always did. She had stayed after Marilyn had delivered to make sure she was all right, and there were no complications after the birth, but everything was fine.

She left them a little while later, after giving Marilyn medication for the pain. She had been through a lot. Brian was going to stay at the neighbors'. Billy had said he'd stay at Gabby's, and Jack was going to spend the night at the hospital with Marilyn.

He watched her as she slept after that, and looked at their sleeping babies. They were exquisite and pink and so beautiful. It was one of the most perfect nights of his life.

Chapter 8

Everyone came to visit Marilyn and the babies while they were in the hospital. Brian was the first, early the next morning, driven by their neighbour, who said she had never seen anything as beautiful as their daughters, and that they looked so different from each other.

Brian took turns holding them, while Jack took pictures. And Billy arrived at lunchtime with Gabby, who couldn't stop looking at them and touching their little toes and fingers. Marilyn asked Billy if he wanted to hold them, but he said he didn't. He said they were too little. Connie and Mike dropped by and brought sweaters and booties that she had been knitting for them for months, and Sean was with them. They said Kevin was away for the weekend with friends, and as Connie said it, Marilyn saw a cloud pass across her eyes, and she looked at her with concern.

'Is he okay?' she said softly. Kevin had seemed distant and distracted the night of the graduation barbeque, but he had left quickly and she hadn't gotten a good look. She knew Connie had been worried for a while.

'I think so,' Connie said quietly, and then went back to admiring the babies. Izzie walked in while they were there, and Andy came just as they left. And then Judy appeared at dinnertime with a stack of gifts, with Michelle and Gabby. Everyone said they'd never seen anything cuter than the twins. They had constant visitors for two days. Jack's boys were away with their mother, so they hadn't seen the babies, but Jack sent them dozens of pictures with his phone.

At the end of two days, Marilyn said she wanted to go home so she could get some rest, and Helen said it sounded like a good idea to her. She was very pleased with how all three of them were doing. And she discharged them at nine o'clock the next morning. Marilyn was going to try to nurse both of them, with some supplements, but her milk hadn't come in yet. Helen thought it might be better for her if she were at home when that happened. There were too many people visiting her in the hospital for her to just calm down and get used to her babies. But Jack was being terrific, as always, and when they got home, he helped Marilyn get settled, and Brian wanted to do whatever he could with his sisters too.

Marilyn heaved a sigh of relief when she slipped into their familiar bed.

'Wow! Everything happened so fast, it doesn't seem real yet.'

'It's real,' Jack assured her, as both babies started crying at the same time, and they both laughed. It was going to be crazy for a while, and Marilyn's mother had offered to come and help her. But she was in her seventies, not in good health, and she would just be one more person for Marilyn to take care of, so Marilyn had asked her to come later in the summer, and for now she and Jack were going to try to manage on their own, with a little assistance from Brian. She insisted that she didn't want a baby nurse. Jack had offered and he could afford one, but Marilyn knew these would be her last babies, and she didn't want to miss a minute of it, and she was determined to do it all herself, with Jack, and he had agreed. But she was surprised by how exhausted she felt. Just walking across the room, to where the babies were sleeping in their bassinets, seemed like a lot of effort, and she wasn't even nursing yet. She and the twins were just getting used to each other.

Brian had gone out with friends, and she had just lain down for a nap that afternoon, after settling the babies in their bassinets, when the phone rang. Marilyn could tell from her caller ID that it was Connie, but there was no sound when she answered the phone. Marilyn thought the phone had been disconnected and was about to hang up when she heard a long, low howl that sounded more like an animal than a human. At first, she didn't know what it was as she listened, and then she suddenly heard her friend's voice and her blood ran cold.

'Kevin' was the only word Connie was able to say to her, and for the next many minutes all she could do was sob. Marilyn didn't know if he'd been injured, had an accident, had a fight with them, or been arrested again. All she could do was wait until Connie caught her breath.

'Take it easy, I'm right here . . . do you want me to come over?' For an instant, she forgot that she'd given birth three days before, but she'd have gone over anyway. 'Connie – tell me what happened.' She waited as Jack walked into the room, and he could see from his wife's face that something terrible had occurred.

'Who is it?' he whispered, and she mouthed Connie's name, as Connie continued to sob into the phone.

'I'm coming over,' Marilyn said, unable to stand it anymore. She knew she could get to her house faster than it was taking Connie to tell her over the phone what was wrong.

'He's dead,' she said, and then howled the same agonizing sound Marilyn had heard when she answered the phone.

'Oh my God . . . oh my God . . . I'm coming over. Are you alone?' Connie was incoherent, and Marilyn leaped out of bed so fast that her head swam for an instant, and then she ran toward the bathroom, still holding the phone, as Jack watched her. 'Where's Mike?'

'He's here. They just called us,' Connie managed to choke out between sobs.

'Just hang in there. I'll be there in five minutes.' Marilyn disconnected the call with a shaking hand and stared at Jack in disbelief. 'Kevin O'Hara just died. I don't know how it happened. I have to go over there. You stay with the babies. If they wake up, give them one of the bottles of water they gave us at the hospital – they'll be fine.'

'You can't drive,' he said, looking frantic. 'You just gave birth.' She was already calling Billy, and he answered right away.

'Where are you?' she said quickly.

'I'm at Gabby's. What's the big deal?' He could hear that his mother was wound up about something, but he didn't know what it was.

'I need you to come home right away.'

'Why?' He sounded suspicious and annoyed.

'I need you to drive me to the O'Haras'. Something happened to Kevin.'

'I'll be right there,' he said immediately, and hung up. He was at the house by the time she was dressed and downstairs. Jack kissed her goodbye and told her not to overdo it. She looked pale and upset, but she wanted to go to her friend. The unthinkable had happened.

Billy drove her to the O'Haras' in less than five minutes, and Marilyn hurried to the front door as fast as she could with Billy right behind her. Sean was standing in the entrance hall, staring at them, and he dissolved in sobs in Billy's arms, as Marilyn rushed upstairs to find Connie. She found her and Mike in their bedroom, holding each other and sobbing, and the moment she saw them Marilyn burst into tears, and sat down on the bed with them and put her arms around them.

'He was shot doing a drug deal in the Tenderloin,' Connie said in agony, as Mike just sat on the bed shaking and sobbing. 'They said he was buying to sell, and he owed the dealer money. They got in an argument, and the dealer shot him . . . My baby . . . my baby . . . they killed my baby.' She was inconsolable, and Mike was distraught, as Marilyn sat with them. She had no idea what to say or do for them, except be there, with her arms around her friends. She held Connie and rocked her in her arms, and then finally she got up and went downstairs to get water and tea. When she came back, she asked Connie if she wanted her to call their doctor, and she shook her head.

'We have to go and identify the body,' she said, dissolving in sobs again. 'I'm afraid to see him . . . I can't . . .' She was incoherent with grief, as Marilyn made her take a sip of water, and tightly squeezed Mike's hand. Billy and Sean walked into the room then, and Marilyn was shocked to realize that Sean was now their only son. No matter how hard they had tried to save Kevin from himself, and how much they had loved him, he had outfoxed them in the end. They couldn't stop him. Sean looked as heart-broken as his parents, and Billy was standing close to him, devastated for his friend. Kevin had been Sean's hero as a little boy, and now he had been murdered in a drug deal, while buying drugs to sell them. Connie had been right when she'd thought he was slipping again. But he was elusive and never able to resist temptation for long, no matter how well he had appeared to be doing. It was frightening to realize how fast things could go wrong, and this was what it led to: grieving parents, and a child they had loved who was dead. Both parents and kids were so much more vulnerable than they knew.

Mike got up and shuffled aimlessly around the room as both women stared at him. They had to go to the morgue, and Marilyn couldn't even imagine it.

'Do you want Jack to go with you?' Marilyn offered, and Mike shook his head and stared at her with eyes that looked like his soul was bleeding through them.

'No, I'll do it,' he said softly, as Sean went and stood next to him.

'I'll go with you, Dad,' he said bravely. He was shaking, and looked small next to Billy, although he wasn't. And there was a shocking look of maturity in his eyes now. He wasn't a boy, he was a man. Connie lay down on the bed and moaned softly, at the mention of identifying her son.

'I don't want to see him that way,' Connie said, whimpering. 'I can't – it will kill me.' Mike picked up his car keys, and Sean followed his father out of the room, as Marilyn looked down at Connie.

'Why don't you come home with me, until they get back?' Marilyn couldn't bear to think of where they were going and what they'd be doing. 'You can help me with the babies.' Connie nodded and got up. She moved like a robot when she did, as Marilyn led her out of the room and down the stairs. She was glad that Connie was willing to go with her. She seemed docile and broken.

Marilyn helped her into the front seat, got in behind Billy, and he drove them back to their house, and as soon as Marilyn walked in, she heard both babies crying, and Jack appeared at the top of the stairs, holding one in each arm and looking frantic.

'They've been crying since you left,' he said, and then he saw Connie, and Marilyn hurried up the stairs, as she realized what had happened. Her milk had come in, and the whole front of her shirt was wet. Connie came up slowly behind her and followed them into the bedroom, while Billy went to call the others and tell them what had happened. It was the most shocking news any of them had ever heard. Marilyn was grateful that Brian was still out, and she asked Jack to call the parents of the boy he was with to keep him for a while, till dinnertime at least, until things settled down at the house, and Jack agreed. They wanted to do all they could to help Connie, Mike, and Sean.

Marilyn climbed into their bed, as Connie sat down in a rocking chair with a devastated expression. Marilyn opened her shirt, unhooked her nursing bra, and Jack handed both crying babies to her. She hadn't gotten the hang of doing it with two of them yet, but she knew they needed to be fed, and she was the only one who had what they wanted. The babies' timing was exactly what they had expected – they just hadn't expected this tragedy to happen. Kevin O'Hara was dead at twenty-five.

Jack gently covered Marilyn with a blanket in case Billy walked in, and Connie sat watching her, crying softly. She could still remember nursing Kevin as though it was yesterday, and now he was gone. She just sat there and sobbed, and then at Marilyn's invitation, she climbed into bed with her and sat next to her while she nursed her babies. It was comforting to Connie just to be there, and she gently stroked Daphne's head while she lay at her mother's breast and finally fell asleep. Jack took them from her as she finished nursing them, burped them, and set them down in their bassinets, and then he came to sit on the foot of the bed with the two women.

'I'm so sorry, Connie,' he said, as she nodded and continued crying, and Marilyn hugged her again. They sat there until Mike and Sean came to the house. Mike looked ashen after identifying Kevin. Sean hadn't seen him, but both father and son had sobbed all the way back to Marilyn and Jack's house to pick up Connie. They sat talking for a while, and Sean went to find Billy and then they went home. Marilyn told them to call if they needed anything, and she promised to come over in the morning. She was going to help Connie make the funeral arrangements. She couldn't imagine living through it, or how devastated Connie must feel, and for a shameful moment, which she admitted to Jack later as she nursed their babies again, she had been grateful that it wasn't one of her children. She couldn't imagine losing Billy or Brian.

Brian came home after dinner and was shocked when they told him about Kevin. Both boys were sad and silent that night. None of their friends could believe it, nor could Marilyn and Jack. She called Connie again that night to see how she was doing. She still couldn't stop crying. She said she'd been in Kevin's room trying to pick a suit for him to wear in his casket, and she dissolved in sobs again as she said it. Marilyn felt terrible that she couldn't be at the house with them that night, but she couldn't leave Jack alone with the twins when they needed to be nursed. In the few hours since her milk had come in, they were ravenous, and it wasn't fair to leave him with starving babies who wouldn't be satisfied with anything he had to give them. The timing was terrible, but Marilyn was determined to manage it somehow. She called Judy and asked her to come to Connie's with her the next day. She had just heard from Gabby what had happened, and she couldn't believe it. It was horrifying to think about and had shocked them all.

Billy's phone had been ringing all night as friends

called him, and a little while later he went back to the O'Haras' to stay with Sean. Izzie came over and sat and cried with them, and then Andy came by, and drove her home.

Billy was still at the house when Marilyn got there in the morning. Judy had picked her up and helped her with the babies, and they took turns manning the phones and doing whatever they could for Connie. She and Mike had to go to the funeral parlor that morning to pick a casket and make the arrangements. But there was so much more to do, people to call, among them the florist, the priest, and the newspaper about the obit. Connie did what she could while they were out. There was going to be a rosary, they had to write a notice of the funeral, and Connie said it was going to be at St. Dominic's, which was their parish and where Kevin had received his first Communion and been confirmed. It was unthinkable to any of them that they were talking about Kevin's funeral, and when Marilyn glanced at Mike, he looked like a broken man.

Sean was sitting on the front steps with Billy, who wore a woe-begone expression. Gabby had come over, and Izzie showed up a little while later, and Andy called several times. No one knew what to do to help the O'Haras. They couldn't bring Kevin back, and all they could do was be there for their friends. Marilyn couldn't imagine living through it, but Connie was a strong woman, and by the time they left for the funeral parlor, she was able to stop crying at least for a few minutes. She was carrying Kevin's suit with her on a hanger, and a white shirt and a tie, and she had socks and his dress shoes in a shopping bag. She looked sadly at Marilyn as she got into the car with her husband and reached out to hug her friend. The two women stood embracing for a long moment.

'Thank you' was all she was able to say without sobbing again.

'I love you' was all Marilyn could say, and from the bottom of her heart she meant it. 'I'm so sorry.' Connie nodded and looked at her.

'I know,' she said, and with that, Mike started the car and they drove away, to the funeral parlor where their beautiful older son would be washed and dressed and have his hair combed for the last time.

Chapter 9

Kevin O'Hara's funeral was unbearable, unthinkable, intolerable for the entire group. The parents sat there listening to the eulogy, horrified, and at the same time grateful that it hadn't happened to their own child. The friends he had grown up with came to mourn him and remember what a sweet kid he had once been. Connie, Mike, and Sean sat in the front pew, looking like they'd been struck by lightning, as the closed casket sat in front of them, like a warning to them all.

The message was one that no one wanted to hear, parents and kids alike: 'Be careful. Be watchful. Be smart. This could happen to you.' It had happened to them, and no one could wrap their mind around it. It was easy to say that Kevin had gone wrong somewhere, that he had been arrested, wound up in rehab, and spent two years on probation, but once upon a time he had been a little boy, an innocent child with the same chance at life as anyone else. Was it his fault? His parents'? His destiny? Life? What warning had they not heeded, what danger signs had they ignored? Why was it Kevin in the box at the front of the church and not someone else? Others had taken the same risks and hadn't died. As she went over every minute of his life, as she sat in the front pew, Connie was no longer sure of anything. All she knew was that he was gone, and it was an agony beyond belief. A pain so enormous and intense that she felt as though her eyeballs were melting and her heart was on fire, and at the same time she felt ice cold.

Connie didn't know what she felt anymore except a searing pain as she watched her husband and younger son and six of Kevin's classmates carry his casket out of the church and put it gently in the hearse to take to the cemetery, where they would put him in a hole in the ground and bury him. She wanted to throw herself in with him, she had loved him so much when he was born, but she couldn't do that to Mike and Sean now. She had to be there for them, and be strong. She didn't know how to do it – all she knew was that she had no other choice. Kevin had left her to hold up his brother and father, and she had none of the answers anymore. A piece of her own flesh had been shot and killed in a drug deal in the Tenderloin. It really was unthinkable. And they had no idea who had done it to him, only that he was dead and what drugs were in Kevin's possession at the time. There was no one to punish, no one to avenge it, but even if they had found the killer, it wouldn't bring her son back now.

They drove out to the cemetery in the limousine they had hired, and stood at the graveside as the priest said a few words, and then Connie touched her son's casket for a last time, the one they had picked with the white satin in it. He was wearing his suit and tie and best shoes, and they were going to leave him there, along with a part of her heart. She was too devastated to even cry on the way home, and everyone who had been at the funeral was waiting for them when they got back.

Marilyn had come to the house to greet them, and Jack's restaurant had catered it, like a bar mitzvah or a wedding, only it wasn't, it was a funeral.

Afterward Connie couldn't remember who had been at the house. All she remembered was that Marilyn had set pictures of Kevin all around the living room and in the front hall. And when it was all over, Mike and Sean were sitting in the study, looking like survivors of a shipwreck.

Sean's friends had stayed to support him, and the young people went upstairs to hang out in Sean's room. Connie and Mike, and Marilyn and Jack, and Judy and Adam sat there staring at each other, unable to believe what had happened. All they knew was that Connie and Mike's son Kevin was dead, but what did it mean? How did you come to understand that you'd never see a child you loved again? It was beyond imagining, and Connie kept expecting him to come downstairs any minute in his suit and tie and dress shoes and tell them it was all a joke. Only it wasn't. It was all too real. His room would be empty forever. His trophies would gather dust and mean nothing. His clothes would hang in his closet until she had the courage to give them away. All Connie understood as she looked at Mike was that they'd never be the same again.

'You two need to get some rest,' Marilyn said softly. They both looked exhausted, and Connie said they hadn't slept since it happened.

Jack's staff had left the kitchen impeccable, and there was food for them to eat in the fridge, if they got hungry, but Connie couldn't imagine their ever wanting to eat again. Her clothes were already hanging on her and felt too loose after only a few days.

Marilyn and Jack finally left the O'Haras' at dinnertime. The others had gone home long before. And Sean was still upstairs with his best friends. After they played some video games, Billy took out a flask and passed it around. There was bourbon in it, which was all he'd been able to take from his parents' bar when no one was looking. Gabby and Izzie turned it away after one sip, but Billy, Sean, and Andy took long swigs until it was gone.

'That's not going to help anything,' Izzie said quietly, always the voice of their conscience in the group. 'It'll just make you feel worse.' Andy looked sheepish when she said it, Billy shrugged, and Sean lay down on his bed. He had nothing to say, and he was tired of people saying how sorry they were. They weren't sorry, they didn't even know. How did they know what it felt like? Even his friends. He would never see his brother again. He was suddenly an only child.

'Do you want to stay at my place tonight?' Billy asked him. He could only guess how much his friend was hurting. He could see it in his eyes.

'I should probably stay here,' Sean said with a sigh. It had been an exhausting day. 'My mom and dad are in pretty bad shape,' he said matter-of-factly. The contents of the flask had helped to take the edge off. He no longer felt quite as raw, as though barbed wire had been tearing through his skin all day. With the help of the bourbon, he no longer felt the pain. And being numb felt good.

Andy was the first to leave – he had promised to have dinner with his parents. And then Gabby and Billy left, and only Izzie stayed.

'You're going to be okay, you know. I know this must be horrible, and I've never had a sister or a brother, but somehow you're going to make it through this. You'll be okay.' If she hadn't been a girl, he would have wanted to hit her, but even thinking it made him want to cry.

'I'm going to stop things like that one day,' Sean said quietly, as they lay down side by side on his bed, and looked up at the ceiling. Sometimes he thought she was his best friend in the whole group, depending on the day.

'How're you going to do that?' she asked, sounding curious, as though they were little kids again and she was asking him how to catch a fish, or how a submarine worked, or what made the fog roll in.

'I'm going to work for the FBI when I finish college, and I'm going to arrest assholes like the one who killed my brother.' Neither of them said that Kevin shouldn't have been there in the first place. There was no point now, he was dead.

'You always used to say that when you were a little kid.' She smiled at him.

'Well, now I will.' He sounded certain, and she almost believed him. She knew he meant it at that moment.

'You might change your mind when you get out of college. Maybe you'll want to do something else.' She was always the voice of reason, and the most practical of the five.

'No, I won't. I always knew I wanted to do something like that. I just didn't know why. Now I do.' He turned over and lay on his side and looked at her then. He wondered what it would be like to kiss her, but he didn't really want to, she was his friend.

'I'm going to miss you when you're away at school,' Izzie said simply, and he nodded.

'I'm going to miss you too,' he said sadly, more than ever now. Losing Kevin would make being away from his friends even harder, and he hated to leave his parents after this. He could already feel it.

'I wish you were coming to L.A.,' Izzie said wistfully.

'I'll see you at Thanksgiving and Christmas,' he said, and rolled slowly off his bed. 'Come on, I'll drive you home.'

They said very little in the car – it was just nice being together. She was trying not to think of what it would have been like if the funeral had been for one of them today. She couldn't imagine it and didn't want to. And she wondered if Sean would really join the FBI one day. It still seemed like a dangerous idea to her. And he had new responsibilities to his parents now, as an only child.

He dropped her off at her father's house, and she told him she'd come by the next day. And he went back to the house that seemed so dead now. His parents' bedroom door was closed when he got home, and the house was dark. He walked past Kevin's bedroom on the way to his own, and for a minute he wanted to go in, and instead he walked into his own room and closed the door, lay down on his bed, and cried.

Izzie and the others came to visit Sean every day, and most days Billy brought the flask with him, with whatever he'd been able to steal from his parents' bar, when his mother was busy with the twins. They still annoyed him, but once they started smiling a little, he had to admit they were kind of cute. He even held them a couple of times. And Brian acted like he was in love with them. He had learned how to change their diapers and helped his mother put them to bed, which was something Billy had no desire to learn. But Gabby thought they were cute too. Billy was glad she was on the Pill and couldn't get pregnant. He couldn't have handled an accident of that kind, and knew he wouldn't be ready for kids of his own for at least another ten or fifteen years.

On the one day he couldn't steal booze from his

parents' bar to put in the flask, he had gotten a homeless guy to buy him two six-packs of beer. Sean and Billy managed to get drunk every day for most of June. Originally it was in Kevin's honor, and after a while it was something to do. All of them were bored, although some of them had summer jobs. Sean was helping his father a few hours a day, Izzie was working at a summer day camp at a community center, and Gabby was busy getting ready to leave and not working, and neither was Billy. Jack and his mom were giving Billy a break and said he didn't have to work his last summer before college. He and Sean sat around drinking every afternoon instead. Andy had a summer job where he had to work mornings, but at lunchtime he came by to see his friends. He was working in a lab, and his mother had gotten him the job. They never let him do anything interesting at the lab, although they were impressed that he was going to Harvard and would be pre-med. But all they let him do anyway was take out the trash or hand forms and clipboards to the patients when they walked in. He wasn't drinking as much as the others, but he took a sip now and then.

It was Izzie who finally called them to order and called them a bunch of losers halfway through July.

'What are you going to do when you're in college? Sign up for AA? You're turning into a bunch of drunks. You're a drag to be with, and all you ever do is drink and play video games and feel sorry for yourselves. You make me sick.' She looked straight at Sean when she said it, and he hung his head. His brother had been dead for only five weeks, and everyone else had given him a pass, but not Izzie, and he knew she was right.

'So what are we supposed to do?' Billy looked at her as Sean handed the flask back to him. This time he hadn't taken a sip, for the first time in weeks.

'Why don't we go to the beach or something?' Izzie suggested.

'Because it's freezing,' Billy said practically. The fog had been in for days. San Francisco was always chilly in July and often dreary and gray, which didn't help their mood.

'So what? It's something to do. Better than sitting around here drunk doing nothing.'

So the next day, after they finished work at noon, they crossed the Golden Gate Bridge and went to Marin. They went to the state beach at Stinson, and had hamburgers, and then sat on the beach in the chill wind. But they all admitted they felt better when they got home.

Izzie stayed and talked to Sean again after the others left. 'Are you going to be okay when you go away to school?' She was worried about him, more than she was willing to admit. His parents looked terrible, but in some ways Sean looked worse. He had dark circles under his eyes and said he couldn't sleep. He kept thinking about his brother and what must have happened when he died. It was driving him insane.

'Yeah, I guess I will,' he answered Izzie, but he didn't sound convinced.

'You have to be now, for your parents' sake,' she pointed out to him. 'You're all they have left.' It was a heavy burden for him. For her and Andy, as only children, it was the situation they'd been in all their lives. But their parents had had only children by choice. In Sean's case, he was an only surviving son, which was considerably worse and more complicated. His parents would miss Kevin for the rest of their lives, and Sean knew he had to make it up to them somehow. It was all he could think of late at night. 'Are you sure you still want to go east?' You could transfer to UCLA, and then you'd be closer to them.' But he just shook his head. Now he really wanted to leave. He couldn't stand it here anymore, knowing that Kevin wasn't in his room and never would be again, and hearing his parents cry all the time. All he wanted to do now was get out. Izzie understood. It was hard even for her now being in this house, and she wasn't living there.

They spent the next two weeks hanging out together after work, but Sean stopped drinking at least. The only one who drank from the flask now was Billy, and he seemed to be drinking less too. He knew he had to get serious about school.

He was the first to leave, in early August. He had to start practice three weeks before school started. Gabby left San Francisco the weekend after he did, to look for an apartment in L.A. with her mom. Before they all left, the five friends had dinner together one night, and then went out to the beach. They promised to call each other often, and they were going to come home for Thanksgiving, but after being together every day for thirteen years, it seemed aeons away. And they all promised to go see Billy play at USC.

Izzie went to Gabby's house the morning she was to leave. They had breakfast together. And Izzie noticed that Michelle seemed thinner again, but she didn't say anything about it. She figured they all knew, and Michelle was clearly struggling with her eating disorder. Izzie wondered if Gabby not being there would make it better or worse. It was hard living in Gabby's shadow, no matter how much the two sisters loved each other.

She and Michelle stood on the sidewalk and waved as Gabby and her mother drove away, and they were both crying. Her mother was driving a van, and Gabby was taking half her wardrobe and her most precious possessions for the apartment they were hoping to find. Gabby wanted to rent a place in West Hollywood. She had been looking for furnished rentals online, and there were three they wanted to see. She was sad but excited as they drove away, and Izzie went back inside and talked to Michelle for a while. She was going into junior year and was nervous about it. And after that Izzie went to see Andy. She wanted to spend time with him before he left too.

And after seeing Andy, Izzie went back to visit Sean. His mother was cleaning out closets, and she cried every time she came across Kevin's stuff. It had only been two months. The house felt like a tomb, and Connie treated Kevin's room like a shrine. Nothing in it had been touched.

Andy was the next to leave. His father was flying to Boston with him, and he was planning to live in a dorm. He saw Sean and Izzie the night before he left, and he texted Izzie right before he got on the plane: '*Be good. I'll miss you. Love, A.*'

Fortunately Izzie and Sean were both leaving San Francisco on the same day. Neither of them wanted to be left behind. It would have been too hard.

Izzie had to have dinner with her father the night before she left, but she went to say goodbye to Sean after dinner, and his mom gave her a big hug.

'You take care of yourself in L.A.,' she said with a serious look. 'Be careful. I want to see you all back here for Thanksgiving in one piece. And don't give your heart away the first day.'

'There's no chance of that,' Izzie said, and laughed. 'I'll be too busy with school.'

'You're going to have every boy in L.A. after you, if they have eyes in their heads.' Izzie had never felt as pretty as Gabby, and none of her guy friends had ever mentioned her looks. She never thought about it herself. They were just friends. Her mother had never taught her all the tricks that Judy taught Gabby, to look sexy for a boy. And no one had gone shopping with Izzie in years. She just took all her same old school stuff to L.A. Her father hadn't even thought of it, and she didn't want to ask. She had enough. But Connie had been shipping things to the dorm for Sean for weeks – sheets, towels, a pillow, bathroom supplies, two posters, a bedspread, a rug. She had gotten him all new stuff, just as she had for Kevin when he went to Santa Cruz. And this was a much bigger deal, since Sean was going so far away. His parents were dreading what it would be like when he was gone.

Connie had told Mike a few days before that they would just have to pretend that both boys were away at school. And she had promised to help Marilyn with the twins, which she thought would be fun. They were an incredible amount of work. Marilyn said she had forgotten how much energy it took. She was beginning to feel old and said she never caught up. And she was doing everything times two.

Connie and Mike flew to Washington with Sean, to get him settled and set him up. The O'Haras flew back the next day on a late flight, and dreaded entering the silent house.

Jeff drove Izzie to L.A. and spent the whole day setting up her sound system and computer, and a small fridge in her dorm room at UCLA. She had a roommate who seemed nice and had sent her an e-mail before she got there. Her parents were there too, and when Jeff left, the two girls went to look for the cafeteria together, since they were on the same meal plan. And she called Gabby, who loved her new apartment. They'd found one on Alta Loma off Sunset. Izzie went to see it that weekend, and it looked very grown-up to her. It was in a building with a doorman and a pool. The furniture was basic, but Gabby had put some of her own things around. And they'd shopped a little and added to it.

'Wow, you're already living like a movie star,' Izzie teased her and Gabby said Billy came by every night, from his dorm at USC. She said he was going to move in with her next year, when he could leave the dorms, and her parents thought it was okay. Gabby's apartment was about ten times the size of Izzie's room at the dorm.

Her father had given her a car, a black Land Rover from his dealership, and it looked beautiful and new. All Izzie had brought to UCLA was a bicycle to use at school. Her father hadn't given her a car, and couldn't afford to, and her mother thought she was too young to own one. So she was planning to get around off campus by cab and public transportation.

Judy and the girls always had nice cars, thanks to Gabby's father and the dealership he owned. Michelle had just gotten a Land Rover that year when she turned sixteen. And Izzie would have been jealous of Gabby's new car if she didn't love her so much.

Izzie came by to visit her the next day too. Her roommate was busy with her friends at school, and Gabby's apartment was going to be a great place to hang out, when she had nothing else to do. Billy was going to be at practice a lot of the time, and he wouldn't be able to get out every night during football season. So the girls were planning to spend time together whenever Gabby was free, and Izzie could do her homework there. It was exciting to be away from their parents and anyone else's rules. It felt so grown-up.

Sean texted Izzie from Washington D.C., that night. He said the campus at GW was cool, and he had already started classes. He said he hadn't heard from Andy, and Izzie hadn't either. He was busy moving into the dorm and getting situated, as they all were. Gabby had appointments to get an agent. She was going to sign up at a modeling agency, if they'd have her, and Izzie was sure they would. She was a gorgeous girl. And she was going to take acting classes once she got settled, so she could do commercials, and eventually a screen test for feature films.

The next day Izzie registered for classes, which was a lengthy process. She had come to school a little earlier than she needed to, to consult with her adviser, and figure out what classes she needed to take. Coming down early also gave her more time to spend with Gabby. After meeting with her adviser, Izzie signed up for philosophy, psychology, a basic math class that was a requirement, and art history, which was an introductory course. And she could tell from reading the syllabuses of her classes that it was going to be a lot of work. She looked around as she got familiar with the campus. People were friendly, and the students had a familiar look. The school had a big-city feel to it, unlike San Francisco, which was a small town. And she liked what she saw. At times she felt lonely for her old friends – it was the first time since kindergarten that she'd be going to school without them. But at least she had Gabby and Billy nearby and as she got acquainted with her new city, she felt a confidence she'd never felt before, and thought to herself, *Okay, world! Here I come!* Izzie was off and running.

Chapter 10

The silence in the house was much worse than Connie had expected. She and Mike sat alone and miserable every night, with nothing to say to each other. There were no other voices, no one came and went all day. All the parents of the kids who had left were feeling the emptiness of it, but it was much worse for Mike and Connie, after Kevin's death. And the killer had not been found. There had been an investigation, but the police had admitted they had no idea who had done it, no witnesses had come forward, so there would be no justice in the death of Kevin O'Hara, which made it that much worse. And it tore Connie's heart out to see her husband come home with a vacant look in his eyes every night. Mike O'Hara looked like a broken man, and Connie felt that way herself. They were getting through the days, but barely more than that. Every hour was a struggle.

Connie went over to visit Marilyn often, and loved playing with the babies, who were three months old now and totally responsive. They smiled and laughed and cooed. But no matter how much fun she had holding them, or helping Marilyn to take care of them, sooner or later Connie had to go home to her empty house, and she said it was killing her, and she had no idea how to make it better. There was no road map for what had happened or manual for how to get through it. All she and Mike could do was live it day by day, hour by hour.

She called Sean often in Washington, and talking to him helped a little, but he could hear how sad she was whenever they spoke on the phone. Usually they exchanged e-mails, but Connie couldn't restrain herself and called him daily at the slightest excuse, until he asked her to cut down on the calls. They always caught him at a bad time, e-mail was better. But Connie missed hearing his voice so she called anyway. Mike was more stoic about it, but Connie admitted to Marilyn that she was in agony most of the time over Kevin's death. And she inquired frequently how Billy was doing at USC. Marilyn said so far so good. He said the practices were gruelling but he was learning a lot, and he loved the coach.

'At least he's learning more about football. I'm not sure what else he's doing. Probably nothing,' Marilyn said with a rueful look. 'And he's with Gabby a lot,' she added, which was no surprise to them.

Gabby had already been booked for her first modeling job, through her new agent, and she called home, all excited about it.

It made both women sad that all the kids were scattered. They had known it was coming, but now it was real.

Marilyn admitted sheepishly one day that she had forgotten they would grow up. And at least she still had Brian at home. He had just gone into eighth grade and discovered girls. It was like starting over, watching him with all his crushes. Marilyn commented that ever since she'd married Jack, Brian had someone to play with, and a man to talk to. She confirmed to Connie that he was a really good guy. He was great with the twins too, and helped her all the time. She couldn't have managed them without him. She never heard from Larry anymore, now that Billy was gone. He never even tried to see Brian, who, fortunately, had bonded with Jack.

All the kids seemed to be settling into their various colleges in September. And it was October when Judy realized that Michelle's anorexia was slipping out of control again. She got a call from Michelle's counselor at Atwood, who was worried about her, and she started outpatient treatment and therapy, as she had before, It was an insidious disease. Judy was shocked when they weighed her. She hadn't realized how bad it had gotten, since Michelle always wore loose clothes. She was taller than her sister, and she weighed ninety pounds at five feet nine. This time at her evaluation, they recommended to Judy and Adam that she be hospitalized and treated as an inpatient, until she gained some weight. They were afraid of the strain on her heart, and they wanted her to do group therapy on a daily basis with other girls with eating disorders. When they got home from the meeting, Judy cried and called Connie and Marilyn to tell them. No one was surprised, and she and Adam reluctantly put her in the inpatient program, in spite of Michelle's protests. She threatened to run away, but she didn't. She had to take a leave of absence from school, and they wanted her there for six weeks until Thanksgiving, and then they would reevaluate her. Judy felt like an utter failure when she realized how sick her daughter was, in spite of the help she'd had before.

In the first group therapy session that included parents, Michelle had said that all her parents cared about was her older sister. Both her parents had cried and said it wasn't true. They loved her too. And there were other stories in the group just like hers. Connie and Marilyn didn't say it to Judy, but they both agreed that the only way Michelle could get her mother's attention was by starving, and now finally she was the focus of their world, not Gabby, who was doing so well in L.A. Although it pained her, Judy realized that Michelle was benefiting from being in the hospital, and she already looked better than she had at home.

Judy went to visit her constantly, and there were other girls in the program whom Michelle liked and felt something in common with. And Gabby was calling her from L.A. every day. She even apologized for not paying more attention to her before she left home, but Michelle said it was okay. She was getting what she needed now. And she knew how busy Gabby had been before she left, and understood.

The only thing that surprised Michelle, once she was in the hospital, was a visit from Billy's younger brother, Brian. He was three years younger than she was, but he said he missed seeing her around school, and he liked her. He had taken the bus over to UC Hospital, and he justified it by reminding her that his brother and her sister were boyfriend and girlfriend and best friends, and had been for thirteen years, as long as he'd been alive.

'What does that make us?' Michelle teased him when he came to visit. 'In-laws?' He was a sweet, friendly boy, and he looked up to her as an older, wiser friend. He was a genuinely nice person and was sorry about her long hospital stay. Brian was bright and a good student, tall for his age like his brother Billy, and looked older than he was. He had matured a lot in the last year. He appeared and sounded far more adult than his thirteen years, closer to Billy's age. He talked about how much he liked his stepfather and twin sisters and brought Michelle a box of cupcakes, which she actually ate. She hadn't eaten anything even remotely like it in the past three years, since she started starving herself, but she didn't want to disappoint him. She was touched that he had come to visit her, and during his regular friendly visits they became fast friends, despite the difference in their ages. He was wise beyond his years.

'Maybe one day we will be in-laws,' Brian said pensively as he ate one of the cupcakes with her. He brought her cupcakes every trip, and she seemed to like them, and he bought them with his allowance. 'Do you think Gabby and Billy will get married one day?' he asked her, and she smiled at the naïveté she could see in his eyes. He looked like a man but was just a kid.

'Probably. Neither of them has ever looked at anyone

else, and they're crazy about each other. They act like they're married now.' Michelle had admitted in group therapy that she was jealous of her sister and the relationship she had with Billy. She would have loved to have a boyfriend too, but she didn't think she was pretty enough for any boy to want her. At sixteen, she had never been kissed, and she felt unattractive to boys. The other girls in the group had pointed out to her that if she put on a little weight, she might be more appealing. And when she and Brian talked about how they felt about themselves. Brian admitted that he had always felt like less than Billy too. They had a lot in common as the younger siblings of two 'stars,' which was hard to live up to. They were both better students than their older, charismatic siblings, but in other ways neither of them felt they could compete. And they both took comfort in knowing that someone else felt as they did.

Brian became a regular visitor at the hospital to see Michelle, and he was happy to hear she was going home for Thanksgiving – he thought it would be good for her. He had come to view her as an older sister and friend. He had been visiting her two and three times a week, and when Judy saw Michelle's visitors' sheet, she was surprised to see his name.

'What's he been doing here?' Judy asked her with

astonishment. They were three years apart in school, and she couldn't imagine that they had anything to say to each other.

'He's been really nice, Mom. He's a sweet kid,' Michelle said sincerely. Her other friends had come only once or twice, and after that were too busy with their own lives to return. Judy realized that Brian and Michelle must have felt they had something in common – both had been overshadowed by their older brother and sister. Judy had begun to learn a lot about her younger daughter, her sense of disappointment about life, and the hidden resentments she had. And if making friends with Billy's younger brother made Michelle happy, she was pleased.

Michelle's friendship with Brian was a good addition to her life.

Judy mentioned it to Marilyn the next time she visited her. Marilyn could hardly get out of the house anymore, she was so busy with the twins, and they were on different feeding schedules, which made it even harder. But Marilyn said she was aware that Brian had been visiting Michelle. She said he felt sorry for her being stuck in the hospital, and he looked up to her. 'I think he really misses having Billy and Gabby around. Michelle reminds him of them. They're both lonely without them.' Marilyn said pensively.

'Aren't we all!' Judy said wistfully, thinking of her daughter in L.A. 'At least you have the twins to keep you busy. I never expected this to be so hard when Gabby left.' But it was also helping her to establish a closer bond to Michelle. Judy had come to understand that she and Adam had failed Michelle until now by concentrating too much on Gabby. Judy had apologized to Michelle for it in group, and both of them had cried but felt better after. The therapy sessions had helped them both a lot.

All the kids came home from their various colleges for Thanksgiving, and the holiday had its bumpy moments for some of them. It hit Sean hard when he walked in the front door and realized his brother still wasn't there, and never would be again. The reality of it was starting to sink in. On Friday night Sean stunned everyone and got a DUI, which was totally unlike him; he had always been so responsible. Connie and Mike were incensed. Connie had the distinct impression that he was trying to be Kevin, in order to keep him among them, but she didn't know how to say it to him. She had read something like that somewhere, about someone imitating a sibling's bad behaviors in order to keep them alive.

Connie called their old paediatrician to talk to her about Sean, and she said she wasn't surprised by what he was doing, and the DUI. Sean had suffered a terrible shock with the death of his older brother, and some acting out was to be expected. She thought in time he would calm down again and act like himself. But Connie and Mike took the car keys away from him anyway and told him he'd have to pay the fine himself. And he had to stay on Monday after Thanksgiving for a hearing at the DMV about the revocation of his license. Mike had hired a lawyer to try and get the DUI charges dismissed, but Sean's blood alcohol content had been .09, which was over the limit, so he had to face the DUI charges, and there was a hearing set on Monday for that too. Sean was deeply ashamed by what he'd done. He told the others about it on Saturday. And Izzie told him he was a fool. She couldn't believe he'd been dumb enough to drink and drive, and she told him so. They knew better than that.

She was in a bad mood for the rest of the day, and angry at Sean for putting himself at risk. And then, that night, Izzie's life took an unexpected and most un-welcome turn. She and Jeff had gone to Jennifer's for Thanksgiving dinner with a group of friends at her apart-ment, and on Saturday, Jeff told Izzie that Jennifer was moving in with him. She was stunned. She had never expected that and was horrified at the idea.

'Are you crazy? You hardly know her, Dad. And she's

half your age.' Izzie was furious about it, but her father seemed serious and refused to be dissuaded.

'Not quite,' he said ruefully, and he was honest with her. 'It's lonely here without you, Iz. And your mom's been gone for a long time.'

'Are you going to marry her?' she asked him with a panicked expression.

'I don't know. We haven't talked about it. Not yet, anyway. I think living with her will be enough. That's all I'm ready for right now.'

'And what if you don't like her? How will you get her to move out?'

'She's not a squatter, Izzie. She's a woman I've been dating whom I really like. The first one in a long time.'

When Izzie told Sean about it before she went back to school, he didn't pay much attention. He was too upset about his DUI, and the possible consequences if it went to trial. He felt like a total fool and had been one.

Gabby was startled by her younger sister, when they had a disagreement over the weekend, and Michelle told her that she was tired of living in her shadow, and being treated like an invisible person, while Gabby was always the star and got her way. Michelle had found her voice in the post-treatment program, and she was suddenly much more willing to assert herself, which was a shock for everyone else in the house. And Gabby was even more surprised to see Billy's little brother drop by.

'What's Brian doing here? He's just a kid,' she said to her mother after his visit. Her feathers were still ruffled by some of the things Michelle had said, but it was a sign of Michelle's improving health that she had said them.

'He and Michelle are friends. He visited her in the hospital every few days. He's a really sweet kid.' Gabby knew he was, but it seemed weird to see him hanging around her younger sister, and he was even younger, no matter how mature he looked.

Gabby had left for L.A. three months before, and things had changed. They all felt that way when they came home. Their parents were beginning to adjust to their absence, and although they had missed them, they were settling into new routines.

Billy had to go back to L.A. the day after Thanksgiving. He was playing in a game for USC on Sunday. All of them were planning to watch it on TV, except Gabby, who was flying back to L.A. on Saturday so she could be at the game.

The weekend went by too quickly, and on Sunday night all their houses seemed painfully quiet again. Only Sean stayed till Monday for his hearing for the DUI. In the end the Judge gave him a stiff fine and reprimanded him severely, but he didn't require DUI school, or revoke his license, since it was a first offense, and his lawyer explained that it was a difficult holiday for him after his brother's recent death. Sean was relieved and flew back to Washington, D.C., that afternoon, greatly mollified by his court appearance and hearing at the DMV.

Connie and Marilyn talked about it on Tuesday, while she helped her bathe the twins.

'Sean suddenly seems so much more grown-up and more independent. Except for the DUI. Mike was furious about it. But other than that, he just seems a lot more adult now,' Connie commented with some relief. He had seemed to be heading in a bad direction after his brother's death but was back on track now, despite his slip over the weekend. It had been an agonizing Thanksgiving for her and Mike too, their first without Kevin.

'Billy seems more responsible too,' Marilyn said as Daphne smiled up at her, enjoying the bath. Billy had even helped her with the twins on Thanksgiving, which was a first for him.

'You're lucky you have the twins,' Connie said enviously. 'It'll keep you young.'

'Not exactly,' Marilyn laughed. 'I haven't had a full night's sleep in five months, and I look about six hundred years old.' She thought Connie was doing a little better about Kevin, but she didn't want to ask. She knew the holiday had been hard for her, as was to be expected. And instead of cooking dinner as she always did, they had gone to relatives of Mike's.

'It'll be nice having them all home for Christmas,' Connie said wistfully. 'I miss seeing their friends too.' She missed Sean constantly, and talking to Izzie, and seeing Billy lope up their stairs two at a time, with Gabby right behind him, and Andy with them. She missed all of them. And she still couldn't believe that for the rest of time, Kevin would never come home again. She knew it would take her all of her life to understand that he was gone forever.

Chapter 11

The kids all came home for Christmas, some earlier than others, depending on their schools. They returned to find their homes decorated for the holidays, with lights strung up outside the houses, and a Christmas tree already set up in the living room of each of their homes.

Connie had decorated theirs with a heavy heart this year. Mike didn't even look at it. He usually put lights up outside the house, but he couldn't bring himself to do it this time, and he didn't help her with the tree. She did it quietly by herself one morning, crying for Kevin. But she wanted to have the tree up for Sean when he arrived.

The Westons had a good-looking artificial tree every year, set up by their florist, with beautiful decorations.

Andy knew what to expect, although he always preferred the lopsided, less elegant real trees in his friends' houses, particularly at Billy's.

Marilyn and Jack went all out. They had much to celebrate. It was the twins' first Christmas, and Brian helped Jack with the lights. They even had reindeer on the roof, and a lit-up Santa Claus in the front yard. It was corny, and they knew it, but they loved it, and so did all their friends.

Judy ordered a white-flocked tree every year and decorated it in silver and gold for Michelle and Gabby, and they had a matching white wreath on the door. Judy was in particularly good spirits. She had her eyes done just before Christmas and was very pleased with the result, and Adam said he loved it. Her new Jaguar arrived the week before Christmas. Michelle was doing much better. And Gabby was up for a national ad campaign for a cosmetic line, which would pay handsomely if she got it. Her career as a model was off and running, and she had signed up for acting classes in January.

Brian was still a regular visitor to the house, since Michelle got out of the hospital. She was looking better, and doing well in school. And she seemed less stressed and was even glad that Gabby was coming home. She was surprised to discover that she missed her. The sister who had garnered all of her mother's attention for her entire life seemed like less of a threat now, as Michelle learned to express herself and developed a personality of her own. She and Brian talked about it often, since he had spent his whole life in Billy's shadow too. His older brother was a lot to live up to. He had been playing in every game at USC, even though it was his first season on the team, but they needed him desperately since they'd lost their star quarterback to an injury. It was a stroke of luck for Billy, and all of the families who knew Billy and had watched him grow up, now watched him on TV. He had a big championship game coming up in January at the Rose Bowl. Gabby was planning to be there, and her parents, Sean, and the O'Haras were going, and Jack and Marilyn were taking Brian.

Gabby's life seemed much more grown-up than Izzie's now. She had an apartment, went to go-sees for modeling jobs, and she was focused on her career. She no longer had to worry about mid-terms, finals, papers, or assignments. She had entered the real world. And Billy could hardly wait to do the same. He thought of college as a bridge to his ultimate goal, playing for the NFL.

Billy had to play one last game before Christmas break, and was coming home on his own, and Izzie and Gabby flew up from L.A. together, and shared a cab from the airport into the city. Gabby dropped Izzie off first and wished her luck, as Izzie got out of the cab with a glum expression. Jennifer had moved in right after Thanksgiving, and this was going to be the first time she'd been home since that momentous event. She wondered if everything would seem different, or the same. She liked Jennifer, but she didn't want to go through the same changes as Billy, if her father married her one day, or had babies with her. Izzie had been happy the way things were.

She waved at Gabby as the cab drove off, turned her key in the lock and walked into the house she had shared with her father, and before that both her parents, since she was born. At first, nothing looked different, and then she noticed that the couch had been moved, her father's desk was now in front of a window, the books in the bookcases looked different. There was a new reclining leather chair, and there were vases of flowers on every table. And the decorations on the Christmas tree were different. As she approached it, she saw that none of her favourite decorations from her childhood had been hung this year. They had bought new ones, and as she walked into her bedroom, she felt suddenly displaced and like a stranger in her own home, although her bedroom looked the same. She set down her bag and sat down on the bed, looking for signs of an invasion here too, but there were none.

She got a text message from Sean as she sat there, that he was leaving D.C. in a blizzard but would be home late that night, and he'd call when he got in. She answered, wishing him a safe flight, and then added that she just got home and it felt weird. He didn't answer, and she wondered if he was already on the plane.

Izzie realized then that she didn't have a gift for Jennifer, and she went to Fillmore Street that afternoon to find one. She ended up getting her a sweater from Marc Jacobs, and a picture book of Cuba, which had no particular meaning, Izzie just liked it, and she went straight to her room when she got home. It felt strange sitting in the living room now, as though it were someone else's house and no longer her own.

Izzie heard Jennifer come in late that afternoon, and she lay on her bed and didn't move, not wanting to face her just yet, and a moment later, her door opened and Jennifer started when she saw her. Izzie hadn't made a sound.

'Oh . . . you're home . . . I was just checking to make sure everything was neat in here, and turn the lights on. Are you okay?'

'I'm fine,' Izzie said, sitting up, with a look of embarrassment. She'd been hiding, and Jennifer looked as though she suspected it. 'Just tired from the trip up.'

'Are you hungry?' Jeff had given her a list of all the things Izzie liked to eat, and Jennifer had bought them all. She could guess what Izzie was feeling. No woman had lived in the house since her mother left five years before. This was a big change for her, on her own turf, and she was used to having her father to herself. Jennifer was trying to make it as easy as possible for her. 'I just got some cheese and French bread, and the pâté your father said you like.' Jennifer looked earnest and hopeful, and all Izzie wanted to do was run away.

'No, thanks. I'm fine. I'm going out with friends tonight.' She wasn't, but she didn't know what else to say. All she knew was that she didn't want to be at home. And Gabby had said her family was going to *The Nutcracker* that night, so she couldn't go there. And none of the boys were home yet. She felt stupid being so unfriendly to Jennifer, but she was an intruder in their home. And Izzie knew her father wanted to live with her. And in spite of trying to be reasonable about it, Izzie felt betrayed.

She followed Jennifer back into the living room, and found her putting magazines on the coffee table that she thought Izzie might want to read. Izzie saw two she liked immediately, but she didn't touch them, and went to stand at the Christmas tree, and then turned to Jennifer with a look of accusation.

'What happened to all our old decorations?'

'Your dad put them in boxes in the basement. We got new ones. Some of the old ones looked pretty tired.' They did, but Izzie loved them. She felt like a child as she looked up at the tree, and missed the battered old ornaments she had had since her childhood. The new ones were pretty, but not the same. 'We can bring them up if you want,' Jennifer said nervously. She was wearing jeans and boots, and a black sweater that set off her figure. And she had long, shining dark hair. There was no denying she was pretty, and she didn't look her age. She appeared more like a contemporary of Izzie's than a thirty-nine-year-old woman. She did yoga every day and was in great shape. She sat down on the recliner and looked at Izzie, who couldn't help noticing that she seemed entirely at home there. The new recliner was hers.

'No, that's okay,' Izzie responded to her offer to bring up the old decorations, and sat down uncomfortably on the couch, facing her.

Jennifer decided to broach the subject, knowing that if she didn't, it was going to be a very uncomfortable week until Izzie went back to L.A. 'I know this is hard for you,' she started gently. 'I kind of went through something like this myself. My mom died when I was fifteen, and I was alone with my father. He fell in love with my mom's best friend and married her a year later. She had two kids I'd never been crazy about, younger than I was, and they had two more kids together. I hated it at first, and I hated her, even though I'd always liked her when my mom was alive. And I was really pissed off at my dad for a while. I went away to college, as far away as I could, and I never wanted to go home. But in the end, I realized that she and my dad loved each other, she was good for him, and she and I are good friends today. She's not my mom, and she never tried to be, but she's a wonderful friend, and one of her daughters and I are best friends. And I love my half brothers too. they're a pain in the neck sometimes, and they were when they were growing up, but they're funny and I love them. My dad died last year, but I still go home to see them all whenever I can.'

'Are you and my dad going to get married and have kids?' Izzie asked, sounding nervous.

'I don't know. Maybe not. This is all either of us want right now.' Or it was all she wanted. Jeff had been hinting at 'long term' for a while, but she didn't feel ready, and she didn't say that to Izzie. She knew it would be too much for her to handle. 'I think losing my mom so young made me kind of skittish about getting attached to anyone. I've never wanted to get married and have kids. I think I figured that if I got too attached to someone, they'd die.' She was being very honest with her, as Izzie watched her eyes. They were open and Jennifer was a real person.

'That's sad. You're not too old to have kids.' She looked even younger than she was. 'I never thought my dad would want to have more kids, but maybe he does.'

'We haven't talked about it. We're just living together. It's enough for now. And whatever he does, with me or someone else, you're always going to be his daughter, and someone very special in his life.'

'He thinks you're special too,' Izzie said softly.

'And I think he is too.' She smiled at Izzie. 'That makes three very special people under one roof. Do you think we can make this work, so you're comfortable here too? It's your house, after all.'

'Yeah, maybe.' Izzie still wasn't sure, although she had to admit that Jennifer was making a real effort. It just felt like she didn't belong there. But they'd been dating for a while, and she realized that something was bound to come up if they dated long enough. She had just hoped this would never happen, but at least they weren't married, and Jennifer sounded like she didn't want to anytime soon. Maybe she thought her dad was too old too. At fifty-six, Izzie thought so. Not for dating, he was still a handsome guy, but for marrying a woman seventeen years younger than he was and starting a family. He was a great father to her, but she couldn't imagine him with more kids, or babies around.

'So what do you think?' Jennifer asked her gently. 'Is there anything I can do to make this easier for you' Izzie smiled when she said it, and wanted to answer, *Yeah. Go home!* But she didn't, and she appreciated what Jennifer was doing, and how hard she was trying to reach out to Izzie. It couldn't have been easy for her either, and she was touched by what Jennifer had said about her mother and stepmother.

'I guess I'll get used to it in a while. It's just different,' she said generously. 'I like the new chair, and the flowers look pretty around the house.' Her little touches were everywhere.

'Are you seeing your mom over Christmas?' Jennifer knew from the past year that Izzie didn't see her often. Katherine's home base had shifted to New York, and she traveled more than ever. Katherine's maternal instincts had never developed, and she treated Izzie like someone else's child.

'No, she's in London. She's coming to L.A. in a few weeks, on business. She's taking me to dinner then.' Jennifer nodded and refrained from comment. She didn't want to criticize her mother, but she felt sorry for Izzie that there had never been an important female figure in her life, only her father. It made Jennifer that much more of a threat now.

'Well, I'm going to get some of that cheese and pâté on a plate,' she said, and headed for the kitchen, and a few minutes later, Izzie wandered in.

Jennifer had done a nice cheese platter adorned with grapes. The pâté was on a plate, and there was French bread in a basket with a red-and-white-checked napkin around it, and before Izzie knew it, she had eaten half the pâté, sampled two of her favourite cheeses, and was sitting at the kitchen table, talking to Jennifer about her roommate, and the problems she had with her. She was trying to decide if she wanted to ask for a new one, or wait and get her own apartment for sophomore year. She had thought of sharing a place with Gabby, but Billy was there so often and she didn't want to live with him. They were major decisions in Izzie's life, and Jennifer suggested she ask for a room change when she went back. Why be miserable until June with a roommate she didn't like?

They were talking about it when Jeff walked in half an

hour later, and was pleased to see them chatting in the kitchen. Izzie jumped up the minute she saw him, and threw her arms around her father, who hugged her tight, and smiled at Jennifer over her shoulder. Jennifer nodded at him. She thought things were going well, better than expected. And she was willing to be patient while Izzie got used to her living there.

They had dinner together in the kitchen. Jennifer had bought two roasted chickens, and Jeff tossed a salad and made some of his special pasta that Izzie loved. And they finished the meal off with ice cream, and then went to sit in the living room and admire the tree. With the rest of the lights turned off, and only the tree lights lit, it suddenly felt like Christmas, and her father put on a CD of Christmas carols. They sat there for a long time together, with Jennifer on the comfortable recliner and Jeff and Izzie side by side on the couch. Jennifer was wise enough not to come too close, and allow them the time they needed to be together. It was obvious how much they loved each other, and how Izzie idolized her father.

Izzie finally went to her room, and left Jennifer and her father talking to each other. And as soon as Izzie got into her nightgown, she got a text from Sean that said 'I'm home.' She smiled to herself as she read it, and responded immediately, 'Me too.' And she knew she was, as she turned off the light and climbed into her familiar bed. Nothing much had changed after all, except maybe a little bit for the better.

Chapter 12

All of the families were excited to have their kids home for the holidays. Their houses came alive.

The O'Haras soaked up Sean's visit like sponges, they were so happy to see him and be with him, and have his friends in and out of the house. Mike and Billy talked football. He'd watched all of the USC games, and was planning to go to L.A. with Sean and Connie to see Billy play at the Rose Bowl.

They talked about the various games during the season, and how lucky he was that they were letting him play so early in his college football career, and he'd done well so far as the rookie quarterback on the team. Mike had no doubt that Billy was going to have an important career in football. Everyone who knew him was proud of him. At the Thomases', Michelle and Gabby talked animatedly about the things they wanted to do together, and the Norton house was bursting with life and excitement with Billy home, Brian thrilled to see him, and the twins keeping them all busy. And most of all the Big Five were ecstatic to be together for a week. They had missed each other fiercely.

Marilyn and Jack had a Christmas party and invited everyone, kids and adults alike. The O'Haras came but didn't stay long, and weren't feeling very festive. Judy and Adam were there with Gabby and Michelle, and Billy stayed close to Gabby at the party. Andy came with his mother, since his father was working on a new book and was in seclusion. And Jeff brought Jennifer and Izzie. Marilyn commented later to Connie what a pretty girl Jennifer was, and she was happy to see that she was nice to Izzie, although Izzie admitted that she still wasn't all that happy that they were living together, and she was afraid they might get married and have babies. But she was willing to concede that Jennifer was nice.

The O'Haras lent them their Tahoe house between Christmas and New Year, to go skiing at Squaw Valley. Billy was going back to L.A. for practice before the Rose Bowl, and would come up for only one day. The others were going to spend the week in Tahoe, and Sean had invited a few other friends, mostly girls. Mike and Connie trusted them with the house, and there had never been any bad incidents while they stayed there.

All the kids were happy when they left for Tahoe in two vans, full of people, skis, and luggage. It was a big house with room for all of them, and a dormitory room where they could fit the overflow of bodies. They were a lively group, and everyone pitched in to make dinner at night. The O'Haras' only condition was no drinking, and everyone agreed to abide by the rules, although Billy had flashed the flask in his pocket. Sean told him to put it away, and he did. Sean hadn't had a drink since his DUI.

They sat around the fireplace at night, talking about their schools and roommates, and Izzie and Andy got into a long conversation about Harvard one night. Andy loved it and thought she should transfer, but she said she was happy where she was, and wanted to stay in California. And she liked knowing that Gabby and Billy were nearby in L.A. – it was like having family in the same city. And Andy talked a lot about the rigors of pre-med, but it had never occurred to him for an instant to do something different, just as Billy had always known he'd play football. It was what their parents expected of them. Izzie's mother still wanted her to go to law school.

But for Izzie it was never an option. She liked the psych class she was taking, and had been thinking about that as a career. She was signed up for abnormal psych the following semester, which sounded interesting but a little creepy to her. Her adviser had told her she'd enjoy it. She still hadn't decided on a major. What she really wanted to do was work with the indigent in a developing country for a summer, or do an internship after college. Like her father, she loved helping people. She just hadn't figured out yet know to do it or for whom.

She and Andy were still talking on the second night, after the others went to bed. They found a bottle of wine in a kitchen cupboard and, despite the rules, decided to share some. Sean had already gone to bed – he had brought a girl up to Tahoe with him, whom he wanted to start dating. He had met her at school. She was a champion skier, and everyone agreed she had a hot body. She was sleeping in the dormitory room with some of the other girls, but Sean was hoping to start something with her by the end of the week, and things were looking hopeful. Izzie had seen Sean kissing her that night, in the hallway after dinner, but he hadn't scored yet.

'So, are you still a virgin?' Izzie asked Andy, with a look of mischief, as they finished a forbidden glass of wine, which made it just a little more exciting. 'Any hot babes at Harvard?' She was half teasing, but not completely. Although he was one of her best friends, Izzie had always found him attractive. She had just never wanted to screw up their friendship, and still didn't.

'Funny that you ask,' he said with a portentous look, and then he laughed. 'Yeah, dammit, I am. They give too much homework. I have no time for sex or romance if I want to keep my grades up.'

'That's too bad. I haven't done too well in that department either. There isn't a lot of campus life at an urban school. I haven't even had a date since last summer, although my roommate has turned out to be the slut of the village. She screws everything that moves.' Izzie hadn't had a serious romance yet, and her virginity was beginning to feel like a permanent condition. 'You know, maybe we ought to take care of this situation together. I want to get rid of my virginity. So do you. Maybe it would give us a certain aura of sophistication,' she suggested, after their second glass of wine. They were halfway through the bottle, and in the altitude, it had hit them harder than they knew. Izzie was looking just a little cross-eyed as she tried to focus on Andy, who stared at her in amazement. And she looked sexy and pretty to him with her hair down. She always had seemed great to him, but he had just thought of her like a sister.

Danielle Steel

'Are you serious?' he thought she had to be kidding, but he could see she wasn't. The idea of what she was suggesting excited him more than he'd expected.

'Sure. Why not? Besides, what if we really like each other? More than as just friends, I mean. Maybe we'll turn out to be fabulous in bed, with real natural aptitude. It could happen. Besides, everyone we know is getting laid except us.' That wasn't entirely true, and they both knew it. Sean was still a virgin too, or had been when he left for college in late August, and he hadn't informed them of any change in status. But Billy and Gabby had been sexually involved since they were fifteen, and Izzie knew that most of her classmates were no longer virgins, and hadn't been for a year or two. 'You and I are the last people on the planet who have never tasted the pleasures of the flesh,' she said, with a lustful look at him and a sip of her third glass of wine. Andy had just finished his second. To Izzie he looked sexy and handsome, and she was attracted to him.

'What are you suggesting?' Andy had the only single room in the house – he wasn't sharing with anyone since it was actually a maid's room. Izzie pointed vaguely in that direction. She was bunking in the dorm room, so it was not an option. And before either of them could reconsider, Andy pulled her to her feet, they took the wine and their glasses, and walked softly to the room where he was staying. Andy suddenly felt as though his whole body were throbbing, and Izzie was weaving a little unsteadily as she followed him to his room with a giggle. She wasn't sure what to expect the first time and hoped it wouldn't be too painful. She had heard horror stories from friends, and also good ones.

'I don't have a condom,' he said with a tone of desperation in the dark, after he closed the door to the tiny room. He could see her face in the moonlight, and she looked beautiful. And he wasn't about to miss this opportunity and wake one of the others to ask for a condom. He had always thought Izzie was lovely looking with her big brown eyes, perfect features, and long wavy brown hair, and now she was offering herself to him. It opened a thousand doors in his imagination as she unzipped his jeans.

'I trust you,' she said simply, and meant it about the condom, as she started to take her clothes off, and he stepped out of his jeans. He had long muscular legs, and a body that would never be better than it was at this moment. She pulled her sweater over her head and unhooked her bra, and her small, perfectly round breasts gleamed like snow in the moonlight. They were creamy white as he cupped them with his hands, and they climbed into his bed together and took the rest of their clothes off. He ran his hands all over her body, and had an overwhelming erection, as she wondered what that would feel like once it was inside her. She tried not to think of it or be scared as she closed her eyes, and he felt between her legs. He had gone pretty far with girls on dates before, but never this far, and before he could stop himself or discuss it further with her, he was in her, and had never felt anything as incredible before, and he realized a moment later that she gave a gasp of pain, but he couldn't stop himself now. It was sharp and fast and over very quickly, and he held her for a few moments afterward, wondering if she was sorry. He wasn't. It had been spectacular for him, and all he wanted to do now was tell her he loved her. He looked down at her face and saw that she looked startled, and there was a small drop of blood where she had bitten her lip so as not to cry out.

'Did I hurt you?' he asked, looking worried.

'No, it was fine. Everyone says it's easier the second time.' She pulled him close to her then, and they held each other in the moonlight for a long time. He wanted to make love to her again, but he didn't want to hurt her.

'Are you sorry?' he finally managed to whisper.

'Of course not,' she said bravely, wondering why it had seemed like such a good idea when they started drinking the wine. She had always loved him, but she wasn't in love with him. She was certain of it now. Maybe it had been a good test, but she knew they had started something complicated that night, and he was going to be away, at college and in med school, for a long, long time. 'Are you sorry?' she asked him in the dark.

'How could I be?' he smiled down at her. 'I think I've always been in love with you.' But she hadn't been, and still wasn't. She loved him, as a friend and a brother. And it felt incestuous having sex with him. This was about more than losing her virginity. It was a mistake, and she knew it.

'I'd better go back,' she said after a while. She didn't want the others to see her coming out of his room in the morning, and Andy didn't want that either. He wanted to protect her, and for now, what they had done was nobody's business. He got up to take her to the dorm room, and he stood naked in the moonlight, looking like a young Greek god. Even Izzie wasn't impervious to his beauty, and she wished she felt differently than she did, but she didn't.

And now all she could think of was that she was terrified of getting pregnant. They had used no protection. She wasn't afraid of getting a disease from him, only a baby, which was a major fear. It was all she could think of now. 'Don't come with me,' she whispered, and he kissed her, and then she put her clothes back on, and when she left, she took the wine and glasses with her. She stopped in the kitchen to empty the last dregs into the sink, and bury the bottle in the trash. She washed the wineglasses and put them away, and then she tiptoed back to the dorm room, got undressed again and put her nightgown on in the bathroom after washing the blood off her legs. She was thinking about Andy and wondered what would happen now. Their parents would be devastated if she got pregnant, especially his, but hers wouldn't be happy either. She couldn't even think of the relationship they might or might not have, and probably shouldn't, only the baby that would ruin both their lives. Andy had just turned nineteen and had ten or eleven years of study ahead of him, and she was eighteen.

She lay down in bed and pulled the covers up to her chin. The others hadn't woken up when she came in, and she tried to remember what it had been like making love with him, but she didn't really want to. She just wanted to float away and be someplace different, on a beach somewhere, all by herself. The room was spinning slightly as she closed her eyes, and she felt a little sick, and a moment later she was sound asleep.

* * *

Izzie didn't see Andy again until breakfast the next morning. The girl Sean had brought with him was helping him and Gabby make breakfast. No one particularly liked her, she talked a lot and was a little giddy. She was chattering loudly, and Izzie walked in looking like she'd been dragged behind a horse all night. She squinted her eyes in the morning brightness and had a fearsome headache. The wine and the altitude had hit her hard. And as soon as she'd woken up, she remembered what had happened the night before. And so did Andy. He strolled into the kitchen, looking like the king of the universe, and smiled at Izzie.

'Hi,' she said absently, and went to sit down with a cup of coffee.

'Are you okay?' he asked solicitously, but no one noticed. They were always nice to each other, and this was no different, except to her. She wanted to tell him she was sure she was pregnant. She had heard stories like that before, of girls who had sex for the first time, and bingo they were pregnant. And his mother would be delivering her baby nine months from now. The thought of it made her head spin, and her hangover didn't help.

'I have a headache,' she said, without explaining more, and he nodded. He did too, from the wine, but he didn't care. He was so excited about what they'd done, and his feelings about her, that he felt like he was flying. Izzie felt more like she was crawling around on all fours, and would have liked to. Flying was not on the cards for her today.

Andy helped himself to an enormous breakfast and sat down at the kitchen table with the others. Gabby started putting sunblock on her face, to get ready for a day of skiing. She couldn't afford to get some weird tan that would make her ineligible at a go-see, and she always took good care of her skin and got regular facials, just like her mother.

The sun was shining, and the snow looked spectacular. Everyone was in a good mood and ready for the slopes, except Izzie. She went to put the rest of her clothes on and a little while later Gabby walked into the dorm room and looked at her, sitting on the edge of her bed, with a devastated expression.

'Are you okay?' Gabby asked her, and she was about to say yes, and then shook her head and started crying. Gabby sat down next to her and put her arms around her. They were alone in the room, since the other girls were still at breakfast.

'I did something really stupid last night,' Izzie said in muffled tones into her friend's shoulder.

'How stupid?' Gabby looked worried. There were no

new guys on the scene to do anything stupid with, so she was instantly afraid it might be drugs.

'*Really* stupid,' Izzie said miserably. 'I had unprotected sex.' Gabby pulled away from her and looked at her in confusion.

'You did? With who?' There was no one there to sleep with except their old familiar crowd of friends, and Gabby couldn't imagine her doing that with any of the boys, but apparently she had. 'Sean?' It was the only possibility she could think of, although even that seemed unlikely. But Izzie had always been closer to him than to Billy or Andy. And Gabby knew Sean told her everything, and she had been very supportive after Kevin died, and she really liked his mother. But Izzie shook her head.

'Andy.'

'You did? Wow . . . I never expected that, although he's really handsome. He just seems like such a kid to me. I guess he isn't anymore.' Gabby smiled at her. Billy was the only one who had looked like a man for years, and their long-standing affair with each other had matured both of them. In a lot of ways, she seemed older than Izzie, who was still a kid, and a student. Gabby was a woman, and out in the world, particularly since graduating from school. 'So are you crazy about him?' Gabby asked with a motherly look.

'No more than I was before,' Izzie said honestly. 'It was a stupid thing to do. It's going to screw everything up with us. And what if I get pregnant?'

'You didn't use anything? You're not on the Pill?' Izzie shook her head miserably, and Gabby dove into the toilet bag she had brought with her and came out with a box of pills. 'Take this. It's a morning-after pill. It'll keep you from getting pregnant. Once in a while I screw up on my Pill, or have stomach flu or something. If you're on an antibiotic, birth control pills don't work. This will. It'll cover you for a slip.' Gabby was an encyclopaedia of information, and Izzie took it from her hand and swallowed it instantly with a grateful look. She didn't want to waste a minute.

'Thank you. I was ready to jump off a cliff somewhere.'

'No problem. So what are you going to do now? About Andy?'

'I don't know. I think I have to tell him that it was a mistake, for both of us. I love our friendship the way it was. We all grew up together. You and Billy are different, because you've been a couple for years. For the rest of us, it would be a dumb thing to do. And besides, he's going to be away at school for a million years.' Gabby nodded. She didn't disagree. They were like brothers and sisters now, except for her and Billy.

'What are you going to say?'

'I don't know. I'll figure it out as I go along. I think I'll stay home today.' She didn't want to tell her she was hung over too. What she'd admitted to was bad enough, from her point of view. 'The whole thing was my idea. I suggested it to him, so we could both get rid of our virginity. But it's not quite as simple as that. It gets complicated very quickly.' The fear of pregnancy alone had brought her back to earth in an instant. And the fear of ruining their friendship was nearly as bad.

'He probably feels that way too,' Gabby reassured her.

But as it turned out, he didn't. He was thrilled with what had happened the night before and was already telling himself he was in love with her, and all day while he was skiing, he fantasized about making love to her and nearly hit a tree, he was so distracted. Sean had shouted a warning to him and gave him hell for not paying attention. Andy was on cloud nine, and he looked at Izzie with disappointment in his eyes when she told him that afternoon that she thought what they'd done the night before was a big mistake.

'Was it that bad for you?' He looked crushed and as though he had failed abysmally in his first sexual venture.

'Of course not. It hurt a little, but they say it doesn't

the second time. I just don't want to screw up what we have. You're like my brother, and you're going to be in med school for the next hundred years.' He knew it was more than that. She just wasn't attracted to him but she wanted to spare his feelings. She continued, 'And if we have a romance that doesn't work out, or we hurt each other's feelings, we could wind up hating each other, and I don't want that to happen. You mean too much to me. I don't ever want to lose you.' What she said was flattering in a way, about how important he was to her, but it hurt his feelings anyway, and he felt it like a reflection on his sexual performance. 'You're beautiful,' she reassured him. 'You have a gorgeous body. You're great in bed, or going to be. I just don't want to trade our friendship for meaningless sex.' He looked insulted again when she said it.

'Was it meaningless for you? It meant a lot to me.'

'It did to me too. But we were both drunk last night, and I still think we were stupid. I want to protect our friendship. Forever! Not trade it in for sex. That's a bad deal.' She was being more sensible than he was, and in some ways more mature, given the direction they were headed. And she was right, he was going to be gone for a very long time. A ten-year long-distance relationship wasn't likely to work. He knew it too. He just didn't want to let go of what they had just discovered, at least not quite so soon.

'Why can't we have both?' he asked stubbornly. 'Friendship and sex? Isn't that what love is?'

'I already love you. I know that. I don't need to have sex with you to figure it out. And what if you cheat on me while you're away at school, or I do in L.A.? Then what? We wind up hating each other. I don't want to do that, Andy. Last night was good, and very special, but it was a mistake, for both of us.' She was adamant about it, and he went to bed early that night, and stayed away from her at dinner, looking hurt. Sean noticed it and asked her about it later on.

'Did you and Andy have a fight?' If so, it was rare for any of them in their group of friends. Even if they disagreed with each other, they never got into arguments, or said hurtful things to each other. It had been a sacred bond between them for thirteen years.

'No, just a policy disagreement about something. It's no big deal.' But Andy had looked upset that night, and they both knew it.

'You owe my parents a bottle of wine, by the way,' Sean said casually, and Izzie looked instantly mortified. 'You know the rules.' He looked stern for a minute.

He had seen it in the garbage when he took out the trash.

'I'm really sorry. I was going to replace it. I took it last night.'

'Is that what you and Andy were arguing about?'

'Yeah, he saw me take it and drink it. He gave me a big lecture about it. I told him I wouldn't do it again.' It was the perfect excuse for the tension between them, and Sean believed her.

'Andy always does the right thing. Anyway, don't do it again. My parents probably won't notice, but I'll have someone buy it for us before we go home.'

'Thank you.' She handed him a twenty-dollar bill a few minutes later.

She and Andy didn't spend much time together for the rest of the trip, and he finally stopped to talk to her again on the last day.

'I'm sorry, Izzie. I was just disappointed by what you said. I've been thinking about it all week, and you're right.' He threw his arms around her and hugged her then. 'I love you. I don't want to screw that up either.' He whispered in her ear, then, so no one else could hear. 'You have one hell of a hot bod, though, if you ever change your mind.'

'I won't,' she reassured him, and she laughed and then

got serious again. 'We shouldn't have done it.' He didn't entirely disagree, although an affair with her would have been very appealing in a lot of ways. She was smart, beautiful, and he loved her, but their long years of friend-ship complicated things and made it feel incestuous, to both of them. He knew she was being smarter than he was about calling a halt to it right away. But he had loved the way he felt when he was with her.

'I'm glad we did it anyway,' Andy said, looking at ease again. He had gotten over his initial disappointment and brief anger at her. 'At least we're not virgins anymore, and if I was going to lose mine to someone, I'm glad it was you. Better to a friend.' She didn't entirely disagree with him, although it no longer seemed like such a big deal to her, nor a burden, whether she was a virgin or not. Now that she wasn't, it didn't matter anymore. And maybe it was okay that Andy was the first. At least they loved each other, even if only as friends, but it wasn't a hot romance for her, even if it might have turned into one for him. She just didn't feel sexual about him. She knew that now. It had been all about the wine.

By that night they were good friends again, and nothing more. Izzie wanted to put it behind her, although Andy was feeling tender toward her, in a way that he hadn't before, and he knew he would always remember his first time with her. Izzie was just grateful that Gabby had given her a pill that would keep her from getting pregnant, and she had narrowly missed a disaster that could have ruined both their lives.

They were all in good spirits when they drove back to the city again on the day before New Year's Eve. Sean hadn't been as successful as he would have liked with the girl he brought, but after several days he found her so irritating he no longer cared. And they were going to L.A. the next day, to see Billy play in the Rose Bowl game on New Year's Day. Billy's father had rented a party bus and was taking a group of friends, and the others were flying. Marilyn and Jack were giving a New Year's Eve party for the parents at their hotel, but they knew Billy couldn't be there the night before the game. Andy, who was heading back to Boston on New Year's Day, would miss it.

In some ways Izzie was glad Andy wasn't coming. She wanted to put a little time and distance between them and the stupid thing they'd done in Tahoe, in case either of them wanted to do it again. She didn't completely trust herself – Andy was a very handsome boy, and she didn't want to slip with him again.

The whole crew from San Francisco arrived in time to celebrate New Year's Eve together. Some of them had taken rooms in hotels in Pasadena, and Sean and his parents were staying at the Beverly Hills Hotel. Gabby and Izzie met Sean for dinner at the Polo Lounge. Billy was with the team that night. He said he had a million plays to learn for the game, and Gabby knew how stressed he was. He had to be in bed by ten o'clock that night, back in his dorm. And after dinner at the Polo Lounge, Izzie, Gabby, and Sean went to the hotel where Marilyn and Jack were staying. And their small, festive party was well under way. The anticipation of seeing Billy play in such an important game was incredible. Everyone was talking about it and hoping Billy would do well. This was a moment he had waited all his life for, and everyone was proud of him. The next morning the O'Haras rented a van and picked up the others to see the Rose Parade in Pasadena. Brian couldn't sit still and Gabby was nervous for Billy. At least the parade was a good distraction for everyone and afterward they went to see the intricate floats along Sierra Madre and Washington Boulevard.

They were all in their seats well before the game. Izzie knew from Marilyn that Larry would be there, probably with several friends and a flock of young girls. Marilyn had whispered to Jack that she hoped Larry wasn't blind drunk and wouldn't do something to embarrass her boys. It was a beautiful sunny day and the weather had been warm. Izzie and Gabby were chatting with Michelle, and Brian kept jumping up to buy souvenirs, while Mike bought drinks and food for everyone. The wait seemed interminable until the familiar scarlet and gold uniforms of the Trojans appeared on the field, and the crowd went wild. Cheerleaders were dancing, music was playing, people in the stands were blowing horns. The fabulous Rose Bowl floats from the parade that morning were parked off to the side. The team from Alabama looked impressive as they came on the field too. Both teams were a gorgeous sight as the game began. USC took the lead quickly, and then Alabama scored twice in the second quarter. By the fourth quarter, they were tied.

They had spotted Larry by then several rows below them, and he was going nuts cheering for his son. There were young girls on either side of him in short white skirts and halter tops who looked like cheerleaders, and he was talking to a whole row of the men friends he had brought with him. They were all screaming encouragement at the players. Larry had lived for this moment, and Billy was making all his dreams come true.

There was a blimp hanging over the stadium, filming the action on the field, and in the final quarter, with a brilliant play the coach had designed, Billy scored the winning touchdown. He won the game for USC, and the Rose Bowl Player of the Game Award for himself, which was an enormous honor. It was truly a moment none of them would ever forget as they handed him the trophy. Marilyn was crying as she watched him, and Jack was hugging her. Sean and the girls were jumping up and down and yelling, and Brian had run into the aisle and was screaming his brother's name. It was pure joy for all of them who had watched him grow up. It was a day of glory for Billy, those who loved him, and the team. Larry even turned back toward where Marilyn was sitting and waved at her. It was one of those perfect moments that happen only a few times in a lifetime, if that.

Billy's family and supporters filed out of their seats with almost ninety thousand fans, and they went to wait for him outside the locker room. They wanted to congratulate him for playing an incredible game. There were victory celebrations scheduled for that night that he had invited Sean, Izzie, and Gabby to. The rest of the group was going to have dinner together in L.A. They were ecstatic over what they'd seen. And when he finally came out to them nearly an hour later, Billy was beaming. His mother hugged him first, and then everyone else hugged and kissed him, and he kissed Gabby hard on the mouth and told her he loved her. He swept her into his arms right off her feet. It was the happiest day of his life, and theirs. Everyone was proud of him and thrilled to know him. Larry had tried to force his way into the locker room, and had then left early on his party bus. But he had shouted his congratulations to his son.

The team had been drug-tested before they left the locker room, as was standard procedure for the championship game, and they were all smart enough to stay clean before it.

Billy had to go back to school with the team. They had them on big luxury buses, and there was an atmosphere of wild celebration as they drove back to L.A. It had been Billy's first championship game, hopefully the first of many more to come.

Sean, Gabby, and Izzie didn't see him again till they met up at a victory party at the Empire in Hollywood at eleven o'clock that night. It had been held there once before, and they were as excited as he was. Billy kept Gabby tucked under his arm all night, and it was two in the morning when he stopped in the bathroom with Sean before they left the last party. They stood at the urinals side by side as they had a thousand times in school, and Billy slipped a small vial of white pills out of his pocket and held it out discreetly to Sean. There was no one else in the bathroom with them, and at first Sean didn't know what it was. Billy didn't say anything, he just looked at him inquiringly and offered it to his friend. From the clandestine way he offered it, Sean understood instantly that it was an illegal substance of some kind.

'What is that?' Sean asked him with a shocked expression. Billy zipped up his pants and laughed at him. Sean zipped his up too and turned to face Billy. 'What is it?'

'It's Ecstasy, man. Don't get excited. They tested us after the game. I'm cool.

'No, you're not,' Sean said, grabbing at his friend by the lapels and slamming him into the nearest wall. Billy had nearly a hundred pounds on him, but Sean got him there with no trouble, and held him pinned. Billy was shocked. 'You're not cool at all,' said Sean. 'Don't you get it? My brother died from shit like that. He got shot buying drugs to sell them. Every time you buy something like that, you're supporting a whole industry of bastards who kill people, and it'll kill you too. Did you like what happened out there today?' They both knew he did, he had spent his whole life training for it and living for that moment, and he was going to go a lot further. He had the talent to do it. 'If you did like it, don't fuck it up, for you and everyone else. I love you, man. Now throw that shit away.' He grabbed it out of Billy's hand and threw it in the garbage. 'Don't fuck your life up like my brother. If I

ever see you do something like that again, I'll kill you!'
Sean was shaking with rage.

Billy stood there calmly, watching him, and realizing
what had happened.

'Everybody does it,' he said quietly. 'you just have to
know when, after they test you.'

'You're going to blow it,' Sean said with an agonized
expression. 'Please, please, please don't.' He was begging
him. Billy put an arm around his shoulders and led him
out of the bathroom, still shaking. The girls were waiting
for them, and Izzie would see that something had
happened, but Gabby didn't seem to notice. She only had
eyes for Billy, and they were going back to her apartment
before he went back to the dorm.

They dropped Izzie at her dorm first and then Sean at
his hotel, and the two boys who had grown up together
hugged each other hard. All the love Sean felt for him,
and the fear he had for him, was in their embrace, and
then Sean got out of the car. He had said everything he
had to say to him in the men's room when he threw the
Ecstasy away. Billy knew how much he cared about
him, and he loved Sean too, but he lived in another world
now, a world of fast lanes, fast people, and big money
that was going to come his way. He could hardly wait to
get out of school and play for the NFL. The

championship game had only whetted his appetite for more.

The sports pages were full of Billy the next day. There were some fabulous photographs of him scoring the winning touchdown, and the *L.A. Times* named him the hottest rookie on the planet. Marilyn was making a scrapbook of all the press on him.

Sean called Izzie that morning before he left. He was flying back to Washington D.C., from L.A. He had a paper to write before classes started again, and he needed time to do the research.

Izzie had an odd sense that some kind of tension had occurred between Sean and Billy the night before, and she was curious about it. She had seen that Sean was upset.

'What happened with you and Billy last night?' Izzie asked.

'Nothing,' he said offhandedly. 'Just guy talk.' He didn't want to tell her that he had delivered a message from his dead brother, but he hoped he had. Kevin had been gone for seven months, and it had changed his life forever. There was no room for leeway now, for halfway measures, or compromises or exceptions. What Billy had wanted to do the night before in the men's room killed people. People died for it, and because of it and from it.

And as far as Sean was concerned, the people who sold it were killers and had to be stopped. He was worried about Billy. There were so many temptations in his world now, of all kinds. But he didn't say that to Izzie. He just told her again to take care of herself. She was a sensible girl with her feet on the ground, and he knew she would. Billy lived on the edge. Ever since the flask had appeared when his parents separated, Sean knew he was at risk, just as he had known it about Kevin.

'Are you coming home for spring break?' Izzie asked him.

'Maybe. Some of the people in my study group are going to Peru on a mission to study the government. I was thinking I might go with them. I don't know yet. I know my mom wants me to come home.'

'Yeah. Me too,' she said softly. She always missed him. She missed them all. At least she saw Gabby all the time. But Andy and Sean had gone so far away. It felt like another planet sometimes, with them in Boston and Washington, D.C.

'I'll let you know what I'm doing,' Sean promised. They hung up then, and Izzie already missed him. She was smiling to herself as she thought about him, and about Billy winning the game the day before. It was a beautiful January day, and all was well, when she went to meet the others for lunch. They were still on a high from Billy's big victory. This was only the beginning for him, and for all of them. And when she saw Billy walk into the restaurant, she was so happy for him, she had tears in her eyes. He looked like the happiest guy in the world.

Chapter 13

A week after USC won the Rose Bowl game, Gabby got confirmation that she had been chosen for the national ad campaign for the cosmetics company. Her agency was sending her out on more go-sees, one of them for a Victoria's Secret ad. She was learning the business.

Billy had stayed with her the night before, and had left for the dorm early that morning, to work out at the gym. They were planning to have dinner together that evening.

She slipped into a short, skinny black dress and a pair of strappy high heels. Her skin looked terrific, and her long straight blond hair was perfectly blow-dried. She had just had it colored, and she was wearing it a little lighter, which looked right in L.A. She had very little makeup on – her agency liked her fresh, with a girl-next-door wholesome look, and so did Billy. After he won the championship game, he had given her a promise ring to replace the one he'd given her in high school, which he'd had engraved with 'I love you.' This one was a narrow band of diamonds with a small diamond heart on it, and she was wearing it on her left hand. It wasn't an engagement ring yet, but she knew it would be one day. He had said as much to her. He had just turned nineteen and she was eighteen, and they had time. He said he wanted to marry her by the time he went to the NFL. They both wondered if he'd stay in school for all four years. After the championship game, she doubted it. The lure of the NFL would be too tempting if they flashed big money at him when he turned twenty-one. Gabby knew that would be hard to resist, but she didn't care. As long as she was with Billy, he could do whatever he wanted. She was behind him all the way.

Her three go-sees that day went well, and she was pretty sure she'd get all three jobs. She had a drink at the Ivy with one of the models after the last one. She liked her and they had worked together a few times, most recently on a shoot for *Vogue*. They talked about how tough the business was, and how lucky they had been. The other girl had come out from Salt Lake City six months ago, and like Gabby, she was doing well. A lot of the girls weren't, but Gabby and her new friend had the look everybody wanted right now. The girl from Utah had just been asked to shoot a commercial in Japan, and she said she was going to do it.

Gabby called Izzie from her BlackBerry as she left the Ivy, but it went to voicemail, so she figured Izzie was still in class. She just said that she called to say hi and tell her she loved her, and then Billy called to say he loved her and ask how her day was. She told him about the go-sees, and he promised to be at the apartment an hour later – he had the keys.

Gabby still had her phone in her hand as she stepped out on North Robertson to hail a cab. She saw one and put her arm up, a beautiful girl in a short black dress, with her long blond hair flying in the breeze. Just then a car came around the corner so fast, she couldn't even see it or step back. Gabby never knew what hit her. She flew into the air when the car struck her, and then smashed onto the windshield. The car was going so fast that she fell off again, headfirst onto the street, and lay there like a rag doll as cars were honking and people screamed. The driver of the car that hit her drove up onto the sidewalk and nearly ran down someone else. He jumped out of the car and started running, and someone grabbed him and pinned him to the ground. Police were on the scene immediately, and two ambulances seconds later. The fire department came. The driver who had hit her was taken into custody. One of the policemen found her phone and put it in a bag as evidence. Her modeling portfolio was spilled all over North Robertson. Traffic was stopped, and they put Gabby on a gurney and covered her. The ambulance drove away in silence as people stared after it. They didn't put the siren on. People shuddered at the grim scene. Gabby Thomas was dead at eighteen.

Chapter 14

The police came to the Thomas home in San Francisco to tell Gabby's parents. As soon as Judy opened the door to them that night, she knew that something terrible had happened.

Billy had been calling Izzie for the past several hours, wondering if she knew where Gabby was. Izzie said that Gabby had left her a message while she was still in class. She said she had sounded fine, had said she loved her, and would call back later. It was a standard message, and Izzie said she was sure nothing was wrong.

'I talked to her at five-thirty. She said she was on her way home,' Billy said, sounding worried. It wasn't like her not to call him if she was delayed. They talked to each other constantly, or texted, throughout the day, even if just to say 'I love you,' or where they were.

'Maybe her agency sent her on another go-see, and she didn't have time to call you. Or she doesn't have service where she is.' There were always funny pockets where cell phones didn't work. It was eight o'clock by then.

'I think something's wrong,' Billy said in a choked voice, and Izzie smiled. The two of them were attached at the hip.

'That you'd know. She'd call you if something happened. Trust me. Or she'd call me. She didn't. Just give it a while, and relax. Maybe she lost her BlackBerry, or it fell out of her purse, or the battery is dead.' There were a million reasons why she might not have called, all of them benign. But in this case, it wasn't.

At that exact moment, the police were walking into the Thomases' living room, and Judy's heart was in her throat. She sat down, and they told her as gently as they could. They said that Gabby had been hit by a drunk driver and killed. He was a freshman at USC, the alcohol level in his blood on arrest was 1.9, and he was in custody. Their daughter had been killed on impact. Judy sobbed hysterically when they told her, and Adam held her, crying too.

Michelle came out of her room as soon as she heard her mother scream, and she knew the minute she saw her.

'Gabby!' Michelle shouted in anguish. Judy nodded, and Michelle put her arms around them as though trying to protect them from the news. She felt a knife-stab of guilt slice through her for every time she had been jealous of her sister, and there had been many, many times. She had admitted it to Brian, her mother, her group, and even Gabby herself. She had confessed, but maybe her bad thoughts had killed her sister. Michelle was sixteen years old, and like Sean a few months earlier, she was suddenly an only child.

The police told them who to contact at the police department in L.A. He said it would be simplest if they would go there, to make arrangements for the body to be brought back to San Francisco. There were a number of forms to fill out, and they told Judy and Adam how sorry they were and looked as though they meant it. One of the officers said he had a daughter the same age, and he could imagine how they felt. But he couldn't, Judy knew immediately. He couldn't possibly – his daughter was still alive. And her beautiful, wonderful, beloved Gabby was dead.

At first they didn't know what to do. Judy called Connie and told her, knowing she'd understand, and then they both thought of Billy. Someone had to tell him. Connie couldn't even imagine it, but she said she'd call

Izzie, who could tell him in person. She called her while Judy and Adam booked seats on a flight to L.A. the next day. It was too late to catch the last flight, and they were in no condition to travel. Michelle said she wanted to go with them.

Connie had no idea what to say to Izzie and wished Sean were there. Izzie answered her cell phone before she looked – she thought it might be Billy again. She was surprised to hear Connie at the other end.

'Hi, Connie,' Izzie said, sounding happy. She had just gotten back to her dorm room, after picking up a salad for dinner. She didn't want to gain the freshmen fifteen and was careful about it. 'What's up?'

'I've got bad news,' Connie said simply. Very, very bad news. She had told Mike, and he was sitting near her, with a devastated expression. And after Izzie, they were going to call Sean. It seemed hideous beyond imagining that two of these young people had died within seven months of each other, Kevin and now Gabby. And she had done nothing dangerous or risky – all she did was hail a cab. But the boy who hit her had been drinking. And now his life would be ruined too. He had killed a beautiful young woman. Connie could imagine how his parents would feel when they heard. Two lives had been destroyed that night, not just Gabby's, and the lives of all those who loved them, and in Gabby's case, there were many.

'What's wrong?' Izzie asked her. The tone of Connie's voice sounded familiar to her, but she couldn't remember why. She had heard that tone before, something dead in her, as though the end of the world had happened. And for them, it had.

'I hate to tell you this over the phone, but I have to. Izzie . . . I'm sorry . . . It's Gabby.'

'What about Gabby?' Izzie could feel her heart pound, and then she remembered that tone in Connie's voice. *After Kevin.* 'What do you mean?' Izzie felt like she was screaming, but it was only a whisper.

'She was hit by a drunk driver. He . . . she's . . . he killed her,' Connie said on a sob.

'Oh my God . . . oh my God . . .' Izzie felt frantic, and all she could think about was Billy. 'Billy . . . does he know?'

'Not yet.'

'It'll kill him . . . Who's going to tell him? He called me a while ago, and he was worried. She hadn't called him since five-thirty, and she was late.'

'I think that's when it happened. He came around the corner and hit her. I'm not sure where she was. He's a freshman at USC. Judy said he was drunk and tried to run, and a witness grabbed him.'

'What do we do about Billy?' Izzie asked, panicking.

'Someone has to tell him, and not on the phone. Do you think you can do it?' She was the only one there who could, and they both knew it. It was going to be the hardest thing she ever did.

'Does Sean know?' She could use support from him. Or Andy. But it would be devastating for them too.

'Not yet. I called you first.'

'He's at her apartment,' she said, as though to herself. 'I'll go.'

'I'm so sorry . . . I don't think he should hear it on the phone. Neither should you.' But they both knew that was different. Izzie felt like a bomb had hit her when she hung up. She had lost her best friend, who was like a sister to her. But Billy had lost his first love and the girl he wanted to marry and was sure he would. Gabby had shown her the beautiful promise ring the day she got it. Billy loved Gabby as much as any wife – she was his childhood sweetheart.

Feeling disoriented and confused, Izzie took a cab to Gabby's apartment. She didn't take the time to comb her hair or wash her face. All she could think about was Gabby. She rang the doorbell and expected to see Gabby open it and tell her it was a joke. But instead Billy answered, with a can of beer in his hand, and he looked nervous the minute he saw Izzie.

'What happened?'

She couldn't find the words to say it to him, and she flew into his arms and held him. His arms went around her as he started to cry, and the beer was all over the floor in a pool around them.

'Oh no . . . ,' he said. 'Oh no . . . oh no . . .' It was all he could say as they both cried and stood there rocking back and forth. He had known the minute he saw Izzie's face. And finally he asked her how. They were still standing in the doorway, and Izzie gently closed the door and led him to the couch. They both needed to sit down, and she felt like she was going to faint.

'A hit-and-run driver. He was drunk. Some kid from USC.' A wave of rage washed over Billy's face, and then he dissolved in tears again, and they held each other and rocked back and forth some more. Sean called Izzie a little while later.

'Oh my God . . .' He was in tears, but all he could think about was Billy. 'How is he?'

'Not good. I'm here at Gabby's with him.' Just saying her name, a rock the size of a fist lodged in Izzie's throat, and she couldn't speak for a minute.

'I'm coming home on the red-eye tonight,' Sean told her.

'Okay.' She couldn't think of anything to say to him. She felt as though they had all been dropped off a building together. She was glad he was coming home. 'Did you call Andy?'

'I wanted to call you first. I'll call him now. Are you okay?'

'No.' *Of course not.* She closed her eyes and clung to Billy, as much for him as for herself.

'Hang in. We'll make it. We all have each other.' But they no longer had Gabby and never would again. 'I'll see you tomorrow.'

'I want to go home tonight,' Billy said as soon as she hung up. He was crying like a baby.

'The Thomases are coming down tomorrow. Maybe we should wait.' He thought about it and nodded.

'Don't leave,' he said to Izzie as she sat there with him.

'I won't. I promise.' She couldn't have anyway. She needed him just as much. His mother called him, frantic about him, but he wouldn't talk to her, so Izzie did instead, and she said that she was with him. Marilyn was sobbing as much as Connie had been. It was a communal loss.

Billy slept in Gabby's bed that night, the one he had

shared with her, smelling her on the pillows. He opened the closets and inhaled the familiar perfume on her clothes. He howled like an animal as he held them, and slept with her nightgown wrapped around him, while Izzie slept on the couch.

Izzie and Billy were still wearing the clothes they'd worn at Gabby's the night before when they met the Thomases at the police station. Judy was devastated and Adam was crying, and Michelle looked like she was in shock. They all were. And they were told that the drunk driver was still in jail.

'I hope he dies there,' Adam said.

They filled out the forms to transfer Gabby. They had already arranged with the funeral parlor in San Francisco to bring her home. They all went to the airport then. Billy and Izzie had packed nothing. All they wanted was to go home, and the five of them took a noon flight. The Thomases had arranged for a car to pick them up, and they dropped both young people at Billy's house. Marilyn and Jack were waiting for them. Brian was at school, and Marilyn had thought to notify Atwood as well. She thought they'd want to know since Gabby had only graduated seven months before.

Billy folded into his mother's arms just as he had when he was a little boy. He stood there and sobbed, as Jack gently patted him, and they led him into the family room to sit down. He looked like an overgrown five-year-old, and not the championship quarterback he had become.

'How am I going to live without her?' he said to his mother. He had loved her since they were five, all his life. They all had. Izzie couldn't imagine a world without her in it either. It was a devastating loss for them all. They sat and talked for a while, and finally Marilyn took him to his room and put him to bed, and then she looked at Izzie and hugged her.

'Thank you for being there for him.'

'I love him,' she said simply. And then Jack offered to drive her home. Izzie looked terrible, and he could see how she felt. She promised to come back later. Jack drove her to the house, and Jennifer was waiting for her there. She didn't say a word, she'd been there for hours, knowing Izzie would come home, and she held her in her arms while Izzie cried. She felt like she was dying of a broken heart.

'I'm so sorry . . . I'm so sorry . . . ,' Jennifer said again and again, and explained that her father had to be in court with a client, or he'd have been there too. Izzie was grateful that someone was home. She had never felt so alone in her life, as now without her best friend.

Jennifer ran a bath for her, and sat with her while Izzie

talked about Gabby, how much she loved her and the things they'd done when they were little, the pranks they played at school. And then Jennifer made her lie down, but she couldn't sleep. She got up and went into the kitchen, and they had something to eat. And then Jennifer drove her back to Billy's. Izzie hadn't been to see Sean's parents yet, and she wanted to, but she wanted to check on Billy again first. And when she walked in, Sean was there, and he pulled her into his arms and held her tight without saying a word.

'You're okay, Iz . . . You're okay . . . ,' he crooned at her, and she pulled away to look at him and shook her head.

'No, I'm not.' And he wasn't either, but it was the best they could do. Billy was sleeping by then, and Sean went with her to see the Thomases, and then they went back to Sean's house. They went up to his room and lay on his bed. He said that Andy was coming for one day for the funeral, but he couldn't come for longer, he had exams. But he would be there.

'I'm worried about Billy,' Izzie said softly, as she lay next to Sean.

'I'm worried about all of us. I think our generation is cursed. All you ever read about are kids our age who are shot and killed, die in car wrecks, or kill themselves, or do drive-by shootings and kill fifty people. What's wrong with us? Why does this shit happen?'

'I don't know,' she said sadly. She'd never thought of it before, but there was something to what he said. They were a generation at risk, in a very high-stakes game.

Chapter 15

The funeral was beautiful, with enormous white flowers everywhere. It almost looked like a wedding and was a little over the top, but somehow it seemed right for Gabby. The Atwood choir sang 'Ave Maria' and 'Amazing Grace,' and Izzie sat between Sean and Andy, with Jeff and Jennifer in the row behind them. Billy sat with Gabby's parents and Michelle, crying like a child. They almost had to hold him up when the casket was carried out of the church. Jack went to walk beside him, as Billy walked out of the church with Michelle. Everyone knew it was a turning point in Billy's life, and surely not a good one.

They all went to the Thomases' afterward, along with hundreds of people. Everyone who had loved her was there, and Billy was visibly drunk an hour after he arrived. It upset everyone, but Marilyn would talk to him later. Marilyn and Jack took him home and put him to bed. It had all been too much for him. He'd been talking all day about dropping out of USC and forgetting football. Jack had called the coach and explained the situation. They were going to give him compassionate leave for as long as he needed, and it looked like it might be a long time, but it was too soon to tell.

Sean and Izzie sat in the Thomases' garden with Andy. It was chilly, but they wanted to be out of the crowd. Andy was taking the red-eye back to Boston that night.

'I just can't believe this,' he said, looking stricken. 'First your brother,' he said to Sean, 'and now Gabby.' And they all knew that unlike Kevin, she had had no risk-taking behaviors – all she had done was step into the street to hail a cab.

'Where do we go from here?' Izzie said bleakly.

'Back to school, to our lives, to do it better, to live a life they'd be proud of,' Sean said. It sounded idealistic, but he believed it.

'What about us?' Izzie asked in a whisper. 'What do we believe in now?'

'Ourselves, each other. The same things we've always believed in.' Izzie nodded, but she was no longer so sure.

It had been a brutal blow to all of them. It was hard to go on after something like this.

'When are you going back?' Izzie asked Sean with worried eyes.

'In a few days. I want to hang around with Billy. I don't think he's going back to school for a while.'

'On the plane home, he said he wanted to drop out and give up football, that it has no meaning for him without her,' Izzie told him.

'Give him time,' Sean said quietly. 'He'll never totally recover from this, I suspect, but he'll learn to live with it. Like my parents with Kevin. He can't give up at nineteen.' But they knew he wanted to right now. 'We just need to keep him from going nuts.' And he was capable of it – they knew that too. His response to the funeral had been to get drunk immediately afterward, just as it had been after his mother got married. It was an easy way out, and one his father had taught him early on. Sean wanted to tell him it was not an option. He'd probably need to be reminded of it again, by all those who loved him. For a while, it would be an appealing anesthetic, but sooner or later he'd have to face life sober again, if he wanted to have a life.

Izzie and Sean stayed for the rest of the week and spent time with Billy, Michelle, and Gabby's parents. Brian was with Michelle in all his spare time. Izzie and Sean tried to comfort everyone and finally each other. Every time she thought of it, Izzie realized that she'd never see Gabby again and couldn't imagine life without her. It was a horrifying thought, and eventually she melted into Sean's arms and just cried.

'I wish you weren't leaving,' she said softly.

'I have to. I'll come back soon. You could come to D.C. to visit me some weekend. You'd like it. It's not a bad place.' But they were all busy with school, and their obligations. She realized she was going to have to babysit Billy a lot in the coming months if he went back to school, but she was willing to do it. And Sean said he'd come out and see him too.

Billy didn't come back to L.A. for a month, and Izzie was busy with school then, but she checked on him constantly, called him several times a day, met him for dinner at her school cafeteria or his. She went for walks with him, forced him to do his homework and helped him with it, and put him to bed when he'd had too much to drink. All they could hope was that he would find his way again, and finally by June, at the end of the school year, he felt a little better, and he went home. Izzie had gotten him through, and he was well aware that he couldn't have done it without her. He told Sean she was a saint, and Sean repeated it to Izzie.

'Not exactly, but it's nice of him to say.'

'I know better, of course, but I didn't want to destroy his illusions. Mother Teresa you're not. I remember the bottle of my parents' wine you stole in Tahoe.'

'I paid you back for it!' she said, embarrassed. But at least he didn't know she'd had a one-night stand with Andy. They didn't refer to it anymore, and Izzie had heard from Andy a few months earlier that he had just met a girl he really liked, also in pre-med.

None of them had important plans for the summer, although Sean was working for his father again, and Izzie was planning to take a class at USF. They had promised to attend the sentencing of the drunk driver who had killed Gabby. They were all going to L.A. for that, and Judy had involved Mothers Against Drunk Driving to make sure that the 'killer,' as she referred to him, would serve a maximum amount of time in prison. He had already pleaded guilty, and his lawyer had arranged a plea bargain with the DA. He was not supposed to do more than a year in prison, and five years on probation. The Thomases were outraged by how little time he was going to serve, and had sent a flood of letters to the judge. Representatives of MADD were going to be in court.

Izzie, Sean, Billy, and Andy flew down to L.A.

together, and all the parents of the group went down as well. This time even Robert Weston, Andy's father, went. They stayed at the Sunset Marquis in West Hollywood, and they all arrived promptly in court the day of the sentencing. They sat quietly in the courtroom, waiting for the judge to walk in, and stood up when he arrived. The defendant walked in with his attorney and his parents moments later, and Izzie couldn't stop staring at him. He looked fourteen, and was only eighteen years old. He didn't look like a killer, but a child. And his mother was weeping silently as his father held her hand, right behind where their boy sat. As she looked at them, Izzie realized again how many lives had been destroyed by what he'd done, starting with his own, and then Gabby's and all their parents', and Gabby's friends'. It was tragic to watch.

The district attorney read off the charges, and the plea bargain that had been struck, with the conditions and length of sentence. James Stuart Edmondson had pleaded guilty to manslaughter and criminal negligence, and had expressed deep remorse to the probation department and the district attorney. The DA discussed the possibility of his going to rehab for a year instead, and the judge said it was out of the question. He had caused the death of an eighteen-year-old woman. The judge looked extremely stern and asked the defense lawyer and district attorney to approach the bench. They conferred for a moment, and the judge nodded. And then he asked if the victim's family would like to make a statement.

With his own attorney at his side, Gabby's father came forward, wearing a dark blue suit and a somber expression, while Judy cried openly, as did Michelle, and Billy looked so distraught that Sean and Izzie thought he was going to faint or attack someone.

Adam Thomas made an impassioned speech about his daughter, how beautiful she was, how beloved, how successful, the future she had ahead of her. He held out a photograph of her that almost ripped Izzie's heart out. And he even mentioned her relationship with Billy and the fact that they would have gotten married and had children. He mentioned everything that would never happen now because James Edmondson, who looked like a child himself, had gotten drunk and killed her. His attorney claimed that he hadn't had a drink since, and it had been unfortunate freshman behavior that had turned to tragedy when he got behind the wheel of a car after drinking.

By the time Adam Thomas finished, there wasn't a dry eye in the house. Billy was sobbing openly in the front row, and the judge seemed to know who he was. He was the star rookie quarterback at USC, and you couldn't miss him in his dark blue suit, white shirt, and tie.

Then the representative from MADD requested permission to speak, and the judge denied it. He didn't want his courtroom used for a media circus. He was well aware of the gravity of the matter before him, without a speech from MADD. He invited the defendant to come forward, and in a shaking voice Jimmy Edmondson told the judge how sorry he was, and he sounded sincere. It was a tragedy on both sides. He looked like he wouldn't survive five minutes in prison, let alone a year, and his mother looked every bit as devastated as Judy.

With an enormously serious voice, the judge explained again that a young woman had been killed, her life had been cut short, and Mr. Edmondson had to pay the full penalty of the law for killing her. He said somberly that there was no escaping the consequences of what he'd done. The judge stunned the entire courtroom by overturning the plea bargain and sentencing the USC freshman to five years in prison, with two years of probation following his release, the main condition of which being that he not touch a drop of alcohol during that time. His driver's license would be returned to him at the end of those two years – he was not allowed to drive until then. The judge asked him if he understood the conditions and the sentence as Jimmy nodded with tears rolling down his cheeks. He had hoped for far less time, and his lawyer explained to him that he would probably serve three to three and a half years of a five-year sentence. It was a very long time, and it was easy to see how ill-prepared he was for the world he was about to enter, a prison full of rapists and murderers and criminals of all kinds. But he was considered a murderer too, even if to a lesser degree. Gabby was his victim and she was dead.

The judge rapped his gavel, and everyone stood up. A bailiff stepped forward with a sheriff's deputy. They put handcuffs on the defendant and led him away. His mother sobbed hysterically, and her husband held her and got her out of the courtroom. She didn't even look at the Thomases, she couldn't. Her own loss was so great, she couldn't think of theirs now, only of what was about to happen to her son, and just had.

They all filed quietly out of court, and the Thomases were shaken. The boy who had killed Gabby was the same age as she was, and looked more like Michelle's age, and she would have been as ill-equipped to deal with prison as he was, but he had foolishly driven drunk and killed Gabby, and even tried to run away. And however painful it was for his parents, justice had been served.

No one spoke on the way out, and even Billy was quiet. What had just happened wouldn't bring Gabby back, but the boy who had killed her had been punished. It had a bitter taste to Izzie, as she stood in the June sunshine outside the court building. She looked at her friends, and they were as shocked as she was. A terrible thing had occurred when Kevin was killed. And now another terrible thing had happened. James Edmondson would go to prison. It was the way the system worked. They got back into the cars that had brought them, and they flew back to San Francisco that afternoon. For them, the nightmare of the proceedings was over. And for the boy who had killed Gabby, his nightmare had just begun.

Chapter 16

The rest of the summer passed peacefully for all of them. It was a time of healing and reflection. Sean, Andy, and Izzie talked a lot about Gabby, and how strange and empty their lives were without her. Billy was deeply depressed, and his mother was forcing him to go to counseling to talk about it, which was sensible. She was desperately worried about him. They all were. He drank too much, and Sean lectured him constantly about it. His friends were concerned, but as the time came closer for him to go back to USC for practice, he began to seem more like himself. It was possible that he would never fully recover, but football had always been his life as much as Gabby, and they were hoping it would be his salvation in the end.

The others had to find a way to heal and go on. Judy was still devastated, but the tragedy seemed to bring her closer to Michelle. She went to New York with her, just so they could spend some time together and have a change of scene. And when she came back, Judy seemed more like herself.

Andy spent as much time with Billy as he could, in spite of another boring summer job, and he and Sean had dinner often and spent hours talking about what had happened and what it meant to them.

The mothers in the group got together often too. Marilyn was worried about Billy, but also constantly busy with the twins, who were running everywhere and driving her happily insane. No matter what else happened, the twins were the bright spot in her life, and a source of immeasurable joy. Their innocence was like a beacon of hope shining in the darkness. Jennifer and Izzie made friends and got closer to each other. Izzie missed Gabby so much.

Izzie went to Tahoe with the O'Haras, and tried not to remember the night with Andy in the maid's room. She and Sean talked endlessly about everything they cared about. He was talking a lot again about working for the FBI when he finished college. It wounded more like a goal now than a dream.

They went swimming in the lake, played tennis, went for hikes, and fished. His father took them water-skiing. They did normal things, and tried to forget all the hard things that had happened.

By the time Izzie went back to UCLA in September, she was ready to face life again. And Sean was excited to go back to Washington, D.C. Billy had left for practice in early August, and Andy felt ready to face his second year of pre-med. They were all headed in the right direction. Gabby wasn't forgotten – she was a memory they would carry with them forever, the memory of fourteen years of friendship, and the childhood they had shared. In important ways, she would always be a part of them.

Sophomore year was hard for Izzie without Gabby. She had loved having her best friend close at hand. Now she was gone. Izzie had a roommate she liked better than her first one, but no one could replace Gabby. She had been like a sister to Izzie and her very best girlfriend. Sophomore year was brutal for Billy too. It was excruciating. Sometimes the agony of losing Gabby still took his breath away. He was having a tough time keeping up with his studies. Izzie helped whenever she could. The only thing that interested him now was playing for the NFL. He was tired of school.

He spent all the time he could working out and at

practice. He had taken Sean's advice, and his adviser's, and stopped drinking. And he was in fantastic shape when he played his first game of sophomore year. He had a strong winning streak and played a remarkable season. His mother and Jack came down often to watch him play and Larry tried to whenever he could. But by the end of football season and another championship game where he had excelled, Billy knew what he wanted to do. He was certain now. All he had to do was get through another year.

He walked into his adviser's office on January 2 and told him what he was thinking, and his adviser was sympathetic. He told Billy he had to wait until he turned twenty-one to enter the NFL draft, which Billy knew. It was what kept him going now. He had won a second championship game. And he felt ready, but he still had to wait. He didn't care about graduating anymore. There was too much waiting for him out in the world. With Gabby, he might have stayed. Without her, he just wanted to get on with his life and start his career as a professional as soon as he could.

He hadn't dated anyone since Gabby died, and had been faithful to her. She had been gone for just over a year, and he still missed her every hour of every day. Living without her was like living with constant pain.

Izzie wished sometimes that her own career decision were easier and clear. She had a deep need to help others, but still wasn't sure how to manifest it. She switched her major to English in junior year, and talked to Sean about it. He was more and more set on the FBI. His brother's death had made his goals clearer. Gabby's had shaken Izzie and she had felt lost ever since she died.

She tried to explain it to her mother, on one of Katherine's rare trips to L.A.. Izzie and Katherine were not like mother and daughter, and never had been. They were more like old friends now, they weren't close, but their relationship was peaceful. Izzie no longer expected anything from her and hadn't in years.

'I still don't understand why you don't want to go to law school,' Katherine said to her over lunch. She was still a pretty woman, although she was fifty-four years old by then. She didn't seem it, and Izzie suspected she had had some work done, but she looked very good. She had moved to London and was living with the same man she had dated for six years. His name was Charles Sparks, he was older than Katherine, and he was enormously rich and successful. Izzie had met him, but didn't know him very well. Her mother seemed happy, which maybe was enough. Izzie didn't have to love him too. Both he and her mother felt like strangers to her. And sometimes Izzie felt as though she were a stranger even to herself. She still didn't know what she wanted to be when she grew up. Sometimes it was hard enough just being alive, but she wanted to lead a useful life too, not just have a job.

'I don't want to be a lawyer, Mom. I guess that's the best reason. And I don't have a head for business like you,' which ruled out going to business school too. Izzie had considered it, but it just wasn't 'her.' She had good organizational skills, but she didn't know where to use them.

'Don't be a dreamer like your father,' Katherine said with a stern look of disappointment. She had never been impressed by his work at the ACLU. 'He's always championing the poor. You don't make money doing that.' Jennifer shared his ideals, as a social worker, and his deep commitment. Izzie respected them for that even if her mother didn't. They had been living together by then for over a year, and it seemed to work. Her parents' marriage never had – they were just too different, and were even more so now.

'I might teach for a couple of years. Or go to India, and work with the poor.' Izzie looked at her mother apologetically, and felt like she was playing roulette with her life. Andy knew where he was going, Sean was fascinated with the FBI, and Billy had his football career, but Izzie still didn't know what she wanted to do. All she had wanted when she was little was to be a good mother and wife, maybe because her mother wasn't. And in the meantime she had discovered it wasn't considered a career. It was a question of luck. Connie and Marilyn were wonderful mothers, but both had had jobs before that. Motherhood seemed like a vocation, not a career. And she was only twenty years old, way too young to be thinking of settling down with anyone. She hadn't met anyone she cared about anyway. She had dated several people a few times, and was never interested in seeing them again. Unlike Gabby and Billy, she hadn't found true love, and wasn't looking for it. All she wanted for now was to get an education and have some fun while she did and wind up in a job she loved when she graduated.

'You'll figure it out,' her mother said when she kissed her goodbye after lunch. She was going back to London that night, and Izzie had no idea when she'd see her again. It had been that way for years. Her father and Jennifer were the constants in her life, and her friends.

Her English major turned out to be the right one for her in junior year. She enjoyed it, and took several classes in philosophy and added a minor in French literature. She was having a good time, and Connie encouraged her to think about teaching. She had enjoyed it until she married Mike.

In January of junior year Billy filed his application to the NFL for the draft. He was finally going to leave school so his professional football career could officially begin. His application was accepted, and in April he was drafted by Detroit. He said it was the happiest day of his life.

It was exciting for him, even if they weren't the strongest team in the league. It was the best thing that had happened to him since Gabby's death, and a hugely important event in his life. He had hired an agent and a business manager, and he finally started dating soon after that. Gabby had been gone for two years by then. He dated mostly models and young actresses, showy young girls close to his own age or younger. Not one of them was worth Gabby, but they distracted him, and he showed up in the press at various events with pretty young girls on his arm. It unnerved his mother a little, but she knew it was good for him, better than mourning Gabby for the rest of the time.

At the end of Izzie's junior year, her father and Jennifer decided to get married. They didn't want to have babies, but they wanted to adopt one. So there were a lot of changes up ahead. Izzie wasn't upset about it. She liked

Jennifer and thought she was good for her father, although she wasn't sure that adopting a child at her father's age was such a good idea. But it fit with their philosophies about improving the lot of those less fortunate than they were, and they were excited about it.

Izzie turned twenty-one and her mother treated her to a trip to Europe that summer with a Eurail Pass and a backpack all by herself. She met up with Sean and Andy in Copenhagen and traveled through Norway and Sweden with them, and then to Berlin. She wound up in Paris on her own, and went from there to London, where she stayed with her mother and Charles for a few days, and she had a good time, and then she came home. She had been gone all summer, and was excited about starting senior year.

She had lunch with Andy before he left for Boston. He had a serious girlfriend, and couldn't wait to start medical school as soon as he graduated. He was hoping to stay at Harvard for that too, and he looked and acted more like a doctor every day. He seemed so adult and mature, and said he wanted to be an orthopaedic surgeon, and he asked her what she was going to do when she graduated. They had talked about it in Europe, but the conversation had been vague.

'I guess I'll teach for a while. Or maybe join the Peace

Corps. I'd better figure it out this year,' she said with a rueful smile. Her mother had invited her to come to London for a year, which sounded exciting, but Izzie didn't want to do that, she still wanted to do something useful, but had no idea what. 'I feel about as grown-up as I did on the first day of kindergarten when I was dishing up plastic food to all of you. You asked for a turkey sand-wich with mayo,' she reminded him, and they both laughed. He had looked so proper and serious in his button-down shirt and khaki pants. And he had known he wanted to be a doctor even then. None of them had changed much since. Billy was still obsessed with foot-ball, and Gabby would have been an actress if she had lived – Izzie's heart always ached when she thought of it. Sean still wanted to catch 'bad guys' and was fluent in Spanish now and would graduate with a degree in foreign policy, which would be useful in the FBI.

'Maybe you should consider opening a restaurant with plastic food,' Andy teased her, and as he said it, the light finally dawned. It would be slightly different from the path she'd been considering, but suddenly it felt like the right one to her.

'It would be better than my real cooking,' she said looking pensive. 'I thought the plastic doughnuts were particularly cute.'

'So were you,' Andy said with a warm expression and ruffled her hair. They never talked about the night they had lost their virginity to each other, but they remembered, and she knew they always would. She was glad he had found someone he really cared about at school. Her name was Nancy and he had met her in lab. He said he was crazy about her, and they had all the same life and career goals and interests. Who knew? Maybe it would work. Izzie had had trouble having faith in anything, the future surely, and even herself, since Gabby's death. How could you trust anything after that?

Izzie wasn't sure what she wanted relationship-wise either. She had dated someone for three months at the beginning of the year, but had lost interest in him very quickly. She felt like a ship without a rudder with no serious love interest or firm career goals.

She and Sean talked about the future when they had dinner the night before he left for D.C. Life after college was everyone's main worry now.

'You'll figure it out,' he said confidently.

'That's what my mother says,' Izzie said with a sigh. Things were actually starting to come clearer, but she didn't want to tell him yet, until she was sure. 'What about you? State Department? Justice? Still FBI?' A lot of the students at GW went into government, and she could see Sean doing something more international, now that he was fluent in Spanish.

'Something like that,' he said vaguely, as she looked at him, but she knew him better than that. He was hiding something from her.

'What does that mean? What aren't you telling me? He laughed when she said it. She knew him too well, but he knew her too, sometimes better than she knew herself. She couldn't hide anything from him either.

'I don't know. I'm checking something out. It's not a new idea for me.'

'Policeman? Fireman? Sheriff?' She reminded him of his earlier career goals, and he laughed.

'Something like that.' He hadn't told his parents yet, and wasn't ready to tell Izzie yet either, but she was like a dog with a bone.

'So?'

'Okay, okay. Just don't tell anyone yet, until I figure it out. CIA maybe, DEA, Department of Justice maybe. I have an interview for the FBI Academy. I'm hoping they might accept me without work experience first.' It had always been his dream, and now more so than ever. He was desperate to get in.

'What does all that alphabet soup mean?' She looked vaguely worried. She had gotten the drift of what he meant, and some of it sounded dangerous to her, particularly the Drug Enforcement Administration, the DEA.

'I still want to catch the bad guys, like the ones who killed my brother. The only way to do that is at its source, to go after the drug cartels in South America. That's where all that shit comes from. They sell drugs to buy guns and arm terrorists around the world.' His eyes lit up when he said it, just as they used to when he brandished his cowboy gun when they were five. He had arrested her regularly when they had play dates at his house. He always put her in jail in his room, and then went downstairs to get something to eat.

'That's dangerous stuff, Sean,' she said seriously. 'People get killed doing that. I don't want to lose another friend.'

'You won't,' he said confidently, 'and I haven't made my mind up. It's just an idea. I want to see what the FBI is all about. It seems like the most interesting of the lot, to me anyway.'

'It really is true,' she said with a sigh. 'All of you knew what you wanted to do in kindergarten, and I'm still trying to figure it out. Pathetic, isn't it?'

'No, it's not. You'll come up with something by next year. You're smart to keep an open mind.'

'My mind isn't open,' she said ruefully. 'It's just blank.'

'No, it isn't,' he said gently, and kissed her on the cheek as he took her home. 'You've always been the smartest girl I've ever known, and you always will be.' She smiled at him, and they hugged again when he dropped her off. Talking to him made up a little for the void Gabby had left in her life. She knew it was a hole that would be there forever. Just as it would be for Billy, and each of them in some way.

Izzie's father and Jennifer got married the day after Christmas. They had a small ceremony performed by a judge, and most of their friends and co-workers from the ACLU were there. And afterward they had a big friendly lunch at a restaurant nearby. Izzie's friends and their parents were there too. Judy still looked very rocky, and Michelle was very thin again. Maintaining her weight was a constant struggle for her. She was in college now, had gotten into Stanford, and was doing well. And Brian was a junior at Atwood. Billy, Andy, and Sean were home for the holidays. Billy was wearing a leather suit and alligator cowboy boots. He looked just like what he was, a professional ballplayer who made a lot of money, and Izzie teased him about it.

'That's who I am,' he said laughing. And according to

the tabloids, he had a hot new girlfriend who was a dancer in Vegas. She wasn't Gabby, but they were all twenty-two and didn't need to find true love yet. Andy had just been accepted into Harvard Medical School. Sean had never told her what happened when he visited the FBI Academy, and changed the subject whenever she asked him. And Izzie was actively looking for a job and had one in mind. It wasn't a lifetime career, but it appealed to her for a while, maybe a couple of years while she figured it all out. She missed having Gabby to talk to about things. She had always been so sensible and mature about life.

And in May, her father and Jennifer's adoption came through. They adopted a two-year-old girl from China who was the cutest child Izzie had ever seen. Her name was Ping. And they were thrilled. Jeff gave up his study to make a room for her, and Izzie helped them paint it over a weekend.

In June, the big day arrived. For all of them. Andy graduated from Harvard, magna cum laude. Sean graduated from George Washington, with honors in Spanish. And Izzie graduated from UCLA as an English major. And the week before she graduated, she had been told she had got a job as an assistant kindergarten teacher at Atwood, where they had all gone to school. It was exactly the job she wanted for now, and her father said he was pleased for her, although she knew her mother wouldn't be. But Izzie was sure she was doing the right thing. Finally. And she was planning to go to Europe again that summer, and visit Venice and Florence, Padua and Verona, and some of the cities she hadn't gotten to the year before.

The ceremony at UCLA was serious and moving. Sean came to her graduation since his had taken place a month before, but Andy was still in Cambridge moving to a new apartment. Billy showed up and caused a major stir when people recognized him. He signed autographs for everyone's brothers. And her dad and Jennifer brought Ping with them. And her mother had come too. It was one of those moments when Izzie missed Gabby terribly, but she felt her there in spirit. It was hard to believe she had been gone for almost three and a half years. The time had passed so quickly, and Billy was doing well now too.

Her father and Jennifer gave her a graduation lunch at the Hotel Bel-Air. It was a beautiful sunny day, and all of them enjoyed each other's company, and laughed a lot at old stories of when they were younger and the things they did then, and the mischief they got into. Sean and Billy told about the first day in kindergarten when she had served them lunch at the picnic table with plastic food.

'And we've been friends ever since,' Sean said, looking at her warmly.

She told them all about her new job then as the assistant kindergarten teacher at Atwood. Her father looked proud of her, and her mother gave her a disapproving look.

'I think you'll have fun with that,' Sean said quietly. 'You're good with little kids.' He had watched her often with Billy's twin sisters, who were four now, and going to the same nursery school Billy and Brian had, and would probably go to Atwood in another year.

'I don't plan to do it forever,' Izzie said softly. 'Just for a couple of years. What about you?' She asked him directly, as the others went back to talking to each other. 'You still haven't told me what happened with the FBI.' He hesitated for a long moment, and then answered her.

'I signed up. By sheer miracle they waived the previous work experience. I figured that was a sign that it was meant to be.'

'You did?' She looked at him in surprise. 'You never told me.' And it didn't sound like a miracle to her.

'It's what I always wanted to do.' She knew that was true.

'I hope they don't give you dangerous assignments,' she said, but they both knew they would and it was what he wanted. 'That seems so risky,' she said with a worried look. 'When do you start?' She'd been hoping he'd be home for a while.

'In August, in Quantico, Virginia. I'll be there till January.'

Her mother got up, ready to leave then. She had a plane to catch to New York. The others were all leaving that night. Izzie had already shipped her things back to San Francisco, moved out of her dormitory, and was staying at the hotel with her father and Jennifer. Sean was flying back with them. Billy had recently been traded to Miami, but he said he was planning to come back to San Francisco to see his parents in July. And he always visited Gabby's parents when he did. Michelle had just finished her sophomore year at Stanford, and Brian was going to be a high school senior. Izzie had already promised to help him with his college applications. He was excited that she was going to be working at Atwood and he could see her anytime.

Sean and Izzie talked quietly on the plane back to San Francisco that night. They were talking about Billy and the life he led. They were both relieved that he seemed to have calmed down in spite of the temptations around him every day. Izzie wondered if he and Gabby would have been married by then. She suspected that they would. Without her, he had less to anchor him, and he was known for the pretty women he went out with, apparently hordes of them. He had never been interested in other women when he was with Gabby, but now they were a status symbol for him, like his expensive suits, his alligator cowboy boots, and the gold Rolex he had on his wrist with diamonds around the face. But even with the fancy trappings, he was still the same boy they had grown up with, the little boy who had put his football in the cubby at Atwood, and had fallen in love with Gabby the first time she took the building blocks away from him. Izzie knew, as she looked at Sean sitting next to her, that in spite of everything that happened, some things would never change.

Chapter 17

When Izzie walked up to the familiar door on the first Wednesday after Labor Day, this time she let herself in with her own key. She had seen that door for thirteen years of her life, and walked through it thousands of times, but not like this. She walked into the kindergarten classroom and turned on the lights. The name tags were on the desk, ready to be handed out to the students on the first day of school, which was today. In an hour, they would all be here. Her name was on one of the tags too.

She looked at the familiar corner with the building blocks, and nothing had changed. The building blocks were new, but the set-up was the same. They had a new play kitchen, in the same location, with a bright pink stove and fridge. And it looked like there was more plastic food than there used to be. She walked over to look at it, wanting to see the plastic doughnuts with sprinkles, but there was a chocolate birthday cake instead, divided into pieces, with pretend candles on it.

There was a dress-up corner, with princess clothes, police and fireman uniforms, and a cowboy hat and holster but no gun. The rules hadn't changed. The classroom looked no different than it had when they were in kindergarten. And if she closed her eyes she could imagine that the five of them were there. She wished she could turn the clock back and start at the beginning. This was where it had all started, when Gabby took the building blocks away from Billy and Sean, Izzie had served them all lunch, and Andy had arrived late in his perfectly pressed khakis and white shirt. He had looked like a doctor even then. She could hear their voices in the silence. And in a little while there would be different voices in that room, new faces, other children. And she was a teacher now, not a little girl in braids. It was a strange feeling, as she put her name tag on, and she expected it to say 'Miss Pam.' Instead it said 'Miss Izzie,' and Miss Wendy had replaced Miss June. It had all happened so fast when nobody was looking. The children of yesterday were all grown-ups now, and some of them were gone. She tried not to think of Gabby in her sparkly pink shoes as she put her coat away and put on an apron. Miss Wendy, the head kindergarten teacher, had showed her where everything was during her orientation. They were starting out with clay today, to get everyone comfortable, not musical instruments, then story time, and recreation, quiet time after that, and then the introduction of letters, numbers, and colors. The format was the same, even if slightly rearranged.

Wendy arrived just as she was leaving for the front door with her name tag on, and the kid's name tags to hand out. She had the attendance list in her hand. She had already memorized their names and needed to match them up with faces now.

'All set?' the older teacher asked her with a broad smile, and Izzie nodded. The pitcher for the juice was set out with the plastic cups they would use. There was a platter of vanilla cookies, no nuts or chocolate. All of a sudden, Izzie could hardly wait. It was exciting to be here. It was her first day at school too.

'All set,' Izzie confirmed, and then went to the front door to greet her new students at the separate kindergarten door. The older ones would rush in through double doors a few feet away. The kindergarten had its own entrance, just as it had when she went there, and tiny desks and chairs. Izzie remembered some of the mothers sitting there on the first day. Her mother hadn't, but some had stayed, though she no longer remembered who. And she remembered wearing a red shirt and new red sneakers.

She took her place and smiled at each child who came through the door, wondering which ones would form lifelong friendships. As she put on their name tags, she almost wanted to tell them what an important day it was, that the children they made friends with 'forever' would be with them all their lives.

Miss Wendy was waiting for them as they came into the room. And when they had all arrived, Izzie went back to the classroom. Some were playing blocks, some were in the kitchen, and others had already started working on the clay with Miss Wendy's direction. Half a dozen mothers were seated on tiny chairs at the back of the classroom, and she noticed one very pregnant one who looked incredibly uncomfortable. And as soon as she saw her, Izzie remembered that one of the mothers had been hugely pregnant on her first day, and when she thought about it for a minute, she realized it must have been Marilyn with Brian. He was upstairs, starting his senior year in high school at that very moment. It was like a chain of children that went on year after year, and now it was this class's turn. This was their moment. Their big day. And hers.

Miss Wendy signaled to her to introduce herself, and Izzie stood in the center of the room and spoke to all of them. 'Hello, everybody, I'm Miss Izzie. My real name is Isabel, but I like Izzie better, and a long, long time ago, I went to this school too.' She glanced over at the block corner as she said it, and a little girl had just ripped a block out of a boy's hands. It was an incredible déjà vu of Gabby, and she felt as though it were a message from her.

Izzie turned her attention back to the class, and told them they were going to be making things in clay today. Everyone looked interested as she said it, and she asked them to form a circle, and slowly they all approached, and she invited them to sit on the floor. She and Wendy sat down with them, and Wendy had everyone say their name, since they couldn't read each other's name tags, which were for the teachers' benefit, not theirs.

Wendy led them to the clay table after she had them sing a song, and they were busy for the next forty-five minutes making things in clay. Then they all washed their hands and came back to the circle, where Izzie read them a story. It was one of her favourites, and the children were mesmerized. And afterward they sent them outside to play. She noticed that the playground had new equipment, which looked more interesting and more fun than what she remembered. And then they gave the children juice and a cookie, when they came back in.

They read another story, allowed them free play for a little while, and then Wendy had each of them hold the letter that started their name. They had a busy morning, and it seemed like minutes later when she was back at the front door, escorting each of them to their car, where their mothers were waiting for them. And then she walked back into the classroom, looked at Wendy with a smile, and took off her apron. Wendy looked exactly like a kindergarten teacher. She had a big smile, kind eyes, blond hair in a long braid down her back, and she was a little round. She was shorter than Izzie, and she was wearing a smock with fire engines on it that she had made herself.

'So, how was your first day, Miss Izzie?' she asked warmly.

'I loved it.' Izzie smiled at her. She knew she was doing something her mother thought unimportant, but there was a cozy happy feeling to being back in familiar surroundings, like going back into the womb. Izzie felt safe and protected here, in a world where she hadn't felt safe since the death of her best friend.

'We have a good time here,' Wendy said, putting the

toys away, and Izzie helped her. 'I think we'll do musical instruments tomorrow, and numbers. They did pretty well with the alphabet today.' Izzie felt like she was going back to kindergarten herself. It was all fun to her, and the children were very cute. There was a little Chinese girl in the class who reminded her of Ping. She wondered if she would have her in the class one day, and Billy's twin sisters would be coming next year, Marilyn had said. It was hard to believe they would be old enough for kindergarten soon, or that she was the teacher. Wendy said she'd been a big hit with the children, and Izzie was happy to hear it. Half an hour later, with everything tidy and ready for tomorrow, they turned off the lights, left the room, and locked the door. It was only two-thirty, and she had the whole afternoon free.

She decided to stop by and visit Connie. She knew how lonely she was without Sean. When she got there, she told her about her morning at Atwood, and Connie thought her job there was a great idea. Izzie had found a small one-bedroom apartment near the school and could walk to work. It was her first apartment on her own.

'What a happy place to work, with all those cute children. I think that's wonderful.' Connie told Izzie then that she had decided to go back to work herself. She was going to help Mike at the office full time, not just a few hours a week. He needed the help, and with no children to help him, Connie had decided to do the accounting, and she liked the idea of seeing more of him. She was tired of doing nothing at home, now that she had no children to look after. Sean had started FBI training on the Marine base at Quantico a few weeks before, and he would be there for five months and then move to Washington, D.C.

The two women sat and talked for a long time, about Sean's FBI ambitions and his plans. He was finally getting to live his dream. Izzie admitted to being worried about him, and his mother said that she respected what he wanted to do, and she reminded Izzie that he had wanted to go into law enforcement since he was a little boy. Izzie didn't argue with her, but she thought it was much too dangerous work, particularly given the fact that they had already lost one son. But Connie was far more broad-minded than she was, and said she would never interfere with any career path he chose. She was a good role model for any mother, in contrast to her own, who wanted Izzie to follow in her footsteps, and always had, no matter what Izzie thought about it or preferred. The morning she had just spent reading stories to the children and playing with clay would never have won her mother's approval, but she had had a great time.

She stopped in to see Connie whenever she could after that, to keep her company when she and Mike got home from work or on weekends. She visited Marilyn sometimes too. She was busy with her three children and her husband. Judy had Michelle, who came home a lot on weekends. And Helen, Andy's mother, had a career herself, but of all the mothers, Connie was now the most alone, and Izzie had the strongest bond to her, so she made a point of visiting her. She sent Sean text messages whenever she did, reassuring him that his parents were doing well. And he called Izzie from time to time, but he was busy at school.

Andy tried to remember to call Izzie too, but he was so swamped at med school that most of the time he forgot. And Billy called her once in a blue moon from Miami or when he was on the road. He said he liked Miami but was travelling all the time. She kept up with him in the tabloids and *People* magazine. He had a pretty racy life, and these days she never saw any woman with him more than once in any picture. Billy was moving fast.

There were occasional stories too that he had been seen at a party or a nightclub in bad shape, drunk or disorderly, or after a bar fight, and he always had some sexy hot babe in tow.

It was Christmas before Izzie saw her friends again. She

had helped decorate the Christmas tree at home, with Ping this time, and had gone to *The Nutcracker* with her and Jennifer. Sean and Andy came back to San Francisco for the holidays, and Marilyn said that Billy was due home soon too, though probably not till after Christmas, since he was in the playoffs for the Super Bowl, and if he was in it, Marilyn, Jack and Brian were going.

They each spent Christmas with their families, as they always did, and the day after, Izzie, Andy and Sean cooked dinner at Sean's home. Connie and Mike had gone out for dinner. Izzie told them what it was like being a kindergarten teacher at Atwood, Andy talked about the rigors of medical school but it was obvious that he loved it, and they badgered Sean into telling them about the FBI. He was stingy with the details, but he smiled whenever he talked about it. He was almost finished, and then he was going to Washington to work in an office. Izzie was relieved to hear it. It didn't sound too dangerous so far. He mentioned that several of the people in his class had graduate degrees. Two even had PhDs. They sounded like an interesting group.

They had a fun evening, and talked about Billy's latest escapades from what they'd read in the press. There had been a recent story in *People* magazine about a wild party he'd gone to in Miami where someone had been shot.

Sean hadn't been happy to hear it, and was looking forward to seeing him when he got home. Billy had become a superstar, but his closest friends were still the ones he had grown up with.

Izzie and Sean were cleaning up Connie's kitchen, when his father called and told him to turn the TV on. He hung up the minute he said it. Sean had no idea where they were – all he knew was that they had gone out to dinner. He walked across the dining room to the TV in the living room, grabbed the remote, and turned it on, as Izzie and Andy followed him out of the kitchen. They didn't know what to expect, but the minute it came on, there was a picture of Billy on the screen, followed by a film clip of an ambulance leaving Billy's Miami home.

'What the hell—' Sean muttered, trying to figure out what had happened. Then the announcer on the news flash said that star quarterback Billy Norton had died of a drug overdose at his Miami home earlier that evening. The three of them stood mesmerized, rooted to the spot and staring at each other.

'Oh no – oh my God,' Izzie said in a weak voice, sinking into a chair. 'Not again . . . not Billy . . .' Neither Sean nor Andy had said a word, as Connie and Mike walked in with a look of shock on their faces. The five of them looked at each other and didn't know what to say.

They didn't know whether to go to Marilyn's house or not, or if she had heard it. It was all over the news on every channel, so if she hadn't seen it yet, she would any minute, or someone would call to tell her. There might even be TV cameras outside and reporters. Billy's death was going to be news all over the country. Izzie couldn't bear the thought of going through it again. It had been four years since they lost Gabby, and it felt like yesterday. And as she looked over at Sean, she could see he was in a rage. He was smoldering. For him, it was just like reliving losing Kevin.

'It's so fucking senseless,' he said, as he threw the remote across the room, remembering all the times Billy had gotten drunk, and when he'd tried to give Sean Ecstasy after the championship game, because they'd already been tested. Sean stormed out of the room, ran upstairs, and slammed the door to his bedroom, as Connie and Mike looked at Izzie and Andy, and all four of them felt helpless. Another of their friends was gone, and unlike Gabby, who had died so innocently, Billy had taken all the risks, and lost.

'I'd better call Marilyn,' Connie said in a low voice, and when she did, her friend sounded strangely calm. There was no screaming, no crying, no hysteria. Marilyn sounded like she was in shock.

'I knew this was going to happen,' she said grimly. 'He couldn't handle the pressure and everything that went with it.' He was a twenty-three-year-old boy, making millions of dollars, and surrounded by temptations that were too exciting to resist. They had all worried about it with Billy, especially once he didn't have Gabby to ground him. And now this, this senseless waste of talented athlete and a boy they had all loved.

Connie had asked her if she wanted her to come over, and Marilyn said she did. Andy said he'd drive Izzie home. He had picked her up before dinner. Connie called to Sean to tell him they were leaving but he didn't answer. He was still in his room with the door closed, grieving on his own.

Andy and Izzie left quietly, and Connie and Mike drove the few blocks to Marilyn and Jack's home. There were already news cameras outside, and people were pouring out of vans, as reporters stood at the front door, ringing the bell to talk to anyone who was willing to talk to them. Brian had seen the news at a friend's house while watching TV, and Marilyn had told him not to come home. He had been sobbing when she talked to him on the phone, and she was too.

Mike told the mob of reporters gruffly to get back down the front steps and stay there, and when Jack opened the door barely more than a crack, Mike and Connie squeezed in, and they locked it again. The shades were drawn all around the house. They were under siege, and fortunately the twins were asleep. Jack and Marilyn looked ravaged.

'I'm so sorry,' Connie said as she put her arms around her friend. They had been there too many times now, and the two men were locked in a tearful embrace. Billy wasn't Jack's flesh and blood, but he might as well have been – he had loved the boy like one of his own for seven years. And he had watched his career sweep him away like a tidal wave. The lures of the fast life had been too heady for him to resist.

They sat talking long into the night, and at two in the morning Connie and Mike went home. They found Sean sitting in the living room, watching reruns of that night, and clips from some of Billy's most famous games, which were being shown on TV. He had been planning to go to the Super Bowl for the first time in a matter of weeks, and now he never would.

'How are they?' Sean asked. A look of deep concern had replaced his rage. When he'd come back downstairs, everyone was gone, and he'd been watching the news ever since.

'About the way we were when Kevin died,' Mike said

unhappily, looking tired, 'only with news cameras outside. The Nortons are going to have to come out eventually to make arrangements.

'They're going to need police escorts to help them,' Sean said practically. 'Do you want me to take care of it?' he offered.

'Do you know who to call?' his father looked surprised, momentarily forgetting he was in the FBI Academy.

'I can figure it out with a few phone calls.'

'Then I think you should. They have no idea what to do, and they're too upset to think. They couldn't even let Brian come home tonight.' Sean nodded, and picked up the phone. He called information and then started dialing numbers. He started out by giving them his FBI ID number each time and took it from there. In twenty minutes, he had arranged for SFPD officers and patrolmen to be at Marilyn and Jack's house the next morning and stay with them all day. It was all he could do to help them. He hadn't even felt his own sense of loss yet, just his outrage at what Billy had done, and his fury at those who had helped him do it. He himself had seen no evidence of Billy's drugging in recent years, but it was easy to figure out from the occasional news flashes in the tabloids. And now it had come to this. His boyhood friend was gone, and the people responsible for it were scot-free. All Sean wanted to do was kill them, one by one, and very painfully. And soon, he would have the means to do it.

Chapter 18

Billy's funeral was a media circus beyond belief. They had to ask the mayor's office and the police to help with barriers at the church, and officers to restrain the crowds. It was a nightmare they hadn't expected. And when Billy's casket was brought to the funeral parlor from the airport, they had to use riot police to control the crowds, and an armed guard to protect the casket. Marilyn, Jack, and Larry couldn't even get to the funeral parlor to see him. Finally the police escorted them there at midnight in an unmarked car. The press were lying in wait for them, but the fans had gone home by then, once they realized they wee not going to be allowed in. And other grieving families at the funeral parlor were justifiably incensed at the disruption.

In some ways, it made the grief easier to bear, because every aspect of what had happened was a trauma. Marilyn sent Brian to stay with the O'Haras, and Sean kept him company until the funeral. He remembered only too well what it had been like to lose an adored older brother. And Brian had worshipped Billy. None of them could absorb the fact that Billy was dead now, and in such shocking circumstances.

The mayor provided a police cordon for the funeral at St Mary's Cathedral and armed guards for the casket, so the family could at least try to bury him in peace. There were over a thousand people inside, and twice as many standing behind a police barrier across the street.

After the funeral, they had their friends go to Jack's restaurant, where bouncers and police only let close family friends in, from a list.

'Jesus, this is a nightmare,' Andy said, as he and Izzie were escorted in. They pushed through the crowd to find Jack and Marilyn. Larry had gone to a different location with his friends. Sean was standing guard over Brian, and Michelle was next to him. The whole scene was incredibly stressful. And the day after the funeral, Marilyn sought refuge at the O'Haras' with Brian and the twins.

'What are we going to do?' Marilyn asked Connie with a look of desperation. 'We can't live like this.'

'It'll die down soon,' Sean said quietly. He was wrestling with his own feelings about what had happened, but he was trying to comfort her. But the anger he felt at the drug dealers who had enticed Billy, and before that his brother, came through his every word. 'You should stay here for a week or two.' And Jack joined them that night. Jack and Marilyn would be staying in the guest room, Sean was sharing his room with Brian, and the twins were in sleeping bags on the couch in the playroom.

It had only just begun to calm down a week later, when Sean got ready to leave to go back to the FBI Academy. Andy had gone back to Cambridge the day before, and Izzie had dinner with the O'Haras that night. She and Sean sought refuge in the old playroom in the basement, hoping to get a little time together to talk. She hated to see how upset Sean was. They were all devastated by Billy's death, but Sean's rage was terrifying, and it seemed to be getting worse day by day.

'You can't let it eat you alive like this,' she said gently.

'Why not? You don't know the kind of people he was dealing with. I do. They all deserve to die. Billy didn't hurt anyone, he was such a sweet guy.' As he said it, his eyes filled with tears, and Izzie gently took him in her arms. Her gentleness only made it worse for him.

'You can't go around killing all of them,' she said sensibly. 'And Billy wouldn't want you tormented like this.'

'He had no defenses to protect him from what they did.' But he also knew that Billy could have tried harder to resist, and he was angry at Billy too. Now his entire family would suffer the agony of losing him, and none of them would ever be the same again. Not even him. 'People like that don't deserve to live,' Sean said, referring to the drug dealers, not his friend, and Izzie understood.

'What are you going to do now? Izzie asked, with a panicked expression.

'Go back to school.' He was almost finished.

'And then?' She knew Sean well. For him, this was just the beginning. It hadn't ended with Billy's death.

'I'll let you know when I figure it out.'

'When do you finish school?'

'At the end of January.' Izzie knew that didn't give him time enough to calm down, if he ever would. He was on a sacred mission now. Revenge.

When they went back upstairs, he promised to call her whenever he could. There were only the three of them now, of the original Big Five. She and Sean and Andy. And Kevin had died too, although he was Sean's brother and not one of their immediate group. Their numbers were dwindling. Everything about the experience had been shocking. She had cried more for Gabby, but she ached more for Billy. It was the third time they had all lived through the agony of loss. And Brian was devastated by the death of his big brother.

She slept on the other twin bed in Sean's room that night, since Brian and his family had gone home. Sean left the next morning before anyone got up. He had already said his goodbyes the night before. And Izzie didn't hear him leave. She didn't know it, but he had gently kissed her cheek before he left.

He texted her when he got back to Quantico, and she didn't hear from him again for several weeks. Jack and Marilyn and Brian and the twins were still dealing with reporters who showed up every few days. The autopsy had shown a lethal dose of Ecstasy and cocaine in Billy's system, and a full investigation was being made of clandestine drug use on the team, to make sure that others hadn't circumvented the drug testing like Billy.

Izzie was back at Atwood, going through the motions in kindergarten, feeling dead inside. Wendy knew that she had gone to school with Billy, and she had told her how sorry she was.

Izzie hardly heard from Sean for the next two months. He had finished his training and moved to Washington for his office job, so she wasn't worried about him. And in March, without warning anyone beforehand, he came home for a visit. He called Izzie on her cell phone when she left school, and invited her to dinner that night. He took her to a quiet, out-of-the-way restaurant known for its hamburgers. He ordered for both of them, and then looked at her from across the table and took her hand in his.

'How've you been?' he asked her with a worried expression. She looked tired and thin to him, and sad, which was how he felt too. It was easier to be angry than to feel the pain of loss again.

'Not so great,' she said honestly. 'Just like you.' Billy had been dead for three months, and Gabby for four years. Losing Billy had brought it all back. And Kevin had been killed less than a year before Gabby, seven months. They had lost more friends and young people close to them in the last five years than her father had in his entire life. 'How is Washington?' she asked. And for a long moment he didn't answer. She could see he had more to say to her, but he was taking his time about it. She had a feeling she wasn't going to like whatever it was, and she was right.

He finally told her after they ate their burgers. Izzie only picked at hers. Every time she looked into his eyes, she could sense what was coming, and couldn't eat.

'I'm going away,' Sean said quietly.

'Someplace bad?' She wanted the truth from him, as much as he could tell her.

'Maybe. I'm not supposed to tell anyone. But I wanted you to know.'

'Did you volunteer for it?' He nodded, and for an instant, she hated him. She couldn't stand to lose another friend if he was killed. 'How long will you be gone?' She remembered all too clearly that he had said he would go to South America one day to fight the drug cartels.

'A year. Maybe less, maybe more. It will depend on where I am and what's happening. If it jeopardizes other agents, or the operation, I can't come out.'

'What if you never come back?' she said, with tears bulging in her eyes.

'Then I was lucky I ever knew you, and that you were my friend.' She nodded. She felt the same way, but hated what he was saying and why. They both knew he might be killed on an assignment. He was willing to take that chance. It was what he knew he had to do, and wanted to. She had no doubt about where he would be going. Colombia most likely, or someplace like it. Maybe Mexico.

'It won't bring Billy and Kevin back, whatever you do

there,' she reminded him, but knew it was pointless. Sean was driven, and very stubborn.

'No, but it will save others. Someone has to go after these people,' he said, looking older than his years. Both his brother's death and now Billy's had taken a heavy toll on him.

'Why does it have to be you?' she asked, her eyes boring into him, as he squeezed her hand harder, knowing how much he would miss her.

'Because that's what I do,' Sean said with a determined look.

'I wish you wouldn't go,' she said softly, and he nodded again, still holding her hand. They both knew he felt he had no choice. It was who he was, and who he had always been. 'Will I hear from you?'

'No. I'll be undercover. It would jeopardize everything. When I come back, you'll know. I'll come home.'

'What about your mom?' Izzie was worried about her too. Connie had already been through so much, and she wouldn't survive losing her only remaining son.

'I told her this afternoon. She understands, and so does my dad.'

'I'm not sure I do,' Izzie said honestly. 'It's not fair to put them through that too.'

'They knew when I went to the FBI Academy that I'd

wind up doing something like this, and why.' It had been about Kevin then. Now it was about Billy too. Izzie knew that much.

They left the restaurant quietly, and he took her home.

'When are you going?' she asked, as she sat in the car with him.

'Tomorrow. Take care of yourself, Izzie. I want to find you in one piece when I come home. We've been through enough of this shit. Billy has to be the last one.'

'Say that to yourself.' She hated him for going, but she knew why he was doing it. It didn't really help. 'I'll visit your mom.' He nodded, and then kissed her cheek, and she got out of the car. She didn't look back at him. She couldn't bear seeing him again. She didn't want to remember him this way – she wanted to remember the good times they had shared, the laughter and the easy days when they were kids. And she was certain, as he drove away, that she had just seen Sean for the last time. He was never coming home again.

Chapter 19

The months after Sean left were infinitely strange. Izzie knew she wouldn't hear from him, but she didn't even know where he was. Neither did his mother. Izzie stopped in to see her, usually on weekends, because Connie was working long hours, helping Mike. She looked older to Izzie now whenever she saw her. Marilyn was still devastated, and Judy had never been quite the same after Gabby died. They belonged to a club of women now, to which no one wanted to belong. Mothers who had lost children. The agony of it stayed etched forever in their eyes.

Izzie and Andy e-mailed frequently too. He was doing fine, and he always asked if she had heard from Sean. She said she hadn't but didn't explain why. Andy had guessed that he must be on an operation for the FBI somewhere, but he assumed that Izzie knew as little as he did, and he seemed confident that Sean would surface any day. He was busy with medical school, and he always said he and Nancy were doing well. She was happy for him. He seemed very far away now and part of another world.

And then, on Memorial Day weekend, she was invited to a barbecue some of the teachers in the middle school were giving. She didn't want to go, but Wendy insisted that she should. And with nothing else to do, Izzie went. She wasn't dating anyone and hadn't gone out much since Billy died. Wendy wanted to help get her moving.

There were about fifty people at the barbecue, mostly married teachers and their spouses, and a few of them had brought kids. Izzie was talking to the art teacher, who introduced her to her brother. He said he was a writer, and had just moved to San Francisco from Oregon. He was in his early thirties and recently divorced. They talked for a while, and he asked for her e-mail address. Izzie didn't know why she gave it to him, but she did. He wasn't scintillating, or particularly good-looking, but he was pleasant to talk to, and intelligent. He had graduated from the writing program at Brown, and was originally from the East.

And the following day he wrote to her and asked her

out to dinner the next weekend. She felt like she was still in shock over Billy, and moving under water, but she hadn't had a date in a year. Both her best friends were away, and she couldn't even talk to Sean, so she said yes. If nothing else, it would be nice to have a friend.

His name was John Applegarth, and he took her to a museum to see an exhibit she had wanted to see, of neo-classic architecture, and then he took her out to dinner at a Moroccan restaurant she hadn't been to in years. She had a nice time with him, and then he asked her out again. He had a grant for the book he was writing, and he told her about it over dinner. It didn't sound exciting, but it sounded interesting, like him. She wasn't crazy about him, but she liked him. They went to dinner a few more times, and when he made his move to get her into bed, she didn't really want to, but she slept with him anyway. It was much better than her experience with Andy, and the two she had had since, but it didn't set her world on fire. She wasn't in love with him, but she wanted to know if some part of her was still alive. She had felt dead for months. And he revived her in a way, but not enough. It was the best they could do for now.

And then her mother came to town, and took Izzie to dinner as she always did. But this time she didn't like the way her daughter looked. She knew about Billy.

Everybody did, but she could see now how hard it had hit Izzie.

'What about the other two? Do you see them? How are they?' she asked about Andy and Sean. She was worried that Izzie seemed isolated and depressed.

'Andy's at medical school, working like a lunatic, and Sean is out of touch for a while.' Her mother frowned when Izzie said it and looked at her quizzically.

'What does that mean?'

'He works for the FBI.' It was all she could say, but it was enough. Katherine wanted to shake her. She could sense that her daughter was drowning, and she needed a strong hand to pull her out of the water before she did.

'Is there someone in your life that you're seeing that you care about?' Katherine asked pointedly. Izzie hesitate for a moment and then shook her head.

'Not really. I'm dating someone, but I'm not crazy about him. He's kind of quiet, and not really my type,' she said honestly, 'but he's nice enough, and smart.

Katherine hesitated for a moment then and looked her daughter in the eyes. 'That's not enough. I want you to listen to me, and think about what I say. You're twenty-three years old. This is the best it's ever going to be. It doesn't get better than this. You're young, you're beautiful. You can do anything you want. You can have any man you want, go anywhere you want. You're not tied down by anything or anyone. You're completely free. You have a job that's below your capabilities. You lead a quiet life, almost no life from what I can see. Two of your best friends died, at a shockingly young age. The other two are far away and you don't talk to them. You live in a small provincial town. And you're dating a guy you admit you don't care about, who doesn't excite you.

'If you let life pass you by now, it won't ever come back. You don't get another chance. Your father did that to himself with his work at the ACLU. He got bogged down helping poor people and forgot about himself, and the career and life he could have had. Work isn't everything, but he was and probably still is a brilliant lawyer. I know he loves what he does, but he could have done better. Izzie, you need passion about life. That's why I took the job I did and got out of Dodge, because life was passing me by. I don't want that to happen to you. I screwed it up with you, but the other decisions I made, about my life and career, were right for me. That's what I want for you. You can have anything you want, if you go out and get it. If you claim it as your own. You have a right to it. Izzie, you need to wake yourself up and take a grab at life. No one is going to hand it to you.

It was a major wake-up call, and in some ways, Izzie

knew her mother was right. Maybe not about her father, who loved his wife and little girl, and his work, even if it seemed unexciting to her mother. But she was right about her, and had been about herself. Her mother had the life she wanted, whatever it had taken her to get it. And Izzie didn't. She enjoyed her job at Atwood, but the rest was a morass of mediocrity, and she knew it, and she was beginning to realize that in some ways she had stopped trying when Gabby died. She had lost hope about her own life. If Gabby could be swept off a street corner and killed instantly, so could she. And what was the point of trying, or living, or even caring about anything, if it could all be over in a minute, the people you loved could die, or you could die yourself? She had protected herself by not trying, at anything. She was living day to day, and just waiting to be hit by a bus, or for lightning to strike her dead, just as it had Gabby or even Billy. Their deaths had hit her hard. And Katherine knew what she was talking about. Although they were different, and Katherine had never been there for her, Izzie respected her. She was accurate in what she said. And Gabby's death, and then Billy's, had impacted Izzie's faith in life, her will to live, and the quality of her life.

'What are you doing this summer?' Katherine persisted.

'Nothing much. I was going to take some classes to help me with work, but I never got around to signing up,' she admitted sheepishly. In truth, she had been too depressed to do it. And she was worried about Sean dying too. She couldn't stand losing another friend, if it happened, but she knew it could any day. She expected to hear the news that he was dead. She had been waiting to hear it ever since he left.

'I want you to do something fun. I don't care what it is. Go to Indonesia, Vietnam, Mexico. The Galápagos. Take dance lessons. Meet people, get out, get rid of the guy you don't care about, and find one you do. You're sinking, Izzie. I want you to wake up. I'll pay for anything you want to do, or anywhere you want to go. But I want you to have *fun*!' She looked earnest as she said it. Izzie could see she meant it, and was touched.

'Do you have fun at what you do?' It was a question Izzie had always wondered about and never asked her.

'Yes, I do. I love my work. I work hard. I play hard. And I love Charles, as eccentric and crazy as he is. We have a good time together. That's what you need. A guy you have fun with. You've already seen the sad side of life. Too much of it, at your age. Now you need to go throw some good stuff in the other side of the scale.'

'I wouldn't even know what to do, or where to go,' she admitted sadly to her mother.

'Figure it out. You've got the time. I've got the money. Go for it!' she said, smiling at Izzie, who suddenly felt closer to her than she ever had. 'Give yourself a week to make some plans, and then *go*!'

Izzie had a lot to think about after their dinner. She hugged her mother close when she left, and she went home to look at some travel magazines, and check some things out on the internet. There were ads for the Caribbean, Morocco, safaris in Africa. But what kept appealing to her was Argentina and Brazil. She had heard that Brazil was dangerous for a woman traveling alone, so maybe Argentina. She looked at some more internet sites then, and got the names of some good hotels. It sounded better and better to her as she read about it. She could learn to dance the tango, she thought to herself, and then laughed out loud. It was an unfamiliar sound, and she realized suddenly that she hadn't laughed since Billy died, and maybe long before that. She was excited for the first time in months, maybe years. She called her mother the next day and told her her plan. Katherine liked the idea, although she warned her to be careful traveling alone in South America and wanted her to get a driver, and Izzie promised that she would. Katherine told her she would gladly pay for it.

'Why don't you meet us in the South of France after that?' We rented a house in St. Tropez.' Izzie felt like a world traveler just thinking about it. But Katherine was her mother, and she could afford it.

The next day she made a reservation to fly to Buenos Aires. It was a long trip, but it would be worth it. And she booked a reservation at a top hotel, which was amazingly inexpensive, and she e-mailed them to get her a car and driver. She planned to stay for a week, and she could extend it if she wanted to. And she booked a flight from Buenos Aires to Paris, and from there to Nice, and a car to St. Tropez, and she planned to stay there for a week too, and maybe a week in Paris after that. She was booked to leave on the Fourth of July, and planned to return sometime in August, depending on how things went. And after that she called her father and told him all about it. He was excited for her, and grateful to her mother for doing something that he couldn't do for her, and he knew Izzie needed it. She needed something. She was stuck. She had seen too much sorrow for too long, and it had sapped the energy out of her, without her even realizing it. She promised to drop by and see them before she left.

And then she called John. He invited her to dinner that night and she decided to go. She wanted to tell him that she was going away, and didn't think they should see each other when she got back.

He took her to a small sushi restaurant in Japantown and the food was good, but she realized as she listened to him that she wasn't interested in what he was saying or in his book. He was ten years older than she was and he had already given up on life. She hadn't yet, even though she had felt that way for the past several months, or even years, since Gabby died. John wanted to take her to Oregon to go camping over the Fourth of July, and she told him she was going to Argentina to learn the tango. Just listening to herself made her want to laugh. She was feeling hopeful again about life. Suddenly it was an adventure and she was willing to try it.

'Argentina?' He looked shocked. 'When did you decide that?' She hadn't mentioned it before, or even thought of it.

'A couple of days ago. I had dinner with my mother. She offered to give me a trip, kind of belated graduation present. I'm meeting her in France after that.' She felt like a spoiled brat as she said it, but he wasn't starving either. He just didn't want to spend his money, because if he did, he'd have to go back to work, and he didn't want to. He wanted to keep his life as small as possible so his funds didn't run out. It was a reasonable decision, but not much fun for her at the moment. She told him that she didn't think they were suited to each other, and dating when she got back didn't seem like a good idea to her. He looked disappointed but didn't argue with her. By the end of dinner, it was obvious to him that she wasn't suited to his life either. A woman who could go to Argentina at the drop of a hat was not a woman who was going to be available to him for the camping and hiking he wanted to do.

He took her home after dinner and she thanked him, for everything. They both knew they would never see each other again, and it didn't seem to bother him. He wished her a good time in Argentina, and she waved as she walked through the door and disappeared. She was out of his life forever and neither of them cared.

She dropped by to see Connie before she left, and Marilyn and Jack, and Brian and the twins. Brian had just graduated and was going to Berkeley in the fall. Izzie felt bad because they were giving him a graduation barbecue on the Fourth of July and she was going to miss it. She called Judy, and e-mailed Andy, who was staying in Boston for the summer, and had dinner with Jennifer and her father and Ping the night before she left, and on the Fourth of July she was on a plane to Buenos Aires, thanks to her mother, who had turned out to be her best friend. She had gotten her moving again and in a very major way.

In some ways, she had saved Izzie's life, which had been bleeding slowly from her.

The city was more beautiful than she'd expected. It looked like Paris, and the hotel was fabulous for very little money. And the driver they gave her was perfect. He even took her to tango bars and escorted her inside to protect her. She danced with strangers. She walked through exquisite gardens. He drove her to an estancia called Villa Maria, forty-five minutes outside the city, she rode horses and swam and had a great time. She wondered, as she walked in the Bosques de Palermo one day, a beautiful park her driver had recommended, if she was anywhere near where Sean was, but she had no way to know, and she forced herself not to think of him. She also went to the Parque Tres de Febrero, much like the Bois de Boulogne in Paris, where she wandered through the rose gardens, along the promenades, and stood by the lake. She sent postcards to everyone at home, and one to Andy.

Then she flew to Paris, spent a night at a small hotel on the Left Bank, flew down to Nice, and went to St. Tropez. Her mother and Charles were thrilled to see her. They took her to restaurants and dinner parties, and dancing at the Caves du Roy one night. It was the most fun she'd ever had with her mother in her entire life. And then, on the spur of the moment, Izzie treated herself to a weekend in Venice on her way home. It was perfect. It would have been better with someone she loved, but she didn't care. She felt free and excited and alive, and she spent four days in Paris on the way back, and then flew to San Francisco. She felt very sophisticated and worldly when she got home. And she felt alive again. Her mother had given her the most incredible gift of all. She had given her back herself. And when she went to work for her second year at Atwood, she told the kindergartners all about it: a place called Argentina, where people love to dance, and Paris – she showed them a postcard of the Eiffel Tower – and Venice, where everyone rode around on boats called gondolas. She showed them a postcard of that too.

'We went to New Jersey to see my grandmother!' a little girl called Heather piped up.

'And did you have fun?' Miss Izzie asked her with a big smile. Izzie looked and felt like a new person. Wendy was relieved to see it. The summer had done her a world of good.

'Yes, we did.' Heather said. 'My grandma let us run around her backyard naked, and she has a pool!' Everybody laughed at that.

It was a special day for Izzie because Daphne and Dana, Marilyn and Jack's twins, started kindergarten that day, and they were thrilled to see her. There was a continuity to their lives.

'Sounds like you had a fantastic summer,' Wendy said as they poured juice and put cookies on a platter.

'I really did.' Izzie smiled at her. 'It was the best summer of my life.' After four of the worst years of her life, or the hardest anyway. She hoped the bad times were over now. And all she could hope was that Sean was alive and well and happy too. For the first time in years, since losing Gabby, Izzie felt alive again. And she was thinking of going to Japan over Christmas. Suddenly, thanks to her mother, the world had opened up to her, and she wanted to be in it.

Chapter 20

The excitement of her summer trip carried Izzie straight through to Thanksgiving. The gift her mother had given her had been incredible, not just paying for it but inspiring her to go. It had been the best summer of her life.

She was still thinking about going to Japan, or maybe India, but she had decided not to go at Christmas. She was thinking about going over Easter break, or maybe the following summer, but she wanted to be home at Christmas, to spend it with her father, Jennifer, and Ping. She had talked to Andy several times after the summer, and he said he was jealous of her trip to Argentina, although Paris, Venice, and St. Tropez didn't sound too shabby either.

'Who's your generous lover?' he teased her.

'My mother. When are you coming home?' She was anxious to see him.

'I can't come home for Christmas. I'm either studying, in class, or at the hospital, constantly, and so is Nancy. We haven't slept in three months.' But he sounded as though he enjoyed it, and he said he'd come home as soon as he could.

Izzie had just started her Christmas vacation from school, when the phone rang on Saturday morning and she heard a familiar voice. Her heart raced for a minute, wondering where he was. But he was alive at least. She hadn't spoken to him since March. It was Sean.

'Oh my God, where are you? Are you okay?'

'I'm fine,' he said, laughing at her. 'Look out your window.' She did, and he was standing there, waving at her, talking to her on his BlackBerry. She opened her apartment door and ran downstairs to see him. He had grown a full beard, and he looked very thin. But he was there, he was alive, and he looked healthy. He was laughing when he saw her and gave her an enormous hug.

'Where have you been for all these months?'

'Colombia,' he said easily, the way anyone else would have said 'L.A.'

'I was in Argentina last summer,' she said breezily, and

he stared at her. She looked better than he'd seen her in years, and happier. He wondered if there was a new man in her life, but when he followed her back in to her apartment, there were no signs of it and she was alone.

'What were you doing there?' he asked suspiciously.

'I went to learn to dance the tango. And then I went to St. Tropez.'

'Did you win the lottery? Did I miss something?'

'My mother treated me. I was depressed after Billy, and worried sick about you. And I was going out with a really boring guy. My mother talked me into dumping everything and going on a trip. It was the best thing I've ever done. How are you?' She was so happy to see him, she couldn't stop talking. His eyes were sunken and dark, and he was very thin under the beard, but he looked great to her. He was alive.

'What happened to the boring guy?'

'I dumped him before I went to Argentina. And I'm thinking about going to Japan this spring. You're not the only one who can travel around the world, you know,' she said, as they sat down in her kitchen, and she poured them each a cup of coffee.

'I wasn't exactly taking tango lessons,' he said drily. 'You're looking good, Iz.' He was pleased to see her so happy. He had worried about her for the past nine months. And he missed talking to her. But he was doing important work.

'How long are you here for?' Izzie asked him as they drank the coffee.

'A week or two. I'm going back in January.' She looked disappointed when he said it, but that was his life now. A week with his family, and almost a year underground.

'Undercover again?' He nodded. They had had some excellent results from his work in Colombia. Now they were sending him somewhere new that was even more dangerous than the last location, but he didn't tell her.

'It's what I do,' he said quietly, and took a sip of the steaming coffee.

'It's hard on your parents,' she said bluntly.

'I know. But they're good about it.'

'They don't need to lose another son, Sean,' she said seriously, but he knew it. He could see that both his parents had aged while he was gone. Losing Kevin, and worrying about him, had taken a toll on them both.

'I know,' Sean said, looking guilty. 'When can I take you to dinner? Will I have to deal with an angry boyfriend?' She looked so pretty and so happy that he was sure there was someone in her life.

'No, I'm single,' she said easily. 'I'm free tonight.'

'I'll pick you up at seven,' he said, and then he got up

to leave. He looked down at her for a long moment and then pulled her into his arms and hugged her tight. 'I missed you, Iz. I hated not being able to call you.'

'Yeah, me too,' she said quietly, but this was how he wanted to live, with no contact with any of the people he cared about, so he could fight a holy war. It didn't seem worth it to her. But it was a choice he had made with his life, at a very, very high price for him and everyone else, even her. He had been part of her sense of hopelessness last spring. She had been sure she would never see him alive again. And she very nearly hadn't, but he couldn't tell her that. It had been a very delicate operation that had nearly gone wrong several times. And then they got him out, just in time.

After he left, she thought about him for a while. She hated his working for the FBI. There were so many things they could have done together, if he had been around. But that wasn't the way he had opted to live, with a home, and a family nearby, a relationship, friends, and a life. He wanted to fight the drug wars for the FBI. It sounded much too dangerous to her. And she was happy, for his mother's sake and everyone else's, that he had come home alive. She knew it couldn't have been easy though, and he suddenly seemed much older than his years. No one would have guessed that he and Izzie were the same age. He looked a dozen years older than she did now, more like thirty-five or -six.

She saw him as many times as was possible and he was willing while he was home. Just like old times. And he had other obligations too, to his family. He drove over to Berkeley and took Brian out and had lunch with him. He took Izzie to dinner several times. They went to their favourite restaurants, for hamburgers and pizza. And once he took her to a fancy French restaurant. He acted like his money was burning a hole in his pocket. But he hadn't been able to spend any of it all year, and he was well paid for his undercover missions, with 'danger pay' to compensate him for the risks he took. He was happy to spend it on Izzie.

He had Christmas with his family, and stayed until almost New Year, and then he had to leave again, and he came to say goodbye to Izzie. He didn't justify his leaving or apologize for it this time. He had already told her that he was leaving for a year, and she was angry at him. She said it wasn't fair to his parents.

He hugged her, and neither of them said anything. There was nothing to say. They both knew that he would spend the next year in constant danger, fighting for his survival, trying to outsmart drug dealers, and trying to glean information for his country. He lived in a permanent state of warfare. The drug money was used to buy arms and finance terrorists.

'Be careful,' she whispered to him. 'And try to come back alive.'

'I'm too smart to let them kill me,' he said, smiling at her.

'And too damn cocky for your own good,' she said, and then he left her. He hurried down the stairs of her apartment, and back out to the street. She was watching him from the window, as he waved at her, got in his car, and drove away. And as he always did, he texted her from the airport. He told her again to take care, and she knew she wouldn't hear from him for a year, or maybe longer. She hated the way he had chosen to live, but she also knew that it was what Sean had always wanted. And if he died there, it was what he would have wanted too, fighting for a cause he believed in. But if he died, Izzie knew it would cost her, and his friends and family, far too much. He was willing to sacrifice them all, and time with them, for what he believed in.

She tried not to let it depress her when he left this time. It was how he was always going to live. He was somebody she was only going to see once in a blue moon now, and they'd catch up on what they'd been doing, and then he'd disappear for another year, trying to stay alive.

And meanwhile the rest of the world would go on without him, and so would she.

She went to a New Year's Eve party, given by a woman she'd met at UCLA, who had just moved to San Francisco. Izzie didn't usually like going out on New Year's Eve, but she didn't want to sit home brooding either. The anniversary of Billy's death had just passed, Sean had gone back under cover and had disappeared, and Andy was stuck in Cambridge, learning to become a doctor. She had no one else to spend New Year's Eve with, so she went to the party.

And she met him almost as soon as she walked through the door. He was the best-looking man she'd ever seen, and he turned with a broad smile the moment he saw her. His name was Tony Harrow, he was a film producer from L.A., and he said he was making a movie in San Francisco.

'And what do you do?' he asked her with considerable interest, handing her a glass of champagne. She had worn a short white satin dress and high-heeled silver sandals. Most of the guests were outside on the balcony, smoking and drinking and laughing. But Tony sat down on the couch with her inside – he said he wanted her to himself.

'I'm a kindergarten teacher,' she said, smiling brightly, sure that he would find her intensely boring. But he didn't.

'And what made you do that?'

'I couldn't figure out what else to be when I grew up. I'm still trying to figure it out.'

'So am I,' he said, laughing. He was wearing an expensive suit, and an open white shirt, and his well-polished black shoes looked expensive. And she knew he had made several extremely successful movies. 'Maybe you could help me find an apartment. I'm looking for something furnished, for a year, with a view.' He looked around at the pretty apartment on Russian Hill. 'Like this one. Maybe we can just get our friend to move out and give it to me.' They both laughed at the suggestion. 'Where do you live?'

'In a mouse-sized apartment near the school where I work.'

'How convenient.' He seemed fascinated by everything she said, no matter how inane. And he was very charming, as well as good-looking. She was flattered that he was speaking to her at all. She never met men like him in her world. Their mutual friend had gone to film school, and had worked for him for two years.

'Would you like to go to the Napa Valley with me tomorrow?' he asked her, and Izzie was so startled, she didn't know what to say. But he looked at her so intently that she nodded. At midnight he was still sitting with her.

He handed her another glass of champagne, and then he leaned over and kissed her lightly on the lips. He barely touched her, which seemed very seductive to her. He was very smooth.

They left each other, and she drove home at one o'clock in the morning. She hadn't spoken to anyone else at the party, and he told her he would pick her up at ten o'clock the next day. And then he had brushed her lips again in the same subtle way, which was incredibly appealing. He was so pleasant, intelligent, and good-looking that he was almost too good to be true. Maybe she had imagined him. But he showed up as promised the next day, at ten o'clock, looking handsome and casual in jeans and a well-cut blazer. He had dark hair and salt and pepper at his temples. She had guessed him for thirty-five, and he told her he was thirty-nine as they drove to Napa. He was sixteen years older than she was, and seemed very sophisticated by her usual standards, but she liked it. It reminded her of Jennifer and her father, who were seventeen years apart. Maybe there was something to being with an older man. He was the first man that much older that she'd ever gone out with, and it was a nice change from boys her own age.

Tony took her to two wineries that were very beautiful, and drove her through the Napa Valley, under handsome old trees that lined the road. Then he took her to the Auberge du Soleil, a hotel and restaurant perched on a hill with a breathtaking view of the valley, with its rolling hills and meticulous vineyards. They ate lunch on a balcony, and when they left that afternoon, Izzie was enthralled. He was interesting to talk to, fun to be with, considerate and thoughtful, and they drove part of the way home with the top down on his convertible, on picturesque back roads.

He told her about the film business and the new movie he was producing. He said he had never been married, but had had several long relationships.

'Why do you think you never married?' she asked him, aware that it was a somewhat intrusive question, but she felt surprisingly comfortable with him by the end of the day. He seemed like a very open person, and had been very free in talking about himself and some of the mistakes he'd made in his business and personal life. He wasn't arrogant or pompous, and she liked that about him, in spite of his obvious success in his industry. He had done very well.

'Scared, I guess,' he said honestly. 'A lot of things. I was having too much fun when I got out of college, then I got too busy building up my business. I was always putting together the next movie. I'm fairly obsessive about my work,' he said honestly, 'and then you get those kickers in life, those blows to the gut that make you decide to play it safe. I was very much in love with a girl when I was in college, my childhood sweetheart. We were sure we were going to get married – in fact I bought a ring and was about to ask her, when she died in a head-on collision. She was driving down to L.A. to meet me when she got killed. It was raining, and her car skidded out of control. I didn't think I'd survive it, but I did. I don't think I ever put my heart out there like that again. I was too afraid to get hurt. I keep just enough distance to avoid any future pain. Maybe you only love like that once in your lifetime, when you're very young.' He smiled at her as he said it, and what he had shared resonated with her, more than he knew.

She took a breath before she said anything to him, but she was comfortable with it. 'I lost two good friends in the last five years, people I grew up with. Not anyone I was in love with, but it kind of had the same effect on me. I feel like I've kept everything at a distance, because I didn't want anything to ever hurt that much again.'

'Love is messy,' Tony said quietly. 'I think if you really love someone, even a friend, you can't avoid the pain. People die, people leave, things change. But sometimes,' he said, smiling at her. 'it all works. I've just never had the guts to try it seriously again.'

'I think I kind of sealed myself off too. I'm not very close to my mother, but I had dinner with her last year, and she kind of woke me up. She said I was letting life pass me by, and it was never going to get any better than it is right now. Because of that, I took a trip to Argentina last summer, and I'm thinking of going to Japan some-time this year. Just getting out of my own little world changed everything. I feel alive again. I think part of me died when my best friends in the world died. It's hard to risk caring that much again.'

'It is,' he agreed, as he got back on the highway, and they drove through Marin. 'But it's worth it, Izzie. Take it from me. It's been the same. I've watched a lot of my friends get married and have kids, and I know it's not for me. I'll prob-ably never take that risk. But you're young enough to do it differently. I'm not sure I am.' It seemed sad to her, but at least he knew himself. It felt like he'd been put on her path to give her a warning. And somewhere in her heart of hearts, she knew she didn't want to be like him. She wasn't Marilyn, or Connie, or Judy, she hadn't lost a child. Or even a love, like Tony. She had lost friends. It was different. She couldn't shut everyone out, or stop taking risks in her life, because of it. He was right, he was a good lesson to her.

And as much as he seemed to be enjoying his life, she felt sorry for him. If he couldn't let himself love someone, he wasn't fully alive. She wasn't sure she was either. She had never been in love in her entire life. But she was young enough to change it. At thirty-nine, it was going to be a lot harder for him to open up again, especially after being hermetically sealed for eighteen years. But he was nice to go out with. She had had a very good time. And when he drove up to her apartment, he asked when he could see her again.

'Do you like the ballet?' he asked her, with a wide, easy smile.

'I've only been to two in my life. *The Nutcracker* and *Swan Lake.*' But she had liked them both. Tony was a man of the world. No one she knew would have invited her to the ballet, although she knew Andy's parents went regularly, but it would never have occurred to anyone to invite her. The boys she dated went out for hamburgers and pizza, and to movies, not to the ballet. It sounded very adult to her.

'Would you like to go to the opening of the ballet with me next week?' he suggested, and Izzie smiled. He really was fun to be with, and she could easily imagine taking tango lessons with him, although he probably knew how to tango anyway. 'There's a dinner afterward,' he explained.

'I'd like that very much.'

'You'll have to wear a cocktail dress. It's black tie for me. But with your looks' – he smiled at her – 'you can get away with something short.'

'That sounds like fun. Thank you, Tony.' She smiled at him, and he laughed and kissed her cheek, barely touching it with his lips.

'Stick with me, baby, and we'll have fun.' She was sure that was true, but with a sudden flash of insight, she suspected that they'd have fun but not depth. He had avoided that in all his relationships for too long. He was a practiced bachelor, and a generous person, but the one thing he no longer gave was his heart. He wasn't like her father and Jennifer after all, who were crazy about each other and madly in love and had adopted Ping. Her father had married the wrong woman, and then found the right one. She didn't think Tony was willing to take that chance. It didn't really matter to Izzie, she wasn't in love with him, but she hoped she would fall in love one day. Tony was still working hard to avoid it and swimming the other way. And she wondered if one of the reasons he liked her and was taking her out was that she was too young to expect anything serious from him, unlike women of his own age, who wanted the whole she-bang, kids and marriage and a commitment he was no longer willing to give. At least he'd been honest with her, so she wouldn't get hurt. They were just passing through each other's lives, like her trip to Argentina. He made no pretense of anything else.

When she went back to her apartment and he drove away, she thought of Gabby with a sharp ache. If she'd still been alive, she could have called her for a consultation about what to wear to the ballet, or borrowed something from her. Izzie called Jennifer instead.

Her stepmother said she should wear something sexy, dressy, and short. She was so much taller than Izzie that she couldn't lend her a dress, but she offered to go shopping with her, which they did the next day. Jennifer left Ping with her father, so they had a real girls' day out. It was the kind of day Izzie had never spent with her mother, but Katherine had given her good advice and trips to Europe and Argentina instead. There was room for both of them in Izzie's life.

They found the perfect dress at Neiman Marcus, it was short and strappy, black chiffon with little black beads on the straps, and they found shoes to go with it. Izzie looked fabulous in it, and very sophisticated. She looked like a woman in the dress, not a girl or a kindergarten teacher. 'You look hot,' Jennifer said with a grin, and Izzie laughed.

'So what's this guy like?' Jennifer asked her when they went upstairs to the restaurant for a bite to eat. 'He must be pretty special if you're shopping for him.'

'I just don't have clothes for the kind of stuff he goes to,' Izzie said, feeling like Cinderella after the ball once she took off the new dress. She was wearing jeans, a pink sweatshirt, and sneakers with holes in them – her standard Sunday afternoon garb. 'He's very smooth, and kind of sexy. He's a movie producer from L.A., he's making a movie here for a year.'

Jennifer looked impressed and intrigued. 'How old?'

'Thirty-nine.' Jennifer frowned at the answer.

'Isn't that a little old for you Iz?' They had sat down and ordered salads by then, and Izzie looked pensive. Jennifer and Jeff were seventeen years apart but gotten involved when they were older, not twenty-three.

'Maybe. I don't know. I don't think he's someone who gets too attached to anyone. He had a heartbreak when he was young. He's more about having fun.'

'Just make sure he doesn't break your heart,' Jennifer warned her wisely. 'Guys like that are easy to get hooked on. They're very charming, and always just out of reach. I went out with someone like that before your dad. I went out with him for six months, and it took me three years to get over him. But I'm a slow learner. You're probably smarter than I am.'

'I don't think I'm liable to get too attached either,' Izzie said softly. 'People die, Jen,' she said as she looked at her with eyes that ripped her stepmother's heart out. She had already seen too much at her age, and had paid a high price for it.

'Not everyone dies young, Izzie,' Jennifer said kindly, and touched her hand to reassure her.

'No, but a lot of people seem to at my age.'

'Why do you think that is?' Jennifer asked quietly. She had thought about it a lot herself. As a social worker, she saw too many tragedies among people Izzie's age, and even younger. Some were accidents, some products of the environments they lived in, but others just seemed to be a sign of the times. She had never seen a group of young people so at risk.

'I don't know,' Izzie answered. 'Maybe we're stupid, or too brave, or we watched too much TV when we were little or something. You watch people get killed every day on the news, and no one thinks about it. And then it happens to someone you know, and it almost kills you. Maybe we're careless or take bigger risks. Like Billy,' she said sadly, and Kevin. All Gabby had done was hail a cab, but the boy who had killed her had been careless and foolish enough to drink and drive. She had heard that he'd gotten out of prison the year before, after three and a half years. She couldn't even imagine what that had been like and didn't want to. And the deaths Jennifer hated most among the young were the suicides, which in her line of work she saw more than most people. It was the second biggest cause of death among youth, after car accidents, and so many parents were unaware of what was happening in their children's lives, or were in denial about it. It broke Jennifer's heart every time it happened to one of her clients. At least none of Izzie's friends seemed to be suffering from depression. Jennifer was always watchful for signs of it in Izzie, after losing her friends. But she seemed to be recovering well, and her mother's gift of the trip to Argentina had benefited her immensely. And now she had a new romance, which was all good, and a hopeful sign, even if it went nowhere. At least it was fun for her, which was how Izzie viewed it. She seemed to have a very sensible outlook about it, and Jennifer was reassured.

'How are Sean and Andy, by the way? You haven't said much about them lately,' Jennifer inquired as they finished lunch.

'There's nothing to say,' Izzie said, shrugging her shoulders. 'Andy's buried at med school, and so is his girlfriend. He couldn't even come home for Christmas.

And Sean is crazy. He thinks he's going to catch all the drug dealers in the world. He did an undercover assignment in South America for most of last year. He can't call anyone or have any contact when he's undercover. It's really hard on his parents. He came home for a week, and now he's doing it again. No one will hear from him for a year, or longer. Except if he dies, I guess.' She looked angry as she said it. She was tired of her friends dying, and he could easily get himself killed. 'I think that's what you meant. Maybe my generation takes bigger risks. Kevin, Billy, Sean. They think they're immortal.'

'All young people think that. Maybe the difference is that your generation acts on it, which is dangerous. That sounds like an extremely risky line of work,' Jennifer said, pained at the look in Izzie's eyes. And she suddenly had the same impression that Katherine had about her daughter the year before, There was no passion there, just pain. Izzie was not willing to throw her heart over the wall for anyone or anything, or care deeply anymore. She knew how high the chances were of getting burned. She had a fireproof wall around her heart. But at least she'd have fun with her movie producer from L.A. for a while. Jennifer could tell from what Izzie said that he was no more willing to risk his heart than she was, which was unconsciously why Izzie liked him.

Izzie promised to let Jennifer know how the opening of the ballet was when they left each other that afternoon, and Izzie went home with her new dress and new shoes in a bag. She could hardly wait to wear them.

They were a big success when she did. Tony went crazy when he saw her. And her face and her figure made the dress look even better. She had a great time with him, and enjoyed the opening of the ballet and the dinner after. They had a very elegant evening, and she felt like a fairy princess. He kissed her goodnight at her door, but didn't ask to come in, and she didn't invite him to. She wasn't ready to, and he was mature enough, and experienced enough, to sense that. But he said he enjoyed her company immensely, and he looked as though he meant it. He smiled at her and kissed her again before he left her.

'I'm going to L.A. next week, by the way. I'll be back on Friday. Saturday night dinner?' She nodded with a shy smile. It had been a perfect evening. 'We'll do something fun,' he promised, and she knew they would. Tony would see to that. Just as he had so far. He hurried down the stairs then with a smile and a wave, and Izzie drifted into her apartment on a cloud, feeling just like Cinderella, before she lost the glass slipper.

Chapter 21

As promised, Izzie called Jennifer the next day to report on the opening of the ballet and tell her how the dress looked.

'It was perfect!' Izzie said, sounding delighted, and grateful that her stepmother had dropped everything to go shopping with her. She had turned out to be a wonderful friend, and never tried to be a mother to her. She was more like a big sister or an aunt. 'Some of the women wore long dresses, but I would have felt silly wearing ones.'

'You're young enough to wear a short one, even to a black-tie event,' Jennifer confirmed, which Izzie had concluded the night before too. The dress they had chosen had been totally appropriate, and Tony had said she looked gorgeous. 'And how was Tony?'

'Handsome and charming.' Izzie giggled. 'I had a great time.' Jennifer was happy to hear it. Izzie gave her all the details of the evening, of the ballet and the dinner after, and as soon as she hung up, Andy called her from Cambridge. She hadn't talked to him since Christmas. She had called him on Christmas Day – he had been working and feeling sorry for himself. He was trying to figure out what to specialize in and was currently considering paediatrics.

'So how are you?' he tried to check in with her as often as he thought of it and had time. They were the only two left in the group now, since Sean was incommunicado in his undercover life for the FBI for a year. And Andy loved talking to her, it was a breath of home for him.

'I'm great!' Izzie said happily. 'I went to the opening of the ballet last night. I didn't see your parents, though. Were they there?'

'Probably, unless my mom was on call last night. My dad usually doesn't go without her. She likes the ballet more than he does. It sounds like you're getting pretty fancy. New guy in your life?'

'Sort of,' she admitted.

'You're holding out on me,' he scolded her.

'I met him on New Year's Eve. He took me to Napa for

lunch the next day, and the ballet last night. He's pretty cool.'

'What does he do? I hope he's not a doctor, you'll never see him. Nancy and I haven't spent a night together in two weeks. Our schedules are never the same. I think she's actually getting tired of it. This is really hard,' he confessed to Izzie, sounding discouraged. 'I don't know how my parents kept their marriage together. We fight a lot when we don't see each other, and we're sleep deprived all the time, which makes her bitchy and me psychotic,' he said, and Izzie laughed.

'You'll get through it. You love each other,' Izzie said, trying to reassure him.

'I hope so. Sometimes I wonder if that's enough.' It sounded like he was going through a rough patch. No one had ever said that medical school would be easy, but it was what he had always wanted. Just like Sean and his crazy life for the FBI. It made her realize that her life as a kindergarten teacher was a lot simpler than theirs, even if it was less challenging.

'So what else is new with you, other than fighting with Nancy and lack of sleep?' She loved talking to him – it was like talking to a brother. It was with Sean too, but he was an invisible brother now, one she could never talk to, and might never again, if something went wrong while he was undercover. She had a constant sense that he might be killed at any moment, and she was sure that Connie did too, her last surviving son. At least Izzie knew that Andy would always be there. Nothing about his chosen profession was high risk. It was safe to love him, and she did, just as she had for eighteen years. They were both twenty-three now.

'There is no "else" in this business,' Andy complained. 'All we ever do is work. Thank God Nancy is going to be a doctor too. No other sane human being would understand it. You were right to bail on me when you did.' They normally never mentioned it, but he felt comfortable with it now, and so did she.

'I think long distance would have been really hard,' she said honestly.

'Yeah, me too. So what's with this new guy? Tell me about him.' Andy was always interested in her life, when he had time.

'Handsome. Older. Movie producer. Nice.'

'Serious?'

'No.'

'Slept with him?'

'Not yet, doctor. You sound like my gynaecologist.' Andy laughed at that.

'Wait till I get assigned to OB/GYN. We can talk

about it then. My mom wants me to be an OB and go into practice with her. I don't think so. So how much older is he?'

'Not that much. He's thirty-nine.' She knew Nancy was a year older than Andy, but in the same year of medical school. She had taken a gap year to travel before starting. But one year made no difference – sixteen years would.

'That's old for you, don't you think?'

'Maybe. It feels kind of grown-up and sophisticated. It's fun for now.'

'I guess, with the opening of the ballet and all that. It's a far cry from my life at the moment. The best we can do is McDonald's, between studying, classes, and rounds at the hospital with our professors, and I fall asleep at the table.' She suspected that he made it sound worse than it was, but she could tell he was stressed, and he had no idea when he was coming home for a visit. 'Well, let me know how it's going. It's nice to remember how the other half lives, people who actually get to go out to dinner, sleep, and even get laid. I'll be too old to do it by the time this is over.'

'I don't think so, Andy. I think you might still be okay.'

'Don't bet on it,' he said ruefully. 'Take care, and call me sometime. I love you, Iz. Don't forget that.'

'I never do. I love you too.'

'Yeah, I know.' It was good to hear, for both of them. They hung up a few minutes later. Izzie decided to clean her apartment, and Andy went back to work. He had an exam the next day.

It was a nasty January day in Boston, and everyone had the flu, and the post-holiday doldrums. There was some kind of virus going around, and half the kids in the hospital were ones they'd admitted for dehydration after days of throwing up. Andy thought if he saw another vomiting three-year-old, he'd scream. There wasn't much they could do for them except give them fluids. And there were some nasty chest infections that had turned into bronchitis and then pneumonia. They had admitted a few of those cases too.

He ran all day, as a second-year student working with the interns and chief resident that day, who was a nasty guy dedicated to making his life miserable, and Andy had a mountain of forms to fill out. Nancy was finally off duty after three days working in the ER, and she was home sleeping. Andy had been up for thirty-six hours, after studying late and working.

He was still relatively fresh at nine o'clock that night, after an eight-hour work day, when a nine-year-old girl came up from the ER, with what they thought was flu and a high fever. She had a hundred-and-four-point-five temperature, and she didn't look good. The resident had seen her and told Andy and the nurses to get her hydrated and give her something to bring the fever down. She was crying and said she felt awful. She looked it. But since it was presumably only flu, they let Andy take her intake history. Her mother had three other kids in the waiting room with her. The child's father was out of town, and their paediatrician was away for the weekend and had only left an on-call nurse to check in with. The nurse had told the mom over the phone to go to the ER. The fever had only come on that day, at noon. But even after they put an IV of fluids into her, the fever continued to get higher and she got worse. Andy knew enough from his studies to worry about the possibility of febrile seizures and called the resident back in at ten.

'I don't like the way she looks,' Andy said calmly, trying to seem wiser than just a second-year student. The resident checked her again and agreed that he didn't like it either, and she was complaining of a stiff neck between sobs. 'What do you think?' he asked the resident.

'Same as I thought when she came in,' he said, sounding impatient. 'Bad case of flu. Let's hope the fever breaks tonight.' They were doing all they could. He left Andy then, to take care of a six-month-old he had to intubate, with a heart problem. It was a busy night for them. Later when Andy looked in on her, the child's eyes rolled back in her head while he examined her, and she lost consciousness. He hit a button on the wall, and instantly a team of nurses and doctors came in at full speed and began working on her, as Andy stepped aside, feeling helpless and inept. The chief resident, who had come from another floor, looked at Andy with a grim expression.

'Looks like meningitis. Did you suspect that earlier?' It was more of an academic question, but Andy felt it instantly as a reproach of his competence. And Andy actually had thought of it, with the stiff neck as a symptom, but didn't want to sound like an alarmist or second-guess the resident on the case.

'I did . . . but I figured it probably was just flu.'

'It doesn't make any difference,' he said tersely to educate him. 'We don't treat it any differently than what you and the nurses have been doing. We can get a tap on her now to confirm it,' he said, and ordered a nurse to call for a spinal tap. The child was still unconscious, and her body was blazing.

The team came in a few minutes later and performed a spinal tap on her, and as soon as they finished, her breathing became labored, and they intubated her, while

Andy watched. They were doing all they could, and were breathing for her, as her blood pressure started plummeting and her heart stopped. Andy watched in horror as they performed CPR on her, then put paddles on her chest to defibrillate her and get her heart going again. The team worked on her frantically for half an hour. Andy felt tears roll down his cheeks, as he observed helplessly. Then the chief resident turned to him and shook his head.

'It was meningitis,' he said, as though that said everything.

'How do you know?' Andy asked, choking on a sob. He felt guilty and responsible for not saving her, but the others couldn't do it either.

'Because she's dead,' the chief resident said. She had lived only twelve hours after the onset of the fever, which was typical in severe cases. 'Nothing moves faster than that. It can kill a kid with the speed of lightning, and adults sometimes too.' They had put a sheet over her after they took all the tubes out, while Andy stared at the little girl they hadn't been able to save, and now they had to tell her mother. Or the chief resident did, and he motioned to Andy to come with him. Delivering bad news was part of the learning process. Andy followed him into the waiting room, while her mother was trying to deal with her three other children, who were seriously at risk now. The mother looked terrified when the two men walked in. All Andy could think of was that it was the worst moment of his life. He had to watch the resident tell this woman that her child had just died. He couldn't imagine anything worse than what had just happened, and telling the little girl's mother.

The chief resident told her, professionally and quickly, as gently as he could, that her daughter had meningitis and that there had been nothing they could do to save her. He said it was a dread disease and lethal in many cases in young children, and even if she had brought her daughter in earlier, it would have made no difference. She had been affected too severely by the disease. He said she could have contracted it anywhere, at school, in a shopping mall, on a bus from a total stranger. And no one was to blame. The chief resident examined the other children while she sobbed hysterically, and then she turned to Andy with a look of fury and beat on his chest with her fists.

'Why didn't you tell me she was going to die? I would have been in the room with her! She died alone because of you! I'm her mother.' Andy wanted to die on the spot as she said it, and he apologized and said they hadn't known, it had only become obvious to them in the last few minutes of her daughter's life, and she had been unconscious.

The mother was inconsolable, and they called a friend to drive her home. The other children were fine for the moment, and it was possible they wouldn't get it. Meningitis was entirely unpredictable as to who caught it, whatever the exposure. They left at two in the morning, after the attending resident and the chief had signed the forms and the death certificate. The child was taken to the morgue until arrangements could be made the next day. And as soon as it was over and the mother had left, Andy stood in a small supply room by himself, sobbing. The chief resident was looking for him and found him. He looked Andy dead in the eye and grabbed both of his shoulders in firm hands.

'Listen to me, we couldn't save her. Nothing you did was wrong. You didn't know what you were seeing, and even if you did, you couldn't change it. I thought she had flu too. And even if I had diagnosed her with meningitis the second she came in, she'd still be dead now. Too often, you can't beat meningitis, particularly in a child that age. She would have died no matter what we did.' He was almost shouting at him. It was the first child Andy had seen die, and he could still feel the distraught mother's fists beating on his chest, accusing him. 'I want you to go home now, and get some sleep.'

'I'm okay,' Andy said, sounding desperate and convincing neither of them. He felt as though he had failed abysmally. And he was convinced he had killed her by not recognizing the signs of meningitis himself. He didn't believe a word the chief resident said – he thought he was just protecting him and trying to make him feel better.

'I want you to get out of here and get some rest,' he said firmly. 'We all lose patients. It happens. Sometimes you just can't win. We're not fixing cars. We're treating people. Go home, Weston. Come back when you wake up tomorrow. You need the sleep.' It was true, but he didn't want to leave now. He had never felt worse in his life. He took off his white coat, and left the stethoscope on the shelf where they kept them, and he called Nancy on his way home. He needed to hear her voice, but she sounded busy when he called. He thought she had been at home, sleeping.

'Where are you?' he asked, confused.

'They had some kind of gang shooting at the fish market. They have four gunshot wounds here. They called me in to help. Where are you?'

'I'm on my way home. I was hoping you'd be there.'

'Something wrong? I thought you were staying late today.' She was confused too. They were both exhausted, and he was nearly hysterical with guilt and grief.

'They gave me a break,' he said vaguely. He didn't add *because I killed a child*, but he wanted to. He didn't have the heart to tell her. It was too awful. Nancy hadn't lost a patient yet, and until tonight neither had he.

'I'll see you later. I have to go back to work. Two of these guys are coding.' He knew that meant 'code blue,' and they were in extremis. She hung up before he could answer. He hoped Nancy would be luckier than he was.

The little girl had coded that night, and they couldn't save her. Her name was Amy. He knew he would remember it forever – and her mother hitting him in grief and fury.

The bed was unmade when he walked in. He could tell that Nancy had left in a hurry. The apartment was a mess because neither of them had been home long enough to clean it in weeks. There was a half-eaten pizza in a box in the fridge, which had been Nancy's dinner, and it could have been his too, but he didn't want it. He went to the bathroom to wash his face and stared at himself in the mirror. What he saw there was a killer, a man who wanted to be a physician and had already failed, a fraud, someone he hated as he looked at him. He always tried to do everything right in his life, for his parents, for Nancy, for his friends, and hoped to for his patients one day.

Always the right thing. Until now. He had killed Amy. He knew he would never forgive himself for what had happened that night. He couldn't be a doctor now. He wasn't a healer, he was a murderer. The Hippocratic oath said to 'do no harm,' and he had. He had killed her, by not knowing what she had, and by not saving her. He walked out of the bathroom with dead eyes. His BlackBerry was ringing, and he didn't answer it. Nancy had just heard what happened, from one of the residents, and she was calling to comfort him. But he didn't look at the phone in his pocket, and he wouldn't have answered it anyway.

There were beams across the ceiling of the apartment they had rented. It looked like a Swiss Chalet with a big stone fireplace, overstuffed couches, and the snow outside. He got a rope out of the supply closet they kept, put a chair under one of the beams, tied the rope to it, and made a noose, just like they had taught him in Cub Scouts. He got on the chair, put the noose around his neck, and jumped off, all within seconds. It was over just as fast as he had done it. It was all he could do now. He owed it to Amy and her mother. Her death had been avenged. And the BlackBerry kept ringing long after he was dead.

Chapter 22

Andy's funeral was a major event. Important people were there – senators, congressmen, doctors, publishers. People stood on line to get into the church. And Izzie was there, the only one of Andy's friends. She sat in the back of the church with Jennifer and her father. The parents of all her friends were there, and each of them had lost a child now. Nancy was sitting in the front pew with Andy's mother, crying inconsolably. Helen kept an arm around her shoulders and cried too. Nancy was the daughter-in-law she would never have now. Andy had been twenty-three when he died, almost exactly five years after Gabby, a year after Billy.

When Andy's father came forward to give the eulogy, his first words were not about Andy, but about himself. No one was surprised.

'I never thought that this could happen to me, to us,' he said, glancing at Helen. 'Losing a child was something that happened to other people, not to me. But it just did.' And as he said it, he started to cry, and finally became human. He stood there and sobbed for a long time, and then he talked about what a star Andy had been, in every way. Star son, star student, star athlete, star friend. No one would have disagreed. Izzie felt a knife pierce her heart as he said it. 'And he would have been a terrific doctor too,' he assured everyone. 'A child died, whom he couldn't have saved, but he didn't believe it. She had meningitis. So Andy gave his life in exchange for hers. To atone for what he believed were his sins,' he explained to everyone, but no one cared.

All they knew was that a wonderful boy had died. He had taken his life, and they would never see him again. It was the cruelest of destiny's tricks, the death of a young person. The death of a child – worse, an only child. Izzie thought her heart would explode in a million pieces, and her head along with it. She couldn't even think. She sat between her father and Jennifer and felt as though her life were over. She couldn't even tell Sean because no one knew where he was. She hated him for being unreachable and for what he was doing. And when it was all over, she stood on the cathedral steps and watched the casket being put into the hearse. She had seen it too often. She didn't even go to the Westons' house afterward, she just couldn't. She didn't want to see anyone, not even the Westons, especially not the Westons, with their shock and grief. Her father wanted her to come home with them, but she wouldn't. She wanted to go back to her apartment and be alone. Jeff and Jennifer left her there reluctantly, terrified that it would be too much for her, that she was at risk now too. But she insisted that she wasn't and reassured them.

She sat in her apartment alone that night, going through old photographs, and stared at one of Andy. He had been such a beautiful kid, and a great friend. She had talked to him on the morning of the day he did it, and they had told each other they loved each other. They always did.

When the phone rang that night, it was Tony. He wanted to invite her to dinner. He had no idea what had happened. He had seen the item on the front page of the paper, but he had no way of knowing that the boy who had committed suicide, from a prominent family of physicians, had been her best friend.

'How about dinner tomorrow night?' he asked her, pleased to hear her voice. She sounded a little strange, and he wondered if he had woken her up. She said he hadn't.

'I can't,' she said in a dead voice.

'What about Tuesday? Wednesday I have to go to L.A., but I'll be back on Friday, if you like that better.' He was anxious to see her.

'I can't. My best friend just died. I think I'm going away.' She hadn't thought of it before, but she liked the idea. Maybe forever.

'I'm so sorry. What happened?'

'He killed himself.' She didn't offer the details, and then he understood.

'I saw it in the paper. I'm sorry, Izzie. Do you want me to come over?'

'No, but thank you. I'm okay. I just need to think about it.' That didn't sound like a good idea to him.

'Are you sure? Let's do dinner next weekend, when I get back from L.A..'

'No, I don't think we should see each other anymore,' she said in a quiet voice, but she knew what she was saying. 'I had fun with you. But I don't think I can do this. Someone always gets hurt. I don't want it to be me.' She knew instinctively that she needed to be with people she loved and who loved her, in order to heal. And Tony was never going to be that person. He could offer her fun but nothing else. He didn't have it to give. He was still running away from his own grief. 'I think we need to let this go, before we start it.' He was shocked when she said it, but he didn't disagree. He could hear that she meant it, and he didn't have anything more to offer her than he had given, a nice dinner, lunch in Napa, and the opening of the ballet. His own heart had been sealed off years before, for the same reasons. He couldn't help her. And Izzie didn't want to end up like him. Slick and superficial, however nice he appeared to be.

'I'm sorry, Tony,' she said seriously.

'No worries. Call me if you ever want to play.' She didn't. That was the difference between them. He wanted to play so he didn't have to feel. Izzie couldn't do that. She was feeling everything and wished that she didn't, but maybe it was better this way. She felt like Andy had been ripped right through her soul and left a hole in it the size of her head, just like the others. She was so full of holes now, she felt like a Swiss cheese. After Tony hung up, she looked in the mirror and tried to figure out what to do.

She asked for a week off from work, and she walked all over San Francisco, thinking. She didn't know where to go, where to be, or even how to be anymore. She went to see Helen Weston and told her how sorry she was, and she met Nancy, before she went back to Boston. And she understood why Andy had loved her. They even looked like each other. Tall, slim, aristocratic blondes with fine

361

features. They would have had gorgeous children, Izzie thought to herself. And she and Nancy hugged when Izzie left her.

She went to see Connie again and saw the strain in her eyes from worrying about Sean. She was helping Mike now, but Sean should have been doing it, instead of chasing bad guys and risking his own life. It made no sense to Izzie, and didn't sound noble to her. It seemed wrong that his parents had to live in constant terror that he'd be killed, and so did she, even as his friend.

She went for a long walk with Jennifer, and they talked about all of it. All Izzie knew now was that she wanted to go away. She couldn't leave until June, the end of the school year. She was stuck in San Francisco until then, except for spring break. And then she remembered the trip to Argentina, and how healing that had been. It had kick-started her life again.

She decided to go to Japan over spring break, and she could figure out the rest of her life later. But she was certain that she needed to get away. From everything. Maybe for a year after that, and then she could go to graduate school, but she couldn't stay here mourning her friends forever. No one was left now except her and Sean, and he was dead to her too, or might as well have been, since she could only talk to him for one week a year.

What kind of life was that, and what kind of friend?

She went back to work, and Wendy told her how sorry she was. She knew Andy's mother and had gone to the funeral too. Izzie hadn't noticed anyone there, just Andy in his casket, and his father standing up in front of everyone, saying he had thought it could never happen to him. It had happened to all of them, the entire community, and was a failure on the part of the community to save him, and for creating a world where young people who had everything going for them would rather die than live. It was a mystery that no one seemed to be able to solve, but it was happening too often to too many, and it had happened to Andy, another casualty of his generation, and of the pressure he and his parents had put on him to always be perfect. Just like Larry's pressure on Billy to be a big football star. In some ways, the expectations had been too much for them. They all had to exceed everyone's wishes for them, or at least live up to them, even if it killed them.

Izzie planned her trip to Japan in April, and she was going to pay for it herself this time. She wanted to visit the countryside, and go to the shrines in Kyoto. She didn't have to renew her contract for school until May, and she was giving herself until then to decide what she wanted to do. She hoped to figure it out while she was in

Japan. She needed to see something new, and wanted to start her life over. Nothing about what she'd done so far felt right to her anymore. And she had no idea what would.

She had dinner with her father and Jennifer the night before she left. She looked serious and quiet, and her father was worried about her, but Jennifer said she was going to be okay. She was doing all the right things, and the trip to Japan was a good sign. She was reaching out for life, although there was no denying that Andy's death had been a terrible blow, yet again. It was a final loss of innocence for her and all his friends, the denial of hope.

She dyed Easter eggs with the kindergarten on the last day of school, and she had had fun with them. She took a cab to the airport to leave on her trip. She checked in, had her boarding pass and her passport in her hand, she had only brought carry-on, and was buying magazines for the flight when her BlackBerry rang. It was Connie, and she sounded breathless.

'Thank God. I thought you were gone.'

'I almost am. My plane leaves in an hour. Why?'

Connie didn't waste any time. 'Sean's been shot.' Izzie closed her eyes and felt the terminal spin around her. 'He's alive. Barely. He took two bullets in the chest and three in the leg. And don't ask me how, but he crawled out through the jungle somehow, and sent some kind of signal. They picked him up in a clandestine operation a week later. They're flying him from Bogotá to Jackson Memorial in Miami tonight. Mike and I are flying out on the red-eye. I thought you might want to be there when he gets to the hospital in Miami.' She assumed Izzie would.

'Why?' Izzie asked her, and Connie sounded shocked by the question.

'Because you love him and he's your friend. You two have always been there for each other, and you're the only one left.'

'He's not there for me, Connie,' Izzie said coldly, 'or for you either, or his father. He's obsessed with killing drug dealers because of Billy and Kevin, but he was obsessed with that before them. He wanted to catch bad guys when he was five years old. Meanwhile he breaks all of our hearts. And next time they'll kill him.'

'I don't think he'll go back after this,' Connie said quietly. 'It sounds like he was very badly injured, and he barely got out.' She was stunned by Izzie's reaction and the harshness of what she'd said.

'He'll go back,' Izzie said with conviction. 'As soon as he can crawl, he'll go back, and you won't know where he is or if he's dead or alive for another year. I don't want to play that game anymore. It hurts too much.' She was trying to get free of it now, even if it meant getting free of him.

'I'm sorry. I thought you'd want to come.'

'I do. I love you, Connie, and I love him. But I think what he's doing is wrong, for all of us, and especially for him. And I don't want him breaking my heart all over again when he dies, and he will. We'll be going to his funeral next. I'm glad he's okay this time, but one of these days he won't be. I have to stop hanging on to it, or it's going to kill me. Give him my love. I'm going to Japan.'

'Take care of yourself,' Connie said sadly, and hung up.

Izzie paid for her magazines and sat down in the terminal, waiting for her flight to board. She felt sick. All she could think about was the condition Sean must be in, and how he had crawled through the jungle for a week, with five bullet holes in him. She didn't know why he didn't die, but next time he might, or the time after. He was addicted to what he was doing, beyond reason, and it cost her too much. She had meant what she had said to his mother. She wasn't even sure she ever wanted to see him again. It was too heartbreaking. They called her flight, and she stood on line to board.

She walked into the gangway behind the others for the flight to Tokyo, and then she stopped before she got on the plane. She couldn't do it. She hated him for it. He had no right to do this to her, even as a friend. She turned around and walked back through the gangway and into the terminal again. She stood there for a long moment, trying to make sense of it, but she couldn't. She walked through the terminal, and bought a ticket for Miami, hating Sean for what he did to all of them.

Chapter 23

Izzie landed in Miami before his parents did, and she was at the hospital when they arrived. Connie looked at Izzie gratefully, and was relieved to see her there. A doctor explained that Sean had just been flown in and was in intensive care. They could see him for a few minutes but not for long.

His parents went in to see him first, and Izzie went in alone after them, and was shocked by what she saw. He looked ravaged, his chest was heavily bandaged, he had tubes coming out of everywhere, and his leg had drains in it and pins from where the bone had shattered when he'd been shot. Izzie couldn't imagine how he had crawled out of the jungle and survived it. He looked twenty years older than he was, but he was alive. His eyes were half closed, but he opened them when he saw her, and he seemed surprised.

'What are you doing here?' he asked her, and gently reached for her hand resting on his bed. She couldn't help herself, and stroked his cheek and then his hair.

'I had nothing better to do, so I thought I'd come to Miami and drop by. It looks like you made quite a mess of yourself, Bozo,' she said, pointing to his chest and his leg. He started to laugh, but it hurt too much.

'Yeah, whatever. You should see what the other guy looks like,' he whispered. He didn't tell her, but he had killed six of them when he left. They had assumed he was dead, and still didn't know he was alive. The FBI was going to have to change his identify for his next assignment.

'You going back?' she whispered back to him. He hesitated, and then he nodded. She wasn't surprised. She had told his mother that he would. 'I figured. You're a crazy bastard, Sean O'Hara. And that's not a compliment, but I'm glad you're alive. Your parents don't deserve to lose another son.' The only one they had left. But she was happy for herself too. It was good to see him, even the way he looked. She didn't tell him about Andy. He was still too sick to know. It would be a hard blow for him too. And for her – the day Sean eventually died, and she knew he would, it would be too much for her. She was already bracing herself for it, particularly knowing he was going back. He had an obsession, and a death wish no one could stop, and she was smart enough not to try.

He closed his eyes then, and drifted off to sleep. He was heavily sedated, but in spite of it, he still made sense, and had been happy to see her. She saw him again the next morning and talked to him for a few minutes, and then she left. She flew back to San Francisco, and decided to postpone her trip to Japan. She had already lost two days of it, and she could go another time.

She let her father know she was back, and she spent the rest of the spring break taking long walks and doing quiet things. She was thinking of what she'd seen in Miami. And two weeks later, once she was back at work, Connie called to say they were home. Sean was still in the hospital, and she said he would be there for a while. He had had some complications with the bullet wounds, but she said that ultimately he'd be fine. *If you can call it that*, Izzie thought to herself.

It was a sunny afternoon in May and Izzie was leaving the kindergarten when she looked up and saw Sean standing there, watching her, in rough clothes, with a full beard, and leaning heavily on a cane. He had trouble walking as he approached, and she wouldn't have admitted it to him, but it made her heart stop to look at him. They were the last two survivors of a universe that no longer existed, another planet that had vanished into thin air with the deaths of their friends.

'What brings you here?' she asked him as she walked over to him and gave him a hug. He looked stronger, and seemed powerful, even with the cane, and he had put on some weight since she saw him in Miami.

'I came home for a visit,' he said quietly, and his eyes were intense. 'I wanted to see you, Izzie, and my parents.'

'Why? Me, I mean. What difference does it make? You'll be dead soon anyway, just like the others.'

'Thanks for the vote of confidence,' he said unhappily. 'I made it through this time.' And even he was surprised. He had heard about Andy by then and was sad about it too. It was such a terrible waste, he was such a terrific guy, with so much ahead of him. A great life, if he hadn't ended it.

'Maybe you'll make it through next time too,' she said, with a look that said she didn't believe it, and didn't want to hope for it anymore.

'Can we have a cup of coffee somewhere?' Sean asked her cautiously.

'Sure. You can come to my place.' She was about to say

it was in walking distance, but it wasn't for him with the cane. But he had brought his mother's car, and he drove her there. He took his time getting up the stairs, and sat down in her living room and looked around. There were photographs of all of the Big Five, together, when they were kids, and several of him alone. He was touched. He wondered why there were more of him, and she saw the question in his eyes. 'You're the only one still alive,' she told him. She sat down next to him, and handed him a mug of coffee. He set it down carefully on a magazine so he didn't stain her table, and looked her in the eyes.

'Izzie . . .' He started to say something to her, but he couldn't finish it. Before either of them knew what had happened to them, he was kissing her and she was in his arms. She wasn't sure if they were fighting each other or making love, or just trying to stay alive. She felt as though an uncontrollable force had taken possession of both of them, and every ounce of his being that he had used to survive was now being poured into her. He was stronger than she expected, and dragging his bad leg, he carried her into the bedroom, and nearly tore off her clothes while she pulled his off just as quickly. They were two desperate people, making love with a passion she had never dreamed of, and she had never felt for him or anyone before, They were alive. They had survived. They needed each other desperately. They were suddenly two halves that made one whole, and they were both breathless when they finished, as she lay in his arms staring at him. She had always thought something like that might happen one day, but she was surprised anyway.

'What was that?' she asked him in a whisper. It was like being possessed. They were like two bodies with one soul.

'I'm not sure. I'm in love with you, Izzie. That's what I wanted to talk to you about. I don't know what to do. You're the only thing that got me out of that jungle, dragging myself by my arms – the thought of seeing you again.' She lay next to him and looked at him with eyes that bored straight to his soul.

'Are you going back undercover again?' It was the only thing she wanted to know. Not if he loved her, but if he was going back. And he was always honest with her.

'Yes, I am,' he whispered back. 'I have to.' She nodded and got out of bed as swiftly as she had entered it, and stood looking at him from across the room.

'Then get out of my bed. And my life. Forever. I never want to see you again. You can't do this to me. I won't let you. All the others took a piece of me with them. If you die, when you die – because you will if you go back – you'll take the rest. I won't let you. I'm taking my life back. You can do whatever you want, but you can't come here, tell me you love me, make love to me, and then break my heart when you go back and they kill you next time. Get out!' Her face was hard as she said it, and he didn't say a word. He knew she meant it, he knew her better than anyone. He got out of her bed and put his clothes on, as she watched him. She was wearing a pink satin robe, and all he wanted was to make love to her again. Worse, she knew that she had found what she was looking for, the passion she had never been able to find about anything in her life. He was it. But her face showed nothing as he stopped in the doorway.

'You're right. I'm sorry. I had no right to do this. Take care of yourself, Izzie. I love you, but that's beside the point.' She said nothing, but she burst into tears as soon as he left. She could hear him limping slowly down the stairs with his injured leg. She lay on her bed sobbing after he was gone. The last time she had seen him, she had thought it would be the final one, and now she felt that way again. She hated him for it. She had no idea how you killed nineteen years of loving someone. But he was a dead man, and she knew it.

She turned her ticket to Japan into one for India, with a departure date in mid-June. She was going to travel for a month or two. And she had signed her contract for the coming school year, but she had told them it would be her last. She was applying to graduate school, maybe in Europe. Other than her family, there was nothing keeping her here anymore. All her friends were gone.

She was looking forward to her trip, and had been reading about all the wonders of India. She was going to rent a car and travel around by herself. She wasn't afraid to do it.

The last day in kindergarten was always a big event. The children would be entering first grade in September, and Wendy and Izzie had prepared them well. These were their last baby days before they entered a more grown-up world. Izzie hated to say goodbye to them and she hugged them all, especially Dana and Daphne, as they left on the last day. She had given each child a book, and written something special in it to every one of them. She still had the book that Miss June had given her on the last day of kindergarten, a dog-eared copy of *Goodnight Moon*.

She and Wendy took their time tidying up after the children left. There was always a moment of nostalgia when the school year ended, and a feeling of new beginnings in the fall.

'Well, we did it,' Wendy said, smiling at her. 'Another year.' She wondered if the next one would really be Izzie's last, or if she would get hooked as she had. For Wendy, it always felt like watching baby sparrows hatch and eventually take flight, but Izzie wasn't sure. There were other things she wanted to do, like her trip to India that summer. The truth was that other than her father and Jennifer, all the ties that kept her in San Francisco had been severed. She felt like it was time for her to go, take flight herself, and find the passion that her mother had spoken of. Sean had almost been it, and could have been, but not with the choices he had made. She had heard from Connie that he had left two weeks before, and was in Washington, doing therapy for his leg, and waiting to be shipped out again in a few months. She wished him well, but she didn't want to be part of his world anymore. It had been hard walking away from him, and sending him away, knowing how much they loved each other. Their afternoon in bed had told them both that. But she knew she had to, and she had no regrets. She wanted Sean and the pain he would have brought her out of her life. She felt sorry for his parents.

'Send me a postcard from India,' Wendy said as they hugged each other.

'I'll do better than that.' Izzie smiled at her. She liked working with her. She was a nice woman, and the two years she had spent in the kindergarten had been good for her. She had grown up herself. 'I'll bring you back a sari.'

She had a whole shopping list of things she wanted to find there – her peace of mind more than anything else. It was going to be a healing trip for her.

After she left Wendy, Izzie walked back to her apartment. She unlocked the outer door, and was just about to go upstairs when she saw him, off to the side, under a tree, in jeans and a camouflage jacket. He had the cane, but he wasn't leaning on it. His beard was trimmed, and she could see he'd had a haircut. It was Sean. She looked at him, but she didn't invite him to come in, and he walked slowly toward her.

'I'm back,' he said once he was standing next to her.

'So I see,' she said quietly. 'I asked you not to come to see me again.' Her eyes told him she had meant it, and he looked wounded, but he couldn't blame her. She didn't look furious with him, just gone. Possibly forever. His disappearance from her life was what she wanted and he didn't. She felt as though her survival depended on it.

'I just wanted to tell you something, in person, not over the phone, aside from the fact that I love you, which may be irrelevant at this point.' He had a terrifying feeling it was, from the look in her eyes. 'I'm back. I'm coming home. You were right about my parents. It's too much for them. The business is too hard for my father to handle on his own now. They never said a word to me, they didn't ask me for anything, but I think I've done enough. We made a real difference this time. It damn near killed me, but it was worth it. We broke one of the most dangerous drug rings in Colombia. Their leaders are dead, we crippled them. There are others, but I can't get them all. I know that now. It's time for me to come home. I resigned from the Bureau two days ago. I just wanted you to know that. In case it makes a difference.'

'Should it?' She looked at him coldly. She was still angry at him, for what he had put them through in his long stints undercover. She knew his parents had forgiven him, but she hadn't. He had a lot to make up for. 'Do you think you can be happy without all that?' she asked him honestly, and he thought about it. They both knew he was addicted to the excitement and the danger.

'Maybe. I don't know. I'll miss the thrill of it, I have to be honest about that. I had a passion for it. But there are other kinds of passion that in the end matter more. I gave what I thought I had to. Now the rest belongs to me, or whoever wants it . . . like you, for instance,' he said in a whisper, 'if you want me. I love you, Izzie . . . even more than I loved working undercover and hunting down drug dealers. I never knew that till I did it. All I thought about when I was down there, was coming back to you and having a life together.' She looked at him hard, trying to decide if he meant it, and if he could do it. He had come from a long way in his heart, to find her. And what he was saying made a difference, a big one. It was all she had ever wanted, and now she knew it. She had known it when he came back the last time. He was her passion, and what had been missing from her life.

She nodded, after listening to him, and didn't answer. There was too much to say to him, rushing over her in waves. 'Do you want to come up?' was all she said, and then she smiled at him, and he followed her up the stairs. He was afraid to even reach out and touch her for fear she would evaporate in his fingers, like a mirage.

She started to put the coffee on, and then he pulled her into his arms and kissed her, with the same passion that had burned between them the last time they had seen each other and had exploded out of control. The same thing happened this time, and the fire that had been dormant but had kept them alive for so long ignited and joined them to each other. They were one flame made of two people, with a love that had endured all the challenges and tragedies of life. But they were still standing, still alive, and still whole. They lay in bed afterward, breathless in each other's arms. Sean smiled when he looked at her. She was the most beautiful woman he had ever seen. She always had been to him, and she was his now. She rolled over on one elbow and looked at him, with the same smile he had fallen in love with the day he met her in kindergarten. He was a happy man as he lay watching her, and she gently leaned over and kissed him, and said the words he had been waiting for: 'Welcome home.'

Betrayal

Danielle Steel

Tallie Jones is a Hollywood legend – an ambitious and passionate film director who creates award-winning productions. But she has little interest in the glitz and glamour of Los Angeles, instead focusing intently on her work and family.

She has close, loving relationships with her daughter, her elderly father and Hunter Lloyd – her co-producer and partner of four years. Completing her trusted circle is Brigitte Parker – Tallie's best friend and devoted personal assistant.

However as Tallie is in the midst of directing her most ambitious film to date, small disturbances start to ripple through her faultlessly ordered world. An audit reveals worrying discrepancies in her financial records, which have always been maintained by her loyal accountant. Receipts hint at activities of which she has no knowledge.

Someone close to Tallie has been steadily helping themselves to enormous amounts of her money. Her once safe world is suddenly shaken to its very core – and Tallie is in shock, trying to figure out who has betrayed her among those she trusts and holds dear . . .

Hotel Vendôme

Danielle Steel

When Swiss-born Hugues Martin sees a small, run-down hotel in New York for the rough diamond it is, he transforms it into a beautiful boutique hotel of impeccable elegance, run with the precision and attention to detail he learned through his hotelier training in Europe.

Renowned for its unparalleled service, the Hotel Vendôme soon becomes the ideal New York refuge for the rich and famous, as well as a perfect home for Hugues' beautiful wife and their young daughter. But when his wife tires of his obsession for the hotel, she walks out on him for a notorious rock star, leaving Hugues a single parent to four-year-old Heloise.

Heloise and her family live happily amid a colourful, exciting and sometimes mysterious milieu of celebrities, socialites, politicians, world travellers and hotel employees – and their inevitable intrigues.

As unexpected challenges arise, the hotel is the centre of their world. And when Heloise grows up, she longs to follow in her father's footsteps and one day run the Hotel Vendôme. The lessons she learned at his side will carry her through it all, in a story no reader will forget.

44 Charles Street

Danielle Steel

Everything is falling to pieces for **Francesca Thayer**. Her beautiful, old house is full of leaks and in need of total restoration. Then her relationship with lawyer Todd collapses and he moves out. As the owner of a struggling art gallery she can't possibly manage the mortgage alone, so she is forced to do the one thing she never imagined she would: she advertises for lodgers.

First arrives **Eileen** – a young, attractive schoolteacher. Then comes **Chris**, a newly-divorced father and graphic designer. Last to arrive is **Marya** – a famous cookery author who is hoping to rebuild her life after the death of her husband.

And so Francesca finds that her house has become a whole new world – and that her accidental tenants have become the most important people in her life. Over their year together, the house at 44 Charles Street fills with laughter, heartbreak and hope.

And Francesca discovers that she might be able to open her heart again after all . . .

Legacy

Danielle Steel

'Someday' is Brigitte Nicholson's watchword. Someday she and the man she loves, Ted, will clarify their relationship. Someday she'll have children. Someday she'll finish writing her book. Someday she'll stop playing it so safe . . .

Then something happens that changes Brigitte's life completely.

Struggling to plot a new course, Brigitte agrees to help her mother on a genealogy project – and makes a fascinating discovery that reaches back to the French aristocracy. Brigitte decides to travel to South Dakota and Paris to follow the path of her ancestor. And as she begins to solve the puzzle of this exceptional young woman who lived so long ago, her quiet life becomes an adventure of its own.

A chance meeting and a new opportunity put Brigitte back at the heart of her own story. And with family legacy coming to life around her, someday is no longer in the future. Instead, someday is now.